He grinned. "I suppose I deserved that, Red."

"Keep on with the Red, and you'll see the nasty side of me."

Brett Atwell was tempted to say he'd like to see any side of her at all, this drop-dead gorgeous woman who'd followed him into the store. His busy imagination conjured up images of all that lush red hair spread across his pillow like wildfire...

"You're staring."

Oops. He needed to shake himself out of the lust that had swamped him and to focus on the job at hand. It wasn't like him to let his mind wander, but then it wasn't every day he met a woman who appealed to him like this one did.

Brett tore his thoughts away from the swell of attraction that had caught his breath. This was a business call. From her questions, he guessed she was a salesperson or the owner. He'd never set foot inside a wedding store before and, having seen all this lace and frilly underwear, he was pretty sure he never would again. He had to admit that some of those cute bikini panties—nothing more than scraps of lace, really—were definitely appealing.

Would be even more appealing on a model. Red, for example. He just loved the way her eyes narrowed and sparked when he used that nickname. She'd certainly got him with that crack about not having a gown in his size. Drop-dead gorgeous and a sense of humor, he amended. What more could a man ask for?

The Bride's Curse

by

Glenys O'Connell

The Wedding Bliss Series

This is a work of fiction. Names, characters, places, and incidents are either the product of the author's imagination or are used fictitiously, and any resemblance to actual persons living or dead, business establishments, events, or locales, is entirely coincidental.

The Bride's Curse

Cover Art by *Jennifer Greeff*

The Wild Rose Press, Inc.
PO Box 708
Adams Basin, NY 14410-0708
Visit us at www.thewildrosepress.com

Publishing History
First Edition, 2021
Trade Paperback ISBN 978-1-5092-3604-6
Digital ISBN 978-1-5092-3605-3

The Wedding Bliss Series
Published in the United States of America

Dedication

To All Brides Everywhere

Chapter One

The silver bells above the door of Wedding Bliss jangled furiously, and Kelly Andrews looked up as a red-eyed and tearful young woman strode into the store. "I want you to take this dress back! The wedding's off!" Susie Lamont declared, thrusting a bulging cardboard dress box at the store owner.

Kelly managed to catch the box before its contents spilled out. Her heart thumped. *Good heavens, this can't be happening again!* Susie would be the third bride in as many months to return this dress, and Wedding Bliss had become a hot topic of conversation in the very worst way. A quiet life as a wedding planner in a small town should have been just what she needed to recover from her stint in the military. Now it looked like the drama was following her even here...

She pointed to the group of elegant Victorian dining chairs that stood near the center of the store. "Goodness, Susie, please sit down and tell us what's got you so upset." Kelly darted a pleading look at her assistant, Noelia Russo, as Susie perched on the edge of a chair. Matronly and calm, Noelia was much better at dealing with customer histrionics than Kelly, who tended to give out impatient *"get over it"* vibes which didn't play well with distressed customers.

Noelia suppressed a smile and stepped into the breach. "Yes, dear," she said. "I'm sure that whatever

1

the problem, we can help fix it. Your big day is only weeks away now! Kelly will go and get us some coffee or a nice herbal tea, and we'll see what we can do."

Kelly took the hint and dutifully escaped into the small office-cum-kitchen space at the rear of the store to put the kettle on for chamomile tea. She had heard that was the most soothing brew, and Susie looked like she needed something to calm her down. Kelly knew firsthand what it was like to be abandoned almost at the altar, and her heart went out to the young woman as she listened to Susie's loud complaints from behind the door. She gathered together three dainty china cups and their matching saucers and dropped chamomile tea bags in each just as Susie loudly proclaimed, "It's that dress. It's bad luck! Mark's having second thoughts about getting married. Everything was just fine until he saw me—he came in when I was trying on the wedding dress."

"Everyone knows it's bad luck for the groom to see—" Noelia started.

"Oh, pish. It wasn't our wedding day and anyway, it was an accident. I wasn't expecting him to come over that evening at all. The dress is so lovely, I just had to try it on with grandmother's pearls..." Susie hiccupped back a sob. "Besides, that's an old wives' tale; no one really believes it. So anyway, he was quiet the rest of the evening, and I thought it was just nerves, what with the wedding being in a couple of weeks. The next day, he phoned—can you believe that? The rat phoned to tell me he wanted to postpone the ceremony." Susie's voice went shrill with hurt. "He didn't even have the guts to tell me to my face."

Kelly shrugged to ease the mounting tension in her

shoulders. Yet another distressed bride had brought back that beautiful vintage wedding gown, insisting that the dress had destroyed her wedding dreams. Kelly had learned by personal experience that inexplicable things happened, that sometimes dark forces shadowed the world as we knew it. But surely it was insane to believe that an inanimate object, a lovely silk and lace designer gown, could have an evil curse attached to it. This whole issue was getting out of hand.

Listening as Susie broke out in a fresh bout of sobbing, Kelly sighed. She had never figured Susie's fiancé, Mark Turner, for a jerk—yet who but a jerk would break off a wedding just two weeks in advance? At least Mark had telephoned and told Susie the bad news himself; her own fiancé, Wayne, had called off their wedding with a brief note...

Noelia muttered soothing words to the distraught bride-to-be, and Kelly uttered a little prayer of thanks that her assistant was so good at consoling brides in crisis.

"Well, honey, I think you were right the first time—it's probably just pre-wedding nerves. Men do get a bit like that before their weddings. You know...all the pomp and everything, the fancy dresses and having to wear a suit and tie." Noelia's soft voice oozed reassurance. "I'll bet you anything he'll be coming around any day now to beg you to forgive him and go ahead with the wedding as planned "

"No, no, he won't. He's gone and signed up for a three-month contract as an engineer on a Mediterranean cruise ship. He's on a plane to Spain right now. Apparently, he wants to see the world rather than be tied down to marrying me."

Kelly's heart ached for the sad young woman. *What a terrible way for a romantic dream to end.* The kettle was whistling loudly, so she couldn't hide in the small back room any longer. She made the tea, added honey and a small jug of milk to the tray, and carried it through to the store. She offered a steaming cup to Susie and told her how sorry she was to hear what had happened. "I'm so surprised. I can't imagine what made Mark behave like that. I've always thought he was one of the good guys." It must have been the wrong thing to say because Susie started sobbing again. Noelia rolled her eyes at her boss while patting the young woman's shoulder.

Susie finally calmed down. Still sniffling, she pulled her pink fleece hoodie around her and took a few sips of tea. "That's the point, really. Mark is a good guy. None of this is his fault."

Susie took a few more sips of tea, and Kelly's stomach contracted at her next words. "It's that darn dress. There's something wrong with it! Everyone in town is talking about it. Everyone knows that two other brides had planned to wear that dress, and that both couples' wedding plans have fallen through. People said that dress was unlucky. You know what they're saying now? That wedding dress is cursed!" Susie's face turned red again, and she began to weep. Kelly's temper rose, and she fought off the sudden desire to slap the girl silly. How could anyone say something so terrible about such a beautiful gown?

"Now wait just a minute…" Kelly burst out, but she was silenced by a signal from Noelia. She knew the older woman was right. Where was the point in chewing the tail off some dumb blonde who'd rather blame an inanimate dress for her failed romance than take some responsibility herself? No doubt that confrontation would be all over town, too, and Wedding Bliss, the most popular one-stop store for wedding paraphernalia in the area, would soon lose enough customers to make the business go broke. Already this crazy sequence of coincidences was hurting their bottom line.

Kelly took a deep, calming breath, trying to ignore the little demon on her shoulder who muttered, "Three failed weddings where the bride wanted to wear that dress? Where there's smoke there's usually fire." Another meaningful glance from Noelia and Kelly clenched her teeth shut. She walked over to the elegant antique cupboard where the cash register stood and took out the store's checkbook from a small drawer.

"Susie, we are so sorry you are unhappy with your dress, even though we don't believe this lovely silk and lace garment is cursed. It's just a dress after all. Anyway, I am so sorry things aren't working out for you and Mark, and of course you can return it," she said in as gentle a voice as she could muster. "I have here a list of receipts from your account. You didn't have us as planners, did you?"

"No, my mom and Gran were doing all the arrangements," Susie said. "My gran is heartbroken because she wanted to see me get married, and she says she's not getting any younger. I did bring everything back—you'll find it all in the box."

"So, let me just take a quick look to make sure everything is okay, and then I'll make out a check for a full refund of everything you spent here. And please, feel free to come back and see us if things change and you and Mark decide to go ahead once he's done his traveling."

Noelia had already opened the box and pulled out the luxurious, oyster-silk dress, elbow length white organza gloves, a bridal garter, and a pretty little purse dotted with hand-sewn seed pearls. She handed the dress over to Kelly, who smoothed the gorgeous, soft fabric over her arm and checked for any stains or tears. Satisfied, she hung the gown up and finished filling out the check.

"Why don't you choose a pretty cami, just a little something to make you feel good? Relationship troubles can make a woman feel so bad about herself." Noelia held out a wispy silken camisole in palest pink. "Just a little gift from us in appreciation of you using Wedding Bliss." She aimed a not-so-gentle warning kick at Kelly's ankle before the store owner could explode with protest.

"That's so nice of you, Mrs. Russo, thank you," Susie said, slanting a sly, knowing smile at Kelly. "I'd advise you to get rid of that dress, though. Send it to a thrift store in some other town if you don't want to destroy it. No one around here would wear it now."

And she was gone, leaving Kelly grinding her teeth. "You rewarded that bimbo with a consolation prize for blaming Wedding Bliss for her screwed-up relationships while ruining our bottom line and our reputation by returning that dress? We really needed that sale." She pushed her long red hair out of her eyes as she glared at her assistant.

"Sweetie, this is a small town, and a business has to be known to be good for its customers or it won't survive. We treated that bimbo, as you call her, with kindness, and that'll get around town, too," Noelia replied serenely, sorting out the items Susie had returned and putting them on shelves.

"Yeah, it'll probably bring in every scam artist from miles around, looking for free silk underwear."

****

Kelly was still fuming silently when she glanced at her watch and gasped. She'd been so busy smoothing the frills and lace highlights of the lovely vintage gown, using a steam iron to gently set everything back in place, that she had almost made herself late for a meeting with one of their wedding planning clients.

"Noelia, can you hold down the fort while I dash over to St. Christopher's church? I have an appointment to talk to the church secretary and get some ideas for decorating for the Montoya wedding. Then I'm meeting Jane Parker, you know, last minute stuff for her wedding next month. We still haven't fixed on flowers or guest favors yet. I'll stop in at the *Marina Grove Telegraph* office afterward and sort out advertising for our new services, see if we can get them to do an affordable 'wedding bells' trade feature."

Noelia raised her eyebrows. "You've got a lot on your plate there, dear. And good luck with the *Telegraph*. Ken Bertram is a lazy old goat, and he'll probably have you running around doing his job for him, trying to get other businesses to take part in a trade supplement." Noelia grinned.

"Well, it might be worth it. We need to be pretty aggressive with our advertising—and slender with our budget—if this nonsense about the cursed dress keeps going."

Noelia turned to greet a young woman who was

just coming in the door. She offered a lovely warm, motherly smile that usually wowed their customers and asked, "Can I help you, dear?"

"I'm off," Kelly said. "Just lock up if I'm not back. See you tomorrow." With a pleasant smile to the newcomer, she dashed out the door.

****

Brett Atwell carried his morning coffee and a stack of old newspapers out to the patio behind his Aunt Mary's Derry mansion. He put both items down on a small table, nodded to his sister who sat on the bench opposite, and then raised his arms above his head to stretch muscles that were still stiff and aching from the long journey home. His last assignment had been working with a non-profit group in sub-Saharan Africa, and he'd flown back non-stop.

Brett loved his job, but there was no feeling in the world like coming home. He sat, stretching his long legs out in front of him, and sipped at the coffee. He savored the drink, enjoying this ritual of the first day back at home, and then opened the oldest newspaper. All the while he was aware of his sister's wary eyes on him. Sasha's behavior was the one irritant in his homecoming.

"So, big bro, are you going to sulk all morning? I told you I had no idea where that damned wedding dress had gotten to."

He wanted to ignore her, but she was, after all, his closest relative other than Aunt Mary, who had taken them both under her wing when their parents died. That didn't dilute his anger at his self-absorbed sister. "Sasha, couldn't you get your mind off yourself for a little while and see how Aunt Mary feels? Hell, after all these years being almost a recluse, you think it's okay to shove her off into a nursing home among strangers? Would it have killed you to take care of her for a while till she was over the pneumonia? And I wouldn't be surprised if you weren't behind that dress disappearing. Though, for the life of me, I can't see why. She's always asking for it, you know."

"Stupid wedding dress. I don't know why she'd want to even see it again after what happened, let alone be buried in it. It's not like she's going to die yet, anyway."

Brett shot her a glare then decided to ignore her. He and his sister had very different attitudes toward family. Sasha sniffed, her left hand playing with the belt on her silk robe. Something else that irritated her brother—he was a morning person, up and at 'em by seven at the latest. Sasha came awake and ready to party in the evening. *How could the same parents produce such different offspring?* he wondered as he folded the local newspaper over at the coming events page.

"You do know that paper is eons old, don't you? All those events are over and done. Why do you waste your time reading old news?"

He sighed. How many times had they had this conversation? "It's not old news to me, is it? I was away, and I like to catch up with what happened while I was gone. Now, are you going to tell me about that wedding dress? Thanks to all the time you left her in that home, Mary thinks she's really sick and going to die. That's why the dress is so important to her. She sincerely wants to be buried in it."

"Come on, Brett. I don't know why you're so

9

protective of her. Auntie Mary has always been a bit strange. Do you remember how she had us believing she was a witch when we were kids? And she had that spell book that she said had been in the family for ages and ages…"

He tried to ignore Sasha's insensitive snort of laughter, although it increased his inward anger. "Give her a break, Kelly. Aunt Mary has always been very good to us, even if she'd been a bit, well, fragile."

"You're kidding me, right? The old lady's as strong as an ox."

"How would you feel if you were in a nursing home with a lot of sick old people, strangers, and no one would tell you when you could go home?"

"She just had pneumonia, and I thought she would be better getting professional treatment…"

But Brett was no longer listening. He'd just run his eye down an advertisement for an estate auction that had taken place three months previously. One item caught his attention.

" 'Lovely vintage wedding gown in perfect condition.' Oh, Sasha, please tell me you didn't."

****

Kelly thought it odd, an old guy in a smart business suit sitting alone on a street bench right across the road from a wedding dress shop. His presence caught her eye as she left the store—it seemed a strange choice to sit here on the street when there was a lovely park right behind him. Was he waiting for someone? Or maybe the poor guy had just lost his job and was filling in time. Surely that would be more pleasant than sitting on the street bench, with a lot more to look at besides the commercial buildings.

He looked so sad and lost and somehow a bit creepy, the way he sat staring so hungrily through Kelly's store window at the bridal gown, honeymoon underwear, sexy garter belts, and other accessories. He didn't look the Dirty Old Man type, but she was pretty sure his presence wouldn't help potential customers feel comfortable enough to come into the store. But a quick check of the time reminded her she had lots to do before she could call it a day, and the old man and his troubles were forgotten as she drove away to her first appointment.

The early autumn day was unusually warm, and the air carried with it a tang of salt spray from the Atlantic Ocean as it waved softly toward Marina Grove bay. The small town on the Maine coastline was slowly settling toward winter as the tourist season ended, and Kelly was able to slip into a usually rare parking spot right in front of the *Telegraph* offices. They were situated right on the main street and faced the ocean across from the wharf where fishing boats were unloading the catch of the day.

She massaged the long scar above her hairline, a parting gift from a Taliban bomb. It ached when she was tired or stressed, and heaven knows, she was both right now. She took a few moments to try and gather her thoughts. This business with the so-called Cursed Bridal Gown was going to drive her crazy and possibly put her out of business. The worst thing was, she couldn't shake the thought that perhaps the gown really was cursed. It certainly wasn't improving her manner, which Noelia frequently told her tended to be a bit abrasive.

"You catch more flies with honey than with

vinegar," her assistant often said. Seemed vinegar was the only thing Kelly traded in at the moment.

Already she had offended the church secretary at St. Christopher's. The slight, gray-haired woman, Debra Moran, had jokingly said that she'd heard Kelly might need an exorcism for a wedding gown that was the talk of the town. Piqued, Kelly had quite nastily wondered aloud if it was blasphemous to joke about such matters in church. The secretary had gone about giving her the information she needed regarding the church's rules on wedding decorations in a tight-lipped, wounded manner.

Her day had continued its downhill slide. It seemed everyone she met had an opinion or a smart comment about the cursed dress. Some were serious, most were witty, but none made Kelly feel any better about the weirdness of it all. News travels fast in a small town. Especially weird news.

Then she had stopped in at the home of Jane Parker and her mother for a consultation on flowers and table favors. The bride-to-be licked her lips nervously as the mother suggested they should get a discount for using Kelly's services, given all the gossip going around.

"But you don't really believe in such stupid nonsense, do you?" Kelly had blurted incredulously, causing the bride's mother to spend the rest of their visit sulkily objecting to every suggestion Kelly made.

Finally, Jane put her foot down and insisted they choose from the flowers Kelly had suggested.

Her mother, a keen gardener, then went on to cast a malicious eye over the list of flowers and deliberately picked the most difficult blooms to find at that time of the year.

The meeting took so long that Jane, noting Kelly casting sly glances at the clock, apologized and asked her to leave the catalogs. "We'll get everything we want firmed up, and I'll be in touch by the end of the week," she promised.

Kelly waited until she was back in her car and out on the road again before she let loose a string of curses on the heads of everyone who thought the Cursed Bridal Gown was theirs to comment upon.

The *Telegraph* was her last stop of the day, and she reluctantly left the calm of her parked car and sought out the advertising manager, Ken Bertram. Her chat with him turned out to be the best thirty minutes of her day so far. He agreed to give Wedding Bliss prominence in a Winter/Spring Weddings trade feature he was planning; the price he named was reasonable and within budget. He even offered a two-column ad in that week's paper at a bargain price.

"Once you get the copy in here for the feature next month, I can get the graphics and layout guys to put the page together," Ken promised.

"I have some great photographs of brides and bridesmaids, as well as of wedding cakes and other items that you could probably use, too." Kelly pulled out a file stuffed with photographs from various wedding paraphernalia companies from her shoulder bag. "I have permission to use these for advertising purposes."

"That's great—less work for us." Ken rubbed his hands together gleefully. Kelly, remembering Noelia's comments about the guy being lazy, suppressed a grin.

Then he asked if she'd mind waiting a moment.

Kelly held her breath, expecting some smart-ass

jokes about the dress, but he merely walked into the outer office and spoke to the newspaper's secretary and general go-fer, Allie McInnis. Moments later, he came back with a smile, shook her hand, and asked if she would call in to the editorial department before she left the building.

Kelly assumed he wanted to have a journalist do a story piece to go with her advertising, which was a welcome surprise. She walked up the steep stairs into the dark, crowded office space where the editorial staff lurked. A small newspaper, the *Telegraph* had a skeleton staff and used a lot of freelance correspondents to fill its pages.

The last straw in her day came when a junior reporter dressed in baggy jeans and a Grateful Dead T-shirt bounced over to Kelly with an earnest puppy expression on his face, notebook clutched in his hand.

"Ms. Andrews? Mr. Bertram said you wanted us to do a story about that cursed wedding dress," the young man, Ronnie Catelli, said as he introduced himself.

Is that what everyone's calling it now? The Cursed Wedding Dress? Kelly was so angry she was sure steam would start hissing from her ears. "What do you mean?"

Ronnie reached for the pen that was lodged behind his ear, irritatingly unaware of the death glare Kelly aimed at him. "I hear that the gown has ruined the romantic dreams of several young couples?"

She dragged in a deep breath, counting to ten for patience. Not wanting to sully the innocence of one so young, she limited herself to a snarled "No" and left the building as quickly as she could before she really lost her temper and aimed some well-seasoned military phrases at him.

****

Kelly thankfully left her car in the small parking space in front of her cottage. She opened the newly painted blue front door of her home, breathing in the soothing atmosphere. Even before renovations, the little fisherman's cottage had held a welcoming feel that called to her. The cottage was only within her price range because it had needed lots of work, but to Kelly it was well worth the hours she had spent plumbing, scraping and sanding the original pine woodwork until it glowed, and painting the plastered walls with soft pastels. She'd added two big, comfortable armchairs and then haunted yard sales and secondhand stores to find vintage kitchen cupboards painted with faded blue milk paint, and a lovely, polished mahogany sideboard which served as a television and stereo stand.

She bent to rub the soft gray fur of Sullivan, the house feline, then paused to enjoy the graceful lines of the shallow staircase and breathe deeply of the salt-tanged breeze that filtered in through the slightly open windows. She loved to sit out on the large back verandah and watch the ever-changing moods of the sea. On hot nights, she slept with the windows open and a cool sea breeze playing over her as the sea's song lulled her to sleep.

Kelly had come to Marina Grove lured by happy memories of a long-ago childhood family holiday in the small seaside town, still a busy fishing port and tourist destination. Here, where no one knew her or her history, she sought healing from two terrible blows. She still had nightmares about the IED bomb blast that had ended her military career and taken the lives of several of her friends in her unit. The ambush had left her physically and mentally scarred, fighting for her life in a military hospital. Her fiancé's desertion during her recuperation had hardly caused a ripple in her emotions after that experience, but it still hurt.

Marina Grove hadn't let her down. As she had regained her physical and emotional health, she followed her dream to open Wedding Bliss, a one-stop wedding planning store to channel all the romantic yearnings of her heart. For other brides, that is. She doubted she would ever trust her heart to a man again.

Sullivan—a rescued tom cat with a checkered history written large in the scars he carried over his face and body—twined around her legs, alternately purring and reminding her with a soft meow that it was dinner time. She rubbed him behind his ears, producing a long, drawn-out purr of pleasure, then loaded his dish with cat chow and refilled his water bowl.

"It's nice to meet someone who doesn't want to lecture me or make jokes at my expense about a silly bridal gown," she murmured to the cat. Sullivan flicked his tail, dismissing her while he wolfed the food.

Kelly made her favorite late supper—a glass of wine, a cup of milky coffee, and a peanut butter and banana sandwich—and settled down on the verandah to watch the twilight glowing over the ocean. She pondered exactly what she was going to do about that dress. The lovely vintage gown that had become the Cursed Bridal Gown.

It was too beautiful to be destroyed or given away. Besides, she'd paid far too much for it at an estate auction in Derry. The jokes and comments were becoming irritating, and she just wished people would forget the whole thing. What really irked her was the negative effect it was having on her business's reputation.

Still, Kelly could understand people having some reservations about a gown that had been returned by three separate brides. With her degree in psychology, she knew people tried to explain things going wrong by finding scapegoats to blame, especially when those failures were very hurtful and seemingly without cause. It was called the Just World Syndrome. If you could blame something on someone's behavior or possessions and you didn't behave that way yourself or have the same possessions, you were safe from whatever bad thing had happened to the other person. A good theory, especially in this case.

But three different couples splitting up after they'd gotten as far as buying a wedding dress? Surely, that must be unusual, especially in a small town like Marina Grove. Given the fact all three brides had purchased that one gown, she could see where the gossip arose.

Kelly had never been superstitious herself and found it hard to believe a gown, especially a truly expensive and beautiful one, could possibly be cursed.

But then, she hadn't believed restless spirits existed, either, until she saw them for herself. She had woken in a hospital bed, disoriented and confused, after the bomb had exploded. She had been reassured to see several men of her unit standing around her bed. Snatches of questions the men were asking filtered through her brain, and she had been overwhelmed with a sense of helplessness before drug-induced sleep had once more claimed her.

It was only later, as Kelly healed, that she

discovered these men had died in the same ambush that had left her wounded. The doctors were quick to tell her a brain injury had left her with hallucinations that would pass as she healed.

Kelly wasn't at all sure she believed them. But she hoped with all her heart that they were right.

"But if dead friends can visit you, isn't it possible that a wedding gown could be cursed?" she asked Sullivan as he settled down to sleep on her feet. The cat answered with a gentle snore.

Chapter Two

Kelly sighed, closed the laptop, and pushed back from her desk. Doing the month-end accounts had never been her favorite part of business, but this was awful. She'd known business had been a bit slow, but the accounting software said it all. She rubbed her tired eyes and bit her bottom lip as she considered the figures she had just run. A comparison between last year and this showed that her business was unusually slow for the time of year.

Was it just that there were fewer brides in need of wedding planning services, or were the ugly rumors about the vintage dress that had become the Cursed Bridal Gown really keeping the customers away? Certainly, Kelly had fewer inquiries about Wedding Bliss's services, and the few drop-in customers had all seemed to want to eyeball "that dress" without buying anything.

Kelly believed the best way to fight gossip and misconception was to face it head on. First thing the next morning, dressed in jeans and an old sweater, she found herself scrambling about in the broad window of Wedding Bliss, reorganizing all the pretty trinkets so she could put the allegedly cursed dress out there for everyone to see.

Maybe if they could see the glorious antique silk and lace confection in the cold light of day all this weirdness about dark forces would come to an end. At least she hoped it would.

Those hopes were dashed as Noelia came in while she was putting the finishing touches to the scalloped hem and flowing train of the dress.

"What on earth are you doing?" The sharp question startled Kelly, and she stuck a pin in her thumb. Sucking the blood from the wounded digit, she climbed out of the window display and faced Noelia with a scowl.

"Look what you've made me do. I'm bleeding," she snapped, waving her hand around.

"What do you expect? Seems everything connected to that dress results in someone being hurt."

Kelly gaped at her assistant. The usually calm and competent Noelia was ruffled and dark-eyed with fatigue. "What are you talking about? The dress didn't prick my finger. I did after you startled me. Or maybe it was the pin that did it. Are you going to say the pin's cursed? Are we about to experience an invasion of cursed bloodletting pins now?"

She'd intended her words to be humorous, an attempt to disperse all this talk about hexes and other nonsense. Instead, they had the opposite effect. Noelia looked as if she was going to burst into tears.

"You need to get rid of that gown. I don't care what you say, Kelly, there's something wrong with it." Noelia blew her nose noisily, a ruse to stop her boss and friend from seeing she was close to tears.

Mortified, Kelly hugged the other woman. "Oh, Noelia, I'm sorry. I didn't realize how seriously you were taking all this. Come on, sit down, and I'll make us a cup of coffee. Then we'll talk this through."

A few minutes later, they sat facing each other on the Victorian dining chairs, coffee mugs in hand and a plate of Noelia's favorite chocolate digestive biscuits between them. "I know you think this is all too weird, Kelly, but I couldn't sleep for thinking about it last night. In Sicily, where my family comes from, people believe in the evil eye and other black magic. My grannie often talked about what it was like when she was a girl before the family came to America. Yes, I know, for an All-American twenty-first century girl, it's easy to dismiss these things, but the old people knew a lot. My grannie used to say there are more things in Heaven and Earth than this world dreams of."

Kelly bit her lip. If only she could tell Noelia, who was her friend as well as an employee, the truth about her own personal demons. Or spirits. For a brief moment, she was tempted to confide in the older woman about the Taliban bomb blast, the noise, the flying shrapnel, the choking dust, the cries, the pain…the visions. The moment passed before she could pull together the courage to try to explain the inexplicable.

"I keep thinking, over and over, what would happen to you if this store should go out of business? I know it means so much to you, much more than just a way to make a living." Noelia softened her words with a smile.

Kelly smiled back, but her eyes filled with tears at her friend's concern. "I hate to see you so upset. Tell you what… I'll put the dress way at the back of the store where only someone really looking will find it. That way, maybe if there is a curse, it will be the dress choosing the bride it wants to be worn by, and the unlucky spell will be broken."

Noelia nodded gratefully. "Put it way to the back, though. Hide it so it can't be found except by someone it chooses. I know you must think I'm a silly old broad, but—"

"Not at all. You're my friend, and I hate to see you upset. Are you sure the dress was the only thing you were losing sleep over? Are your children okay?"

That brought a big smile. "Yes, they're fine. I think Alex might announce his engagement soon. He's been going out with this lovely girl for a year now, and they're very good together."

Kelly smiled. "That's wonderful, really. Just know that Wedding Bliss's services will be there for you at a deep discount—like zero cost—when they're ready to tie the knot."

"That's very sweet of you. Thank you." Noelia snagged the last cookie, then gathered up the pretty china plate and cups to wash and put away in the small kitchen area in the store's back room.

True to her word, Kelly draped the vintage gown on a padded hanger and tucked it away in a shaded corner of the store farthest from the door.

"That's a good spot—no one can actually see the dress unless they're really looking. I just hope that dress is out of here before—"

The silver bells above the door jangled as a customer came in, and Noelia's words were lost.

The customer was model slim, her dark hair perfectly styled in the just-out-of-bed fashion that takes hours to arrange and wearing a designer suit.

Oh my gosh, look at the red soles on her shoes! Kelly was so busy wondering how anyone could walk in those heels that she jumped when Noelia nudged her and whispered, "Customer alert."

As if she read Kelly's mind, the newcomer grinned and said, "I know what you're thinking…it takes practice not to fall off these heels. I can't wait to get home and put on my flip flops."

Feeling dowdy in her dusty jeans and sweater, Kelly appreciated the young woman's sense of humor. "One of the joys of small-town living is people actually think you're being uppity if you dress too well." She felt a blush climb up her cheeks as she realized her words could be misinterpreted as a criticism of the other woman's dress.

But obviously this smart young woman was far too self-assured to take offense. She held out her hand to Kelly and then to Noelia. "I'm Daria Welcome, and my company, Welcome Home Realty of Derry, is representing a group of developers negotiating to buy the old cannery building."

Developers were looking at the old disused cannery? Visions of sprawling housing and commercial developments came to Kelly's mind. Such a project would change the quaint nature of the town she loved.

"They're going to develop the cannery? What are you planning on constructing?"

Daria smiled reassuringly. "You must be Kelly Andrews, the owner of that lovely little cottage I pass on the way into town? I've watched over the past few months as you've completed the renovations. It's a jewel now."

"Thank you. It's coming along but still a work-in-progress. But what's going to happen at the cannery? I know it's an eyesore but…"

Daria raised her hand. "Don't worry—we're looking to gentrify the building and create some beautiful condominium apartments. It will probably increase the value of properties in the area rather than diminish it."

"Well, that's a relief. I think the government has owned that building since…er…"

"Since the previous owners' demise?" That thousand-watt smile again. "Yes, the government did take the cannery and other portions of the Peterson family estate after they were indicted for money laundering. The Feds are not the easiest of clients to negotiate with, I can tell you." Daria rolled her eyes. "I'm spending a lot of time here in Marina Grove, searching records, reading reports, and overseeing contractors and architects. You're not thinking of selling your cottage, are you?"

The question came out of left field, and Kelly blinked before answering. "Not for a moment. I love that old house."

"I can see why. Anyhow, that's not why I'm here. I'm getting married at Christmas, and I'm looking for the perfect gown."

Kelly's smile widened. "Come and take a seat, and we'll discuss what you're looking for. We offer a range of gowns of different styles, including some beautiful vintage dresses from top designers. We are also able to arrange every aspect of your wedding, right down to party favors, mementos for the reception guests, flowers. You name it, we do it."

"Sounds like I've come to the right place—I know what I want, but the details are so time consuming. I could use some help." Daria smoothed the back of her skirt and sat on one of the delicate antique chairs.

"Could I get you a drink while you're chatting?" Noelia asked.

"A decaf latte would be nice."

Noelia suppressed a grin. "I'm sorry—we have a pot of regular coffee on the brew. The boss hasn't yet shelled out for a classier coffee maker."

Kelly flushed and Daria laughed. "That's okay. I probably shouldn't have coffee among all these beautiful gowns and things—I can be a bit klutzy." She turned to Kelly. "I'm looking for that very special dress. The one everyone is talking about…"

Kelly heard Noelia's sharp intake of breath. Remembering her promise to keep the dress out of easy view, she replied, "Why don't you start by taking a spin around the store and looking at all the gowns, get some idea of what you're really looking for."

Daria raised one questioning eyebrow, but gracefully stood and walked around the store. She was obviously a woman who knew what she wanted. She quickly viewed and discarded several dresses. She seemed drawn to the back-wall alcove where Kelly had hidden the Cursed Bridal Gown.

Noelia, frowning, quickly stepped forward to redirect her. "Are you looking for a de la Renta gown? I noticed your suit…"

"Yes, he has beautiful designs. I've looked at his wedding styles, but I do really want a vintage gown. Like that one over there…"

Daria crossed the room and stepped around Noelia as she headed for the spot where Kelly had hidden the dress as if drawn there by an invisible string. "Oh, it really is beautiful." Her brown eyes glowed as she fingered the soft silk. "This is it, isn't it? The gown everyone is talking about?"

"You don't want that one—it's cursed!" Noelia blurted out. For a split second, Kelly wanted to throttle her assistant.

But Daria was unfazed. "I don't believe in curses. Anyway, Drake and I have been together a long time. Our relationship is too grounded for some silly rumor about witchery to affect us."

Kelly took a deep breath of relief. Together with the work in hand, this sale—and any additional services Daria wanted—would put their bank account out of the danger zone. She studiously ignored Noelia's expression of horror and suggested Daria try the dress on.

The other woman glanced at her watch. "Darn, I've got a meeting in twenty minutes. I'm staying at the Captain's House B & B, the former Peterson place. Could you bring the dress over to me tomorrow afternoon? I'll try it on, and you can arrange to do whatever alterations are necessary then…" She stopped speaking as she saw the expressions on the faces of the other two women.

Kelly was the first to speak. "Captain's House?" she stammered.

"Yes, I know about the murders that took place there. Cal Peterson shot his son's lover, the boy turned the gun on himself, and then the old man had a massive coronary. It's a terribly sad story, but the family was deeply involved in organized crime and, well, I guess violence begets violence. Anyhow, like I said, I'm not superstitious about curses and things that go bump in the night."

Kelly swallowed. If ever a place was haunted, it was surely the Captain's House. Long before the tragedy Daria referred to, there were all kinds of rumors about the place and the happenings there, including the suspicious death of one of the early Peterson wives. She wasn't keen to test her status as a magnet for the restless dead, but for a sale of this size she'd gladly walk into the first ring of Hell. Kelly tried to keep the reluctance out of her voice as she agreed to meet with Daria the next afternoon at two o'clock.

"One other thing. While I don't believe in curses, I do think that sometimes bad memories leave their mark behind. Your store gives every indication something bad may have happened here in the past. The entryway feels so chilled. Has anyone mentioned the depressing atmosphere?" Seeing Kelly's stormy look, she hastily added, "I didn't mean to offend you or anything—the store is lovely. I've worked a lot with old buildings, and sometimes they get, well, a feel to them. Maybe you should have a look at the history of this place."

And she was gone, in a whiff of expensive perfume and the clack of designer heels.

Kelly and Noelia sank down on the elegant Victorian chairs, both looking shell-shocked.

"Whoa! That woman's like a whirlwind through your head," Noelia declared.

Kelly just nodded. Relief mingled with apprehension.

After all, she had arranged to meet that whirling dervish tomorrow in a house where very bad things had happened. Had the three victims left the impression of their rage and fear and grief in the walls of the old mansion? Or would their restless spirits recognize

Kelly's special gift and seek to communicate through her?

****

Kelly clambered back into the store window. It looked untidy and bare since she had given in to Noelia's request to remove the vintage wedding gown. She would have to revamp it with another gown and some more wedding paraphernalia.

She shivered as she began her work—maybe the afternoon sun had gone behind a cloud or something because it did seem chilly. A tingle ran down her spine as she recognized that the elderly man was again sitting on the street bench across from the store. He was dressed in a classy looking business suit and seemed to be staring directly in the window at her. A chill enveloped her as she looked at him. He'd been there several times over the past few days, and she wondered if he was new to town and lonely.

Then he disappeared from her mind as the mother of one of the brides whose wedding she was planning came into the store to discuss mother of the bride dresses. After nearly an hour looking at catalogs, magazines, and designer sketches, and discussing what the most appropriate wear was for a middle-aged woman who wanted to look glamorous but didn't want to look like she was trying to upstage the bride, they finally settled on a robin's egg blue linen dress with a matching jacket.

The delighted customer arranged an appointment to come in for a fitting when the clothes arrived, then asked Kelly to put together a selection of jewelry and accessories for her to try as well.

Another happy customer! Kelly was about to return

to her window dressing when the woman turned at the door and said, "You know, it's awfully cold in here—maybe you have the air conditioning turned up too high?"

Kelly stared at her departing figure. It was at least eighty degrees outside, unusually warm for early autumn. Why was it so cold in here? She wrote a quick note asking Noelia to get the furnace guy to check that it wasn't blowing too cold, then slipped her lightweight jacket on, gathered up her briefcase, a pile of brochures and catalogs, and headed out the door.

She was actually going to get home at a reasonable hour for a change. Her gaze was drawn to the empty street bench as she crossed the road. Maybe that old man was having an early night, too.

Chapter Three

He was there again the next morning.

Almost all her customers were female, and Kelly was sure they would react to the old guy's cold gaze in the same way she was—with a shiver. There was something about that concentrated intensity, and the poor man looked so pale…

Sometimes she considered her job to be a bit like the spider and the fly—she created an enticing display in her window and the clients came in and got stuck in a web of beautiful wedding things. But that was the key—first she had to get them to venture into her web.

She seriously doubted that this old man was planning a romantic wedding and unforgettable wedding night. Despite his good grooming, he looked tired and thin, as if he'd been ill for some time.

Maybe she should call the sheriff. She knew Selma Francis wouldn't mind popping over and having a word with the man, just to see what his fascination was with Wedding Bliss and to encourage him to find another perch. Selma had been one of her customers, purchasing some ravishing honeymoon wear from the store earlier in the year. The two women had become friends, and Kelly knew the law officer was capable of talking to the stranger firmly without giving offense.

As she dithered about what to do, Kelly saw yet another customer stop and gaze in the window, move to come inside, and then hesitate, glance around toward the bench, and walk away. *That did it!* She had to do something. Her military training had taught her how to handle difficult situations, but this wasn't some dusty town in Afghanistan. This situation needed tact and gentle diplomacy, which Noelia had pointed out once or twice wasn't really Kelly's strong point. Still, not really being the sort to run off to authority figures, having not always seen eye to eye with authorities herself, she decided to go out and tackle the man on her own. Surely he'd understand if she explained the situation to him calmly?

She poured two cups of hot free trade coffee, liberally doused them with cream, and carried both out to the bench. On closer inspection, the old man seemed younger than he'd first looked. His skin had that kind of pallor that goes with long term poor health, and Kelly felt suddenly guilty about her mission. After all, if he was convalescing and enjoying sitting out here in the sun, what harm was he doing?

She almost turned around and headed back into Wedding Bliss when the old man spoke. His voice sounded rusty and unused, but his question startled her. "Why did you take the dress out of the window? I thought that woman had returned it."

Kelly slopped hot coffee down her shirt as she stared in shock. A shiver ran through her as he made no attempt to take the coffee mug she offered him. "What happened to the dress?" he repeated.

"Why?" she asked, a tremor in her voice. "Did that dress catch your eye? We have many more inside that are just as lovely."

Without looking at her, he answered. "But that one

is special. It's the only one that will do."

"Are you planning a wedding? For your son or daughter, perhaps?"

Still he didn't look at her. "No. But a good friend of mine—someone I once wronged…"

Kelly drew in a deep breath. This really wasn't going as she'd planned, and now she wished she'd waited until a time when Noelia was in the store. The older woman definitely had better people skills. Suddenly, the scar on her temple began to ache, the forerunner of the blinding headaches she'd suffered from time to time ever since she'd been wounded. She slopped more coffee as she tried to hold two cups in one hand while pressing the other to her head.

He finally turned to look at her then, as if he knew she was in pain. "It will go away." His voice, though still rusty, held an unexpected kindness.

"You need to go away!" There was something off about this man—how had he known about the pain in her temple? He gave her the serious creeps, and what little ability she had to be tactful had flown. "You're upsetting customers coming into my store, staring at them as you do…"

Out of the corner of her eye, she saw a tall young man dressed in jeans and a denim shirt enter Wedding Bliss. Not the usual kind of customer for her store. The store was empty because Noelia was taking the morning off, so she had better go and see what he needed. She turned back to repeat to the old man that he had to go away, but he was already gone. He'd left quietly while she was struggling with the sudden headache, she guessed.

Warily, she stood from the bench, feeling woozy.

She hadn't had one of these headaches for a long time, but when they happened she sometimes lost her balance and fainted. The pain seeped away as she walked back toward the store, and by the time she stepped inside, much to her relief, it had gone altogether.

****

Kelly blinked to adjust her eyes to the store's interior after being out in the bright sunlight. She pushed the old man on the bench out of her mind as she stepped forward to introduce herself to the young man who stood in the middle of the store. He looked befuddled by all the lovely frilly, lacy, silky things.

"Good morning. I'm Kelly Andrews. Can I help you find what you're looking for?"

He turned and gave her a friendly smile. Kelly was momentarily dazzled. This guy was hot. Older than she first thought, probably thirty or so, with blond hair and the kind of tan you only get from working outdoors. Briefly she wondered if he'd been in the military like herself, but nothing else about him suggested being in the armed forces.

His eyes widened as looked her up and down, and he gave a low, appreciative whistle through his teeth. "Well, hello there, Red!"

The dazzle swiftly turned to irritation. No one had mocked her red Scottish coloring since she was old enough to make them wish they had never tangled with her. Setting down the mugs and tucking an unruly curl behind her ear, she sidled forward until they were almost nose to nose. Then she rose up on tiptoe, her mouth close enough to his ear that her breath tickled his skin and murmured, "The last guy who called me that is still in the hospital."

His deep brown eyes widened. Then he laughed a low, deep, sexy sound. "Sweetheart, I love a woman with red hair and the temperament that goes with it."

She stepped back a pace and gave him a feral smile. Obviously, he wasn't intimidated by her threat. *The fool.*

"So, all flirting aside, can I help you with something?"

The slow, lips to feet and back again appraisal he gave her made her palms itch to thump him. She reminded herself of Rule #1 of business: Do not slap customers.

"I'm looking for a wedding dress."

"Oh!" Laughter licked through her like a sudden rain. She returned the long, slow, head to toe and back again stare. "I'm not sure we have anything in your size. Maybe your partner…?"

He actually blushed. "No, it's not for me—" He stopped when he saw her laughing. In fact, Kelly was laughing so hard she had to drop onto one of the chairs.

"Oh, lord—you should have seen your face! Gotcha!" *Revenge is so sweet.*

He grinned. "I suppose I deserved that, Red."

"Keep on with the Red, and you'll see the nasty side of me."

Brett Atwell was tempted to say he'd like to see any side of her at all, this drop-dead gorgeous woman who'd followed him into the store. His busy imagination conjured up images of all that lush red hair spread across his pillow like wildfire…

"You're staring."

Oops. He needed to shake himself out of the lust that had swamped him and to focus on the job at hand.

It wasn't like him to let his mind wander, but then it wasn't every day he met a woman who appealed to him like this one did.

Brett tore his thoughts away from the swell of attraction that had caught his breath. This was a business call. From her questions, he guessed she was a salesperson or the owner. He'd never set foot inside a wedding store before and, having seen all this lace and frilly underwear, he was pretty sure he never would again. He had to admit that some of those cute bikini panties—nothing more than scraps of lace, really—were definitely appealing.

Would be even more appealing on a model. Red, for example. He just loved the way her eyes narrowed and sparked when he used that nickname. She'd certainly got him with that crack about not having a gown in his size. Drop dead gorgeous and a sense of humor, he amended. *What more could a man ask for?*

"When you've finished staring at those bridal garters…"

"Those what…?" Her question had brought him back to the present and to his purpose for being in the bridal shop.

"Bridal garters. They're the things brides…"

"I know what they are," he cut in hastily, wondering just how explicit her description was going to be.

"Okay, so you don't want a wedding dress for yourself. Most grooms don't shop for the dress for their bride, so I'm assuming you're not actually looking to buy a gown. Why, exactly, are you here?" Those blue eyes threw off sparks again, and he had to shake himself to concentrate on the matter at hand. Her long-suffering sigh made it obvious he'd better get down to business, and quickly. Who knew what a red-haired woman like her might do if she lost her temper?

The very thought was toe-curlingly delicious in its possibilities.

Red was now at the arms folded, toe-tapping stage. "Would you please stop standing there like you've been turned into a pillar of salt and tell me what I can help you with? You do realize, don't you, that this is a store? It's a place where people come to look for things they want to buy, and if the store owner—that would be me—is lucky, they will actually buy something. Now, are we clear on that?"

"I'm not actually looking to buy anything…"

"Then maybe you should leave. There's a big box store on the highway. They're a bit more sympathetic to people who are just looking to browse."

"I am looking for a wedding gown—just not to buy. This one was bought illegally…"

He could have bitten off his tongue. *What a stupid thing to say!* He could almost see Red blowing steam out of her ears. Why couldn't he stop looking at her like a lovesick schoolboy and kick his mind into gear?

Very quietly—dangerously quietly—she asked, "Are you saying that I illegally procured a wedding gown? That I *stole*—"

"No, it's not that at all."

"Well, fella, you'd better explain exactly what you do mean and what you want from my store. You've got ten seconds…" She glanced at the wall clock, and he got the impression she really was counting those seconds. "Nine…"

"It's a long story. My aunt had this wedding dress.

It's old, and she hadn't seen it in years. Well, my sister, Sasha, she got it into her head that she should sell some of my aunt's stuff. You see, she's going through a divorce and a bit short of cash. My aunt wasn't there at the time. She's in a home and…"

Red stopped tapping her foot and pointed to the door. Stepping right up into his space, she spoke slowly as if she thought him slow on the uptake. "Too. Much. Information. We're not a charity. I don't want to hear your sob story about your aunt. I don't know what your game is, but I think you need to get back to your crazy-sounding family. Or simply get out of my store. Now."

That frown line between those blazing blue eyes told him that she meant what she said. It would be a whole lot safer for him to leave now and come back later when she'd calmed down and he'd got his equilibrium back. Maybe then he could manage to string a proper sentence together. Then again, when had he ever played things safe?

Without even thinking, he gathered her into his arms and captured her mouth in a sizzling kiss. Taken by surprise, she struggled momentarily and then seemed to melt against him, causing his pulse to race.

Then she pushed herself away, both hands on his chest, and snarled, "Why you…you…!"

Seeing her speechless, which he guessed was rare for her, he grinned. He could have sworn sparks flew from that fiery red hair. "I'm Brett Atwell. Here's my card. Maybe we can discuss this further over a drink…?" He placed a small business card on the walnut cupboard by the cash register and picked up one of her cards from the small silver box there. *Kelly Andrews, Wedding Planner.*

"Out!"

"Maybe dinner? Call me. I'm not a man to back down from a challenge." He grinned. "See you later, Red," he said and chuckled at her snort of irritation as he left the store.

****

When Noelia arrived to start work after lunch, she found Kelly scrubbing out the storeroom. Boxes and other stored items were spread out all over the backroom/kitchen area.

"What on earth are you doing?"

"Cleaning out all this junk and rubbish—what does it look like I'm doing?"

"Hallelujah, Hell has finally frozen over."

"You think you're so very funny, don't you?" Kelly, scowling, finally emerged from the small room. Her appearance brought another smile to Noelia's lips. Kelly's clothes and face were streaked with dust, and a long cobweb draped her curly ponytail.

"Whatever prompted this?" Noelia reached over and swatted the web.

"Good lord, I hope its resident wasn't at home." Kelly started running her hands through her hair in search of a recently evicted spider.

"So I take it something happened to upset you." Noelia moved over toward the coffee pot and had poured them both a strong brew before Kelly finally answered. How could she explain the idiot who'd been in her store, claiming to look for a stolen wedding dress and accusing her of being a criminal? A gorgeous, dazzling idiot who had called her Red and sent her pulse into overdrive with one raised eyebrow? Oh, and that kiss. Who could forget that kiss? Kelly brushed her fingers across her lips, still feeling the tingle that Brett's mouth had left there.

Noelia instantly noticed the pink flush that trailed across Kelly's cheeks. "Come on, spill the beans, missy." The older woman handed her a mug. "You're blushing. And you only do cleaning and sorting like that when you're really peed off with someone or something. Otherwise, you just throw more stuff in on top of the stuff that's already there and slam the door shut."

"Very funny. There was a guy in here…"

"A guy, hmm? And in a wedding shop, too. Fancy that. Was he a groom?"

"Are you going to let me tell this story or what? I was out there trying to persuade that old guy who sits on the bench and stares in our window to get lost, when I saw this tall, hunky kind of guy come into the shop. So I came in after him and found him staring at the honeymoon undies like he'd never seen panties before in his life." Although she was willing to bet that man had seen his fair share of panties—or if not, it wasn't for want of ladies offering. She reached over and picked up the card he'd left. Brett Atwell. Just a name and cell phone number. Obviously a guy who didn't give much away. *And one who liked a challenge…*

"Looking at the lingerie? The nasty beast! I hope you gave him what-for!" Noelia stifled a giggle.

"I did indeed. I asked him what he wanted, and he said, 'A wedding dress.' I pointed out that he was a hard size to fit."

"You didn't!" Noelia chose a chocolate-covered biscuit and began to nibble.

"He went all red and stammered a bit. Then he said

he really was looking for a wedding gown that had been purchased illegally. He was calling me a thief!"

Noelia's coffee mug stopped halfway to her mouth, and she looked open-jawed at Kelly. "He didn't!"

"He did. And he called me Red."

"Holy smokes, honey—do you want help burying the body?"

"I wish! I just threw him out. Oh no—is that the time? I'm supposed to meet Daria Welcome in forty-five minutes and look at the mess I'm in!"

****

Forty-two minutes later Kelly parked her car in the gravel apron at the front of the Captain's House Bed and Breakfast. She got out with her arms full of catalogs and samples and a cardboard dress box slung over one shoulder. She paused for a moment to stare up at the mansion's cold gray stone façade. It was a magnificent building that a wealthy and powerful man, a sea captain involved in slavery, had once built for his bride. History had always interested Kelly. Since moving to the town, she had attended several Marina Grove Historical Society meetings and enjoyed reading books about the small town's past life.

So much of that history revolved around the men who had grown rich and influential on the natural resources of the area. She knew a lot about the Captain's House and about the tragic deaths barely a year ago as Federal agents closed in on the family's illegal activities. But stories about the Petersons went back to the very beginning of Marina Grove. The very first Peterson, a legend in the town because of the great wealth he had accrued from local resources, was said to have been so angry with his first wife that he threw her to her death from one of the tall upper windows. If ever a place had restless spirits looking for a living soul to aid them, it would be this house. She shivered just thinking about it and wondered if there was any way for her and her gift—or curse—to go unnoticed there.

Chapter Four

"You look absolutely beautiful!"

Kelly smiled as she watched Daria Welcome swirl elegantly in front of the cheval glass. It was true—the vintage gown fit Daria as though it had been made for her. The oyster silk brought out the woman's creamy, dark coloring, and the style deliciously hugged the curves of her slender figure. "Your fiancé won't be able to say 'I do' and get that ring on your finger quickly enough when he sees you in this. That is, if he doesn't trip over his own tongue."

Daria laughed. "I had a funny feeling that this was the gown I wanted before I even saw it, just from hearing everyone talk about how beautiful it was." She turned this way and that, a smile playing on her lips as she admired the effect in the mirror. Even without her makeup, Daria was a beautiful woman; her slender figure and sweet curves showed the elegant gown off to perfection.

"Even though they also said it was cursed?" Kelly questioned as she knelt to straighten the short train that flowed from the back of the dress to pool softly on the floor.

"Ah! Like I said, I don't believe in that stuff. I do believe that strong emotions can leave an imprint in places and on objects, but they're only echoes of the past. Echoes that can be changed or overlain with happiness, joy, and love. Which is exactly what Drake and I have together."

"Doesn't it worry you that three other brides who had wanted to wear that gown didn't even make it as far as the altar?"

Daria snorted. "If a little thing like a bad vibe from a dress split them up, then perhaps it was better it happened before they were married. Why not just look for a different dress? Sounds like the relationships weren't strong enough anyway to go the distance."

Kelly wanted to hug the woman for her sheer common-sense approach. "Well, thank you for that. You don't know how much you've lifted my spirits. All this talk about curses and dark forces at work in a gown I bought because I loved it, well, it's been getting me down a bit.

"On the subject of spirits, you obviously are sensitive to atmosphere. So how on earth do you cope with staying in this place?" Kelly waved her hand to indicate the Captain's House.

Daria reluctantly slipped out of the dress and dressed again in the tailored slacks and expensive-looking silk blouse she'd been wearing when Kelly arrived. The woman surely had good taste, Kelly thought. Daria continued as she brushed out her wavy dark hair. "Funny enough, most of this house has a wonderful atmosphere. I think that's due to the lovely couple who run it. Have you met Cheryl and Bo? They got married late in life, and they are so obviously in love. I believe their happiness has transformed this house. Except..."

"Except?" Kelly paused in the process of carefully putting the dress on its hanger and waited for her to go on. "I mean, have you felt anything weird around the house? Maybe in the front foyer?"

Daria gave her a long, considering look. "You mean around the entrance to the room that was once the study? Did you know that's where, well, where it all happened? They've changed it into a library and sitting room for guests, but no one ever seems to go there." She gave a delicate little shudder. "Myself, I avoid it like the plague."

Kelly was pretty sure she would avoid that spot, too. She'd felt a sense of cruel cold as she'd walked into the house where the tragic story had unfolded—after all, three people had died violently. She would have liked to ask Daria more about her philosophy, but they were interrupted by a sharp knock at the door.

"That must be Cheryl or Bo. I hope you don't mind. I asked if we could have a light late lunch in my room so that we could finish discussing whatever else might be needed."

"Wow—that's nice of you." It was after three o'clock, and Kelly's stomach announced loudly and embarrassingly that it had been a long time since breakfast. She was famished.

Daria grinned and opened the door to admit a tall woman with gray-streaked dark hair who pushed a tea trolley into the room.

"This is Cheryl, who runs this beautiful place." Daria made introductions as Cheryl greeted Kelly with a warm smile that changed her face from ordinary to beautiful. "It's so nice to meet you, dear. I have heard so many good reports about your store and the lovely things you sell."

"Thank you so much for that." Kelly could have

hugged the other woman. "We've been having some difficulties lately, so it's nice to hear a kind word."

"Oh, that will pass," Cheryl replied confidently as she placed a selection of tiny sandwiches, fruit, and some cupcakes on a small table under the window. She accompanied it with some crockery and silverware, linen napkins, and a flask of hot coffee.

She stood back to study the display, then turned to Daria. "I hope this is enough for you. If there's anything else, just give me a call," she said as she left the room with a friendly invitation to "Enjoy!"

"Isn't she wonderful? I understand she used to be the housekeeper here before everything blew up. If I thought I had a ghost of a chance, I'd try and lure her away to be the housekeeper in the home Drake and I are having built." Daria seemed to notice Kelly's wince at her phrase 'a ghost of a chance' and grinned. "Just a figure of speech. I guess a lot of people are sensitive to what happened here."

"A bit of a silly reaction, I know. It's just that what happened was, well, not something that goes on much in a small town like this. I think it shocked everyone to the core. Anyway, good luck with trying to lure her away. She seems happy enough here, and she's certainly doing a wonderful job."

Half an hour later the table was littered with empty cups, plates, and cupcake wrappers, and Kelly had a notebook full of ideas to explore for Daria's wedding— including lists of items such as flowers and bridesmaids' gifts.

"I'm still amazed that the dress needs no alterations at all. All three brides who tried it on have fit into it well enough and would have needed only minor alterations, but I say again, it could have been made for you. It doesn't need even the slightest tuck or hem. It's by a famous Parisian designer—I should have brought the note that was in the box with it when I bought it because I can't remember the name offhand."

"I'd be interested in seeing that. Drake and I are meeting up this weekend to finalize our plans for the wedding date and location. I can't believe how many small details are involved in such a simple ceremony." Daria walked to the door with Kelly.

"That's what wedding planners are for—to take as much of the burden as possible off your shoulders so you're still able to smile as you walk down the aisle."

****

Kelly managed to scurry from the Captain's House without encountering any of the shades that might be lurking there. Once outside, she took a deep breath of the salt sea air. Perhaps Daria was right and such things were only echoes of the past. Her own experience with restless spirits didn't support that theory, though.

It was good to be back in the calm of Wedding Bliss. Her next appointment with the realtor Daria would be at the store where there was no danger of running into any of the insubstantial figures she glimpsed from time to time. Or at least she hoped that would be the case. She had the awful feeling that one day one of these visions would have the strength to actually make contact and demand something of her. The very thought made icy shivers scamper up and down her spine. She comforted herself with the thought that she had not seen any apparitions in the two years since she'd moved to Marina Grove. "Maybe the doctors were right. Maybe these really were some sort of weird hallucinations," she muttered to herself. But she didn't believe a word of it.

Kelly told her assistant all about her visit to Daria's room, censoring out her anxieties about ghostly figures that could have been lurking in the hallways of the Captain's House. Noelia exclaimed in delight about how well the gown had fit the young woman, and how happy the client had been with the purchase. Noelia's smile grew even broader when Kelly outlined the details of the lucrative wedding planning contract Daria had signed.

"Well done!" the other woman said, hugging Kelly. "That calls for a celebration. Tea, or coffee?"

Kelly laughed. "What? No champagne?"

"Earl Grey or Colombian, that's the best offer today. But I'll sweeten the deal with chocolate cookies!"

While Noelia prepared their celebratory coffee, Kelly busied herself filling out her notes and checking her calendar so as not to miss any deadlines. Despite the problems with that dratted gown and the fall off in people wanting to plan spring weddings, Wedding Bliss was busy enough with nuptials already arranged. Winter weddings seemed popular these days, and several brides were planning to tie the knot before New Year's. They also had two Christmas nuptials. Kelly loved these weddings when the events were made even more special because of the season. Even the possibility of snow and the unpredictable weather didn't detract from the romance of those Yuletide days.

They had just sat down to enjoy the break when a young woman and an older lady who looked like mother and daughter had paused to look in the window.

They appeared to be discussing the 1930s gown that was displayed there and which would look fabulous on the girl, Kelly thought. She crossed her fingers that they'd be interested enough to come into the store.

Then the two of them seemed to shiver as if a cold breeze hit them. They turned and walked quickly away. Noelia and Kelly exchanged puzzled looks.

"It must have gotten suddenly colder out there," Noelia suggested.

But the same cold breeze blew over Kelly, and a strange feeling that they weren't alone prickled at the back of her neck. "Darn it!" she exclaimed, looking out of the window to see the old man was once more sitting on the bench, gazing in at Wedding Bliss.

"That's it! He's wrecking our business," she snarled. She made for the door as Noelia looked up from the orders she was writing.

"Who are you talking about? Not that young man who calls you Red?"

"No, not him." Kelly surprised herself by thinking it would be nice to see him. He gave her shivers of a different kind. "It's that old guy out there on the bench—the one I told you about who sits looking in our window."

Noelia joined her at the window, standing on tiptoe and craning her neck to look out over the window display. "I can't see anyone."

"He's right there on the bench. You'd think he had a mortgage on it, the time he spends there."

Noelia looked again, and then back at Kelly, her expression puzzled. "Honey, there's no one there. The bench is empty."

"I guess he must have sneaked off while we

were…no, he's there. Can't you see him? Push the dress aside a little so that…"

"Really, there's no one there. Maybe the sun is in your eyes and casting shadows?"

Kelly stared, first at Noelia and then at the bench. She could see the old guy as clearly as day. Noelia couldn't see anyone on the bench at all.

That could only mean one of two things. Either she was going crazy or the old guy was a ghost. The first she'd seen since moving to Marina Grove. Her hopes that this was over were dashed.

Kelly shivered and fought back tears. The very idea of these visions starting over again depressed the heck out of her. There was only one way to find out if he was flesh and blood or not. She slipped her short velvet jacket on against the cool breeze and left the store to walk briskly over to the bench.

The old man didn't look up as she approached, but as soon as she stood before him he greeted her in that same rusty sounding voice. "I wondered if you'd come out."

Kelly thought the voice sounded fainter than the first time she'd heard it, and still he didn't look at her as she sat down beside him. Kelly was horribly conscious of Noelia's worried gaze from across the road, and she spoke to the man in barely a whisper.

"I don't know who you are, but just say what you want and go away!"

He was silent for so long she would have thought he had gone if it hadn't been for his pale presence on the bench. And he was getting paler. Stranger and stranger. She now recognized that he was an apparition, and she startled when he finally spoke.

"I want some help. Once, a long time ago, I hurt two people I loved very much. Now I need to make it right…before I leave." The sorrow in his voice tore at Kelly's heart, and her eyes filled with sudden tears for the old man.

"Does this have something to do with that wedding dress you were so fixated on?" Already her anger at him was dissipating, but she had to get to the bottom of why he was there before his presence ruined her business.

"Yes, it does…" His words were cut off as he disappeared before her very eyes. Coming along the sidewalk was Brett Atwell, the hunky guy who wasn't afraid of consequences. The consequences of calling her Red, that is. This was the second time the ghost had taken leave quickly when Brett had appeared. Was it this man's presence that disturbed the ghost so? And, if so, why?

Brett crossed the road toward her. "Hello, Red," he said and grinned widely at her narrowed eyes. "I thought we could maybe grab some dinner together and try and get back on the right foot."

"Just tell me one thing before I kill you. Did you see anyone sitting on this bench as you came toward me?"

He shot her a puzzled look. "No one except your own sweet self." There was that dazzling smile again. So that settled it. If Noelia couldn't see him and Brett couldn't see him and if he could do that weird disappearing act, there was no other answer.

She was being stalked by another restless spirit.

As if it wasn't enough that she was being stalked by a ghost, now she had The World's Most Annoying

Sexy Hunk looking down at her with that self-satisfied smile on his face. The smile she itched to smack—or kiss away.

Get a grip, Kelly girl.

"Let's get this straight. Why do you want to have dinner with me? What do you think I am? A masochist? Do I look like a woman who wants to spend the evening getting indigestion from serious irritation by a stray guy who wants a wedding gown of his own and accuses her of stealing things?"

Brett had the good grace to look embarrassed. "That's one of the reasons I'm asking you to have dinner with me. I need to explain that. I wasn't trying to insult you."

"Only one of the reasons?" She raised an eyebrow and gave him the Death Glare.

"Well, there are other reasons..." Seeing her about to implode, he raised both hands in surrender. "You can't blame a guy for trying, can you?

"Just know this: I'm ex-military, and I learned a few things from the Marines."

"I'll bet there was no shortage of volunteer teachers... Ouch!" He grabbed her wrist in strong fingers as her open hand connected with his face.

"That was play. If I'd really meant to hurt you, you wouldn't be in any condition to even say 'ouch'," she warned, but a playful grin gave her away.

He hung his head in an unconvincing caricature of shame.

"I am so sorry; it's just that, when I'm nervous, I turn into a clown. Actually, I'm quite a serious guy." He even managed a serious guy expression. "Like, I'm seriously asking the most gorgeous woman I have met for years, maybe ever, to have dinner with me while I explain to her why I may have appeared to be a jerk."

"You're telling me that the jerk part was only an appearance? Not for real?"

"Cross my heart and hope…"

"No, that's okay. The cross-your-heart part will do. We don't need the hope-to-die part." Kelly shuddered. Too many great guys she knew had died, and she couldn't bear to hear the words said even lightly. She studied the face of the man before her. He was attractive, with that blond coloring and the dark brown eyes a girl could melt into…and she hadn't gone on a date in so very long. Maybe she deserved to have a little fun. "So, where are we going to dinner? If it's really posh, I might need to go home and change."

The smile he gave her was dazzling, and she felt more lighthearted than she could remember feeling in years. In spite of this guy's foot-in-mouth syndrome, she really did like him.

Funny thing, attraction.

"How about the Midnight Garden? I've heard their food and atmosphere are both great, and there's a Swedish cook."

Yeah, Kelly thought, *and there's supposed to be a resident ghost there, too.* Haunted places were definitely off her fine dining list. About all she needed was to have a counseling session with a restless spirit over some of their wonderful hot chocolate. "To be honest, I'm in the mood for something simpler, like maybe a fish burger and fries at the Marina Café?"

Brett smiled, and Kelly's pulse raced. "Ah, a lady after my own heart. I do so like a woman who eats real food."

****

It turned out the Marina Café was the perfect spot for a first dinner date that wasn't really a date. Or at least Kelly told herself it wasn't a date. Brett seemed to have other ideas judging from the way his eyes lingered on hers and his fingers seemed to creep across the table of their own volition to gently touch hers.

And she didn't mind at all.

It had been a long time since she'd had such fun with a guy who made no bones about the fact that he enjoyed being with her, too. Her ex-fiancé, Wayne's, abandonment had soured her on the idea of love, which was why she channeled her romantic nature into Wedding Bliss. She enjoyed creating the perfect wedding for other brides while hiding the hurt of her own broken engagement and latterly non-existent love life.

She decided to enjoy the feeling while it lasted and focus on the sexy guy sitting across the table from her. Wearing a dark blue polo shirt and jeans, he was definitely worth looking at. They talked about their childhoods, their work, and their dreams. As a bonus, he was well read and opinionated; they found themselves debating current affairs and having some hotly contested opposing views. Then their differences would dissolve in laughter as one or the other quipped and both laughed. And that shared amusement led to sizzling glances and a warm feeling that spread all the way to her toes as they gazed at each other across the Formica table.

Reluctantly, Kelly broke the spell. "This has been lovely, Brett. I almost don't want to spoil the evening by asking you what it was you wanted to explain?"

"Then don't." He reached over and held her hand again, his thumb brushing the tender spot on her palm. Heat flickered along her arm as awareness of the man enveloped her, and she had to shake herself back into reality.

It would be oh so nice to just forget everything and have fun. But his statement at their first meeting in Wedding Bliss about an illegal sale still bothered her, and she needed to clear the air. "You more or less accused me of buying stolen goods or maybe of stealing a dress myself. It's going to niggle at me until I find out what you meant, so spill."

"You're not going to let this go, are you?" He heaved a sighed and reached for his coffee.

*****

How do you explain something like this without making your family sound like nut jobs? Brett wondered, frowning. The last thing he wanted to do right now was to give Kelly a poor opinion of him. The thought that what Kelly thought of him was important startled him. After all, he barely knew the woman and already her opinion mattered? But he found it hard to keep his hands away from hers, and man, that sizzling sensation when he touched her…

Drawing in a deep breath, he started. "I'm an engineer working for a non-profit organization, and a lot of my work is overseas. I've been out of the country for about five months, working in sub-Saharan Africa. When I came home, I discovered my aunt was in a nursing home."

He signaled to the waitress for more coffee, waited until she'd filled both their cups and left a selection of little creamer pots, and then went on. "I should back up a bit. My Aunt Mary is the only relative I have left besides my sister, Sasha. Aunt Mary is my father's sister. When I'm away I usually keep in touch, but where this assignment was, well, let's just say there wasn't much by way of a communications infrastructure.

"Aunt Mary is something of a recluse, and aside from myself and Sasha, she doesn't see many people. Or any people, really. Sasha was supposed to be keeping an eye on her. My sister is, let's just say impetuous, and she's just gone through her second divorce. She decided to move into the family home while she got herself straight."

Kelly was watching him, those lovely eyes of hers a deeper blue; he suddenly had the thought that he could spend hours watching them change from lighter to darker blue and to stormy gray, reminding him of the ocean in all its many moods. He drew in a deep breath and shook himself back into the topic at hand.

"To cut a long story short, Aunt Mary had a bout of pneumonia, and Sasha, not being the nurturing type, decided she should go to a nursing home where she could get proper care while she regained her health. Unfortunately, my sister is enjoying having the house to herself and has left Mary in the home far longer than necessary. My aunt has become quite depressed. She's got the idea that because she's been under nursing care for so long, there's really something very seriously wrong with her and that we're trying to hide it from her.

"She thinks she doesn't have long to live, which is nonsense. She's as strong as an ox, and not really all that old, either. She turned 63 last year and Sasha—my sister—and I wanted to have a party for her, but she went ballistic and said she didn't want to have to cope with a houseful of people she hardly knew poking about. But the idea that she's dying has got into her head.

"Anyway, I'm going to get her home as soon as I can get a proper support system in place. In the meantime, convinced she's about to die at any minute, she's asking me to bring in her wedding dress. She wants to be buried in it." Brett's voice failed him at that thought, and he focused on his anger toward his sister in order to stop tears pooling in his eyes.

"And this dress is the gown you're looking for?" Kelly prompted.

"It seems that my sister—" Anger laced his voice now. "It seems that Sasha was a bit short on cash and thought she'd have an advance on what she expects to inherit from our aunt by holding a little estate sale through a local auction house. The dress, a lace and silk item from a French designer, was one of the items that were sold. And your name, or your store, came up as being the purchaser."

****

Kelly had already guessed, from his description, that he was referring to the dress now known as the Cursed Bridal Gown. Obviously, he wanted the dress back, but Kelly needed some time to think about all this. She couldn't tell him she thought she had the dress, because she'd already sold it to Daria, a woman who knew what she wanted and was unlikely to change her mind. It was a conundrum that needed some thought. "I did buy a vintage gown at an auction in Derry, but whether or not it's the dress you're looking for is a moot point. I need to telephone the auctioneer and see if I can find out where the gown I have came from."

Brett shot her a look that said he wanted to challenge her on this, but then he shrugged.

"Okay, I'll give you a few days to do that, and we'll talk again. In the meantime, how about we enjoy the evening?" He reached across the table and pushed back a curl of red hair, then traced her jawline with his thumb.

The effect was electric—Kelly shivered at his touch and knew she wanted more. At the same time, she was just burning to question Brett about the dress's history. Had it really been cursed? And why? And did she even believe in such things?

This wasn't the time, though. She imagined this mature young man would probably call for a strait jacket if she began to witter on about apparitions and old men on benches and cursed gowns that no recent bride had been able to wear. She thought he was probably far too grounded to do more than say goodbye and escape as fast as he possibly could, should she come out with her theories, so she kept silent.

They finished their coffee and went out into the mild sea-scented evening. Dusk had fallen while they'd been engrossed in their conversation, and lights twinkled on storefronts along the palisade.

"I know that most of the tourists are gone now, but the place still looks like a fairytale town," Kelly commented as she leaned against the railings and took in a deep breath of sea air.

Brett reached out and took her hand. "It's actually my favorite time to be here, when it's quiet and we locals can take our town back again," he said with a smile. "At least, before the winter hits."

"You obviously don't rely on the visitors for your livelihood," Kelly replied. "Still, it is nice to have a quiet time before the Christmas rush."

They strolled hand in hand along Main Street, the breeze from the bay ruffling their hair and clothes, and awareness sparking between them. There was no need to speak as they just enjoyed the moment. When the breeze grew stronger and colder, Brett slipped off the jacket he was wearing and wrapped it around her shoulders.

A gentleman! Kelly smiled her thanks but grew somber as she warned herself not to enjoy being wrapped up in his warm scent too much. After all, they hardly knew each other and, in her experience, even long-term relationships could shatter easily enough.

"It's getting late, so let me walk you home."

"My place is right on the edge of town, too far to walk in the dark," Kelly replied. "But if you want to follow me in your car, perhaps you'd like to stay for a coffee before you head back to Derry? I'm actually on the coast road, so it's not going out of your way."

"Red, I'd be happy to go out of my way for you."

Kelly all but growled. "How many times do I have to warn you about that nickname? Just remember, it's lonely out where I live, and the sea…well, accidents happen, and the bodies are never found."

"Now you're scaring me."

He looked anything but scared, Kelly thought. There was a masculine strength about Brett that suggested there wasn't much that would scare him. "I would seriously doubt that."

They parked their vehicles on the laneway outside

her house and were just walking on the garden path toward the front door when Kelly saw a bright shadow ahead of them, and a sharp pain lanced through her skull. She cried out, grabbed at her head, and slowly crumpled to the ground. Then she was falling, falling as shots rang out all around her under the hot desert sun...

Chapter Five

The world had turned white, completely white, and was so bright it made Kelly's eyes burn. Was she dead? *Was this the famous end-of-life white light people talked about?* She tried wriggling her fingers and toes, and everything felt intact. She doubted dead people could feel like that.

If only that demon, whoever he was, would stop shining that light…

As if her thoughts had communicated themselves to the demon, the light clicked off to reveal a pleasant looking man with café au lait skin and sad eyes. "Hello, Ms. Andrews. I'm glad you are back with us. It seems you had a fainting session. I am Paramedic Abbas Faheem." He offered her a quick smile and turned his attention to the screen on his equipment pack.

Kelly squinted now that the light was gone. She took in her surroundings, realizing she was home and lying on the lumpy settee in her own living room, not that Other Place. The heat, the burning, the unforgiving sand, the sound of gunfire were all gone.

"Can you tell me what happened, Red?" A familiar voice. And an annoying name. She tried for a cutting answer, but all that came out was a croak.

"Unless I miss my guess, it would appear to me that Ms. Andrews is experiencing some recurrent pain from a wound she acquired while serving her country."

Abbas Faheem cast another small smile her way. "I communicated with the doctor on duty at the hospital, who checked your records. You have a history of headaches after a serious head wound. How is your vision?"

"I can see perfectly well, now that you've turned that darned light off." Kelly struggled to sit up. "Abbas Faheem—the clever lion. Abbas is a lion, Faheem is intelligent. Funny the things that stick in your mind. I couldn't remember much of my Arabic, but that came back without even thinking about it. Are you a clever lion, Abbas Faheem?"

"Right now, Ms. Andrews, I'm just a lowly paramedic, once an army medic, who is pleased to see that his patient is well on her way to recovery." He began to pack his medical equipment into a large carrier.

"Why do you think that's a shrapnel wound?" That familiar voice again. *Brett!* Yes, it was the man she'd been walking with...wearing his jacket...holding hands...

"Because I'm sad to say I have seen many such wounds, also while serving this country of ours." The paramedic turned back to Kelly. "Your vital signs are back to normal, but I'd like you to rest, and tomorrow report to your own doctor. He will take blood tests and will likely arrange for you to have x-rays. Sometimes it can happen that a tiny sliver of bone, or maybe metal from the shrapnel, can lodge in the brain and not be easily noticed in the early days following the injury, due to brain swelling. If these fainting events become more frequent, the doctor will get you a referral to a specialist, just to get it all checked out. I wish you both a good day."

Faheem waved a salute and, accepting their thanks with a weary smile, left them.

Kelly was flooded with appreciation for all the caring people in this small town, people like Abbas Faheem, the medic who had served his country like she had, and for Brett Atwell, who stood beside her wearing a concerned expression and looking as if he would be willing to take on dragons to protect her.

****

Brett brought her a cup of strong, sweet tea and a lot of questions she didn't feel she could easily answer. "I'm not sure what happened, Brett." It was the truth. After all, she wasn't sure she really saw a ghost, was she?

They were still in Kelly's eclectically furnished living room. Although she knew it was unfair, she was getting a bit irritated at Brett's hovering over her as if he expected her to pass out at any moment. She caught the ironic thought that she simply wasn't used to being fussed over.

"You were just about to invite me in for a nightcap after our dinner when you suddenly went white as a sheet, grabbed at your head, and collapsed. Fortunately, you had your door key in your hand, so I retrieved it and was able to open the door, and then I carried you inside and called the emergency services."

"Thank you for being so…kind."

Brett shrugged as if it were nothing. "I could hardly leave you in a heap on your laneway now, could I? I was brought up better than that. Of course, I'm used to women falling at my feet but…"

"Don't flatter yourself, buster. How long…?"

"How long were you out?" He glanced at the handsome watch he wore on his left wrist. "Looks like at least one of us got her beauty sleep. It was about ten o'clock when I called the paramedics, and it's two forty-five a.m. right now."

"So long?" Kelly's stomach churned. She had lost more than four hours. She'd never been out as long as that before. *Oh, God, was the damage to her brain getting worse?*

She assured Brett that she was fine, that she intended to rest for a while, and he should leave to get some sleep if he could before beginning his own busy day.

"You're kidding, aren't you?" The frown between his eyes contradicted his bantering tone. "After that little episode? I'd be worried sick about you." He raised her hand to his lips and left a gentle kiss there—a kiss that seemed to tingle on her flesh long after it was over. "Honey, there's no place I want to be right now other than with you."

Kelly lay back on the pillows and allowed herself to bask in the sense of security his presence brought, a feeling that was rare for her. Brett tucked a colorful vintage quilt around her and sat on the edge of the settee, seeming content to have Kelly snuggle into his side.

The tall grandfather clock on the window wall ticked its lazy song, and Kelly thought she had not felt this safe in so very long...not since that fateful day in Afghanistan. Perhaps she had never felt truly safe since the day when she'd looked her own death in the eyes. And lost so many comrades and friends. Perhaps a person never feels completely safe after such an experience, but it's enough to feel cared for right now, she thought, and her body melted into a gentle doze snuggled up against Brett's solid strength.

Sometime later, she woke again as Brett's weight bounced the settee as he settled back down beside her holding two mugs of hot tea. "Drink this, Red. It's supposed to be good for shock."

He handed her one of the mugs and grinned when she snapped back, "Keep calling me Red and you'll be the one getting a shock."

She stretched languidly, raising an eyebrow when she heard the clock strike seven. "I didn't even notice you'd got up. I guess the pills really put me out."

"You needed your rest," he replied, the twin lines of a frown puckering his forehead under the mop of blond hair. "How are you feeling? Any pain?"

She shook her head, wincing as a sharp throb raced through her temple. Brett gently stroked her forehead, checking for signs of fever as the paramedic had advised. The frown deepened as she stiffened when his fingers found the long, ridged scar that ran from just behind her hairline, over her temple, and toward the back of her scalp.

"This is the wound that the paramedic was talking about?" His voice was tight and angry.

Kelly struggled to swallow around the memories that flooded back. Among them one so much more recent—that fleeting glimpse of the ghost of an old man, the old man she'd last seen on the bench in front of Wedding Bliss, standing beckoning to her just seconds before the terrible pain ripped through her skull…

"You know that recently the U.S. government

removed the exclusion of women in combat roles? Well, we were already there in some front-line jobs. I was attached to a ground crew as a driver. We were in a convoy, and there was an armored car before us and another one after us. We felt about as safe as anyone could feel in that situation. It was slow going because the crew ahead of us was constantly on the watch for roadside bombs. Everything was going fine, we were on time with the supplies we were bringing to camp, and we were starting to relax. We were almost there when…when the truck ahead hit an IED, and it was like the whole world blew up in our faces."

Even now, years later, she could still feel the tension, the sick fear, welling up in her belly at the memory. Brett squeezed her hand, and she glanced up at him, grateful for his comforting presence.

"It was just crazy. The Taliban opened fire, and our guys raced to positions to return that fire. There wasn't time to check on the guys in the vehicle ahead of us, but I grabbed a machine gun from an injured soldier and tried to protect him and me by strafing the area. Then I pulled him—fortunately, he wasn't a big man, although bigger than me. I started to drag him toward the nearest vehicle. Funny how God gives you strength in these life and death situations.

"Anyway, he was wounded really bad, but I could hear him moaning so I knew he was still alive. Then another explosive device went off close by, and I guess I was hit by the shrapnel. An awful pain ripped through my head, and I could hardly see for my own blood running into my eyes, stinging. Still, I got myself and the wounded guy into the shelter of the vehicle. I don't remember any more after that until I woke up in a transport plane on my way to the armed forces hospital in Germany."

Brett leaned down and kissed her gently. When he raised his head, she could see the admiration on his face. "I could only imagine what you went through out there, and what guts it must have taken to put your life on the line to save another soldier's."

Tears sprang into her eyes, but she shrugged his praise away. "What I did was nothing compared to the courage and sacrifice of some of the other guys," she insisted. "Three of my buddies died in that attack—they paid with their lives to keep us from being overrun until help arrived. I owe it to them that I survived and was airlifted out to the military hospital.

"Head wounds are funny things, often unpredictable. I was in and out of consciousness for quite a while, and it took some time before my memory came back. I had speech problems, too, but the docs assured me it would all clear up. One thing they couldn't be certain about was the… hallucinations…I was having."

"Like post-traumatic stress disorder flashbacks?"

"Something like that." How could she explain to him that the woman he was caressing actually saw restless spirits? It would be enough to send most red-blooded guys running for the exit.

Suddenly the front door opened, and Noelia Russo came rushing in.

In one hand, she had a plastic container of what looked like soup, in the other a bouquet of fresh flowers. She stopped short at the sight of Kelly lying on the sofa with Brett hovering over her like a protective sheepdog, then grinned.

"Here I was, worried sick about my poor friend who I heard had collapsed and was at death's door, and here she is, cuddled up with a gorgeous guy! If I'd known you were in such good hands…" The head to toe and back again look she gave Brett made her double entendre obvious. "I wouldn't have worried at all."

Kelly struggled to sit up while Brett stood, not sure whether to scowl or laugh at Noelia's suggestive wink.

Noelia shoved the flowers and plastic food container at him. "Make yourself useful, dear, and see to these. The flowers go in a vase filled with water, and the soup goes in a casserole dish and into the microwave for four minutes when Kelly is hungry." She handed them to him and then stood back, looking skeptical. "You will get that right, won't you?"

Brett was quick to recover. "Yes, of course. Flowers in the microwave, soup in a vase."

Noelia laughed out loud. "No need for cheek, young man. Get outta here."

When he was gone, she sat down on the edge of the sofa and gave Kelly a hard look.

"All joking apart, I meant what I said, honey—I really was worried. What happened?"

Kelly quickly filled the older woman in, and then asked, "But how did you get to hear of this?"

Noelia gave her an incredulous look. "Surely you've lived here long enough to know that news travels faster than the speed of light in Marina Grove? And remember, I live next door to Julie Carlson…"

The penny dropped. "The police department secretary? And she heard it from the 911 dispatcher."

"And if Julie knows about it, so does everyone else in town. You'll probably have a store full of visitors before noon. I guess there's no point in telling you that you should take the day off and rest?"

Kelly shook her head, swallowing hard at the sharp pain caused by the sudden movement. "This whole thing with the wedding dress is driving me crazy. Brett is convinced that I bought a wedding dress belonging to his aunt, who wants it back—oh, for a lot of reasons. Apparently, it should never have been sold."

"Oops, that really puts you down the creek with no paddle. I really doubt you'll get Ms. Welcome to let you buy the dress back. She doesn't look the type to give up gracefully something she wants."

Noelia had hit the problem on the head. "I don't even want to ask her until I'm sure what's happening. I need to find out who the dress belonged to and why…well, why it seems to have this weird ability to screw up other brides' wedding plans. I mean, you'd think a wedding gown would carry happy vibes, wouldn't you?"

"If Brett thinks it belongs to his aunt, can't you just outright ask him who she is and why the dress is, well, cursed?"

Kelly chewed her bottom lip, a habit she had when trying to figure something out. Noelia waited patiently for an explanation. "If I ask Brett, first it means I think I might have his dress—and I haven't told him that for sure yet—but also he's very protective of his aunt. She's been ill. More to the point, I think he'd either go ballistic if I asked if she had cursed the gown…"

"…or he might think you're a nut job for even suggesting such a thing." Noelia smiled triumphantly. "You really do like this guy, don't you? Not that I can blame you. He's definitely eye candy."

"Noelia!"

"What? I might be…of a certain age, but I still know an attractive man when I see one…like now. Anyhow, I think I might have something that could help…" Noelia paused and then went on. "I was doing a bit of cleaning up at the store, and there's something I need to show you, back at the shop."

"I hope it's a bill from the furnace guy, saying he's fixed that cold draft."

"Not exactly. In fact, he couldn't find anything wrong."

Kelly struggled to her feet, reaching out a hand to the sofa back to balance herself.

"Whatever. I need to get into the store. If you're not there and I'm not there…"

Noelia gave her a long look. "Maybe you should get more rest. The store is quite safe; it's only eight-thirty, and we don't open for another hour."

Kelly gave her a sheepish grin. "It's just that it's already been a long day…" She gingerly pushed herself away from the support of the sofa, half afraid that the searing pain in her head would recur. To her vast relief, there was no trace of a headache and no dizziness. In fact, she felt just fine.

And part of the reason for that feeling fine just walked back into the room. "Where do you think you're going?" Brett asked, taking the opportunity to drop a quick kiss on her cheek and enjoying the surprised expression on her face.

"To see a man who isn't there. And a woman about a dress."

Small wonder Brett looked puzzled as he watched her make her way carefully up the stairs to dress for work.

****

He didn't want to let her go alone. How could he explain to her what he'd felt as she'd gone deathly pale, screamed in pain, and crumpled like a puppet with its strings cut? The fear that he was going to lose her before even getting to properly know her had burned in his soul. *Dammit, she'd been through enough.*

He wanted to stay by her side and protect her, yet being protected by a man was probably the last thing she needed. Let's face it, she'd shown herself capable of coping in more dangerous situations than he'd encountered in his own work, although there'd been a few close calls in some of the Third World countries where he'd worked for the non-profit organization, negotiating with governments and building schools and wells and whatever else was needed. The idea that this woman, so slender and feminine, had been in such danger had sent adrenaline racing through his system. But the rage quickly faded into admiration that Kelly was strong enough to face down insurgents and save the life of a fellow soldier. He could only imagine the courage that must have taken.

There was so much more he wanted to ask her about the after-effects of her wound, the hallucinations, how it affected the rest of her life. Darn it, he didn't even know if she had a significant other, and here he was, daydreaming that they were so much more to each other than they could possibly be on such a short acquaintance.

What turmoil she'd thrown him into. What did she mean by 'to see a man who isn't there'? And he still hadn't found out for sure whether she had Mary's

70

wedding dress…

Brett smiled. Kelly Andrews was unlike any other woman he'd known. And he really was a guy who liked a challenge.

Chapter Six

Weird as it might sound, the fainting and flashback episode seemed to have cleared Kelly's brain. She was energized and determined to clear up the twin mysteries that had appeared so suddenly in her life—a cursed wedding dress and a restless, enigmatic spirit.

And possibly a third mystery, in the delectable shape of Brett Atwell.

With a lightning flash illuminating the landscape of her mind, she realized the possibility that these weren't separate mysteries but rather they may all be part of the same package. There was a link between the Old Man on the Bench and Brett Atwell—the Cursed Bridal Gown. The ghost did a quick disappearing act every time Brett appeared. The Old Man on the Bench, whom she now reluctantly admitted was a restless spirit, was obsessed with the Cursed Bridal Gown. Brett was searching for that very dress.

He was there again, the old man on the bench. Kelly flashed back to the moment the previous evening when she'd seen him waving to her from right in front of her own home. A shudder passed through her. Had he been inside her house? Was this ghost an invisible presence in many private aspects of her life? And what, in the name of all that was good and sane, did he want with her? She shivered at the very idea of this old man witnessing even her personal moments—and yes, her innermost thoughts.

Sure, she'd met other restless spirits, but it had been like brushing up against cobwebs. When she had awoken in the hospital, the fallen comrades around her bed had seemed real, substantial as in life. She thought that was perhaps because she had a strong connection to them in life. Since then, the contacts with other spirits had been nothing more than a slight, shivery experience, quickly glimpsed figures, barely intelligible words, and then over. So mild, it had been easy to convince herself that the doctors were right, and she was hallucinating. She could dismiss the conversations she'd had with spectral people as figments of her damaged brain.

But this guy, well, he definitely wasn't going to be put off so easily. Had trying to ignore him brought about that awful flash of pain and fear that transported her back to that terrible time in the desert? She shivered with a sudden cold.

Kelly averted her eyes from the bench and its ghostly occupant, hoping against hope that seeing him wouldn't prompt another shard of pain to slice through her head, and hurried into the store after Noelia.

Her assistant was waiting for her by the walnut cupboard they used as a counter. With the flourish worthy of a master magician, Noelia pulled out a vintage white beaded bag shrouded in tissue paper. "Do you remember this?"

Kelly shook her head. It was familiar, but they had handled dozens of these vintage bride's purses. Why would she remember this one specifically?

"This came in the same box as that gown. You know—*that gown*." Noelia gave a little shudder as if she couldn't bring herself to use the nickname they had given the Cursed Bridal Gown. "We know it's a French designer gown from the paperwork that was in the box, but this purse somehow got separated and not entered into the book with the dress. And do you know what I found inside?"

Kelly shook her head again, mesmerized by the show Noelia was putting on.

"Ta-da!" The older woman pulled out a yellowed slip of paper. "This, my dear, is a receipt from a very well-known Parisian design house, dated 1972, and made out to Miss Mary Atwell. No street address, just Derry, Maine. I think we may have found the original owner of the dress."

"Yes," said Kelly, still not seeing where this was going. "The sale I attended was at an auction house in Derry, and Brett's last name is Atwell as well. He said he got the name of the auctioneer from his sister, who was selling off things belonging to his Aunt Mary through that company. He talked to the auctioneer, who suggested the purchaser was Wedding Bliss. It definitely fits."

"We have to find out more about this Mary Atwell and find out why she cursed the dress!" Noelia said.

Kelly stared at her. "Why would you assume she was the one who cursed the dress?"

"Just a hunch. Because you said Brett said she was unmarried. A spinster. She ordered this very expensive and exclusive dress but didn't get married in it. Was the gown for someone else, or did Miss Atwell just not get married? But even if she didn't curse it, she must know who did, and why. It was her wedding dress, after all."

"All right," Kelly said, playing along. "But then

why would *we* need to know that information? The dress has been sold. Daria Welcome is wearing it to her wedding. It's not our problem anymore."

"It is our problem because it still remains to be seen if Daria's wedding will actually happen. Business has already dropped because of the rumors surrounding that dress, regardless of the fact that it's been sold. Imagine if it were returned a fourth time? We'd be doomed. We have to find out more about the dress from this Mary Atwell and find a way to end the curse for good."

Kelly shook her head at the idea that Daria Welcome, whom she liked and who seemed so sure of the love between herself and her fiancé, might find her plans heartbreakingly ruined by the Cursed Wedding Gown. Noelia was right—they had to do some sleuthing and see what could be done to remove the taint of misery from the dress. Now that Kelly knew there was a ghost in town, and said ghost was asking about the cursed dress, she had to admit she was starting to see Noelia's point that they should try and find out what was happening.

"But Brett's not going to let go of this, yet I can't question Brett about his aunt *or* the dress. Not without raising all sorts of questions. I haven't even said for sure that we have the dress he's looking for. He wants the gown back for her, and I don't see Daria Welcome giving it back. I really don't know what to do, other than see if we can defang the curse. If there actually is a curse."

"Oh, there's something wrong, and that's a fact." Noelia folded the receipt and put it back into the pretty beaded bag after noting the details on a pad of paper kept on the counter. "And I can't help feeling we do have some responsibility in all this. If we sell the gown, knowing that there's something wrong…well, it's not like there's a broken zipper or something, but we do have to try and fix it."

Kelly had other reasons why she didn't want to ask Brett about Mary. If she did, she might end up having to explain to him why she was interested in his aunt. And that meant not only explaining the theory of the curse, which would be bad enough, but what about the ghost angle? But what on earth could the connection be between a fifty-odd-year-old wedding dress with a bad reputation and an incredibly irritating ghost who was asking questions about that same dress? Somehow the idea of telling Brett about the recent appearance of a ghost in her life, and how she suspected a connection between the ghost and all the troubles the gown had brought, both amused and embarrassed her. She didn't think their relationship was ready for a trip into the spirit world yet. And what if she was wrong? She doubted if a man like Brett Atwell was given to flights of fancy—or tolerant of those who were. She didn't want to look like a fool in front of him.

"Or we could just forget the whole thing. I'll tell Brett I don't have the dress and I can't give out the name of the client who bought it. End of story." She looked hopefully at Noelia.

The older woman scowled. "You know you can't shirk your responsibilities like that. What about Daria? What if that dreadful Cursed Wedding Gown wrecks her happily ever after plans, too?"

Kelly sighed. Trust Noelia to take the moral high ground. "Are you sure we couldn't…?"

"Absolutely not! However, there are other ways to get information that might help answer the questions about the dress's history," Noelia said. "Now, we—or rather you—must go to the newspaper files and see if you can find out anything about Mary Atwell. She must have been a pretty well-off lady, or from a rich family, to be getting a gown like this for her wedding, even in the seventies. She would have had the kind of wedding that would be in the society pages if you go back to 1971. If there are pictures, you'll be able to tell if the dress we sold Daria really is the dress Brett's aunt wants. If it's not, then you can just tell him that and everything will be fine."

"Except that the dress is still rumored to be cursed because of what happened with the other three brides." Kelly sighed. She couldn't think of anything she fancied less than a day in the basement newspaper 'morgue' going through musty old editions of the *Telegraph*. Or worse, driving into Derry and searching through the local paper there.

Actually, there was something worse—that would be going out and sitting on that bench with her invisible ghost friend and finding out what he needed to make him go away. But it had to be done. She sighed again.

"I can tell you're not inspired by the task I've set you, so I'm going to sweeten the deal with a nice cup of coffee and a couple of chocolate covered cookies," Noelia said, placing a tray on the small table between them. "Of course, coffee making would be even better and quicker if we had one of those fancy new coffee machines."

"Not in the budget, especially with all the lost sales," Kelly retorted.

"And if you—we—solve the problem?"

"Then I promise you a trip to the store to choose a machine with all the bells and whistles."

"Deal." Noelia grinned triumphantly. "Are you going to the newspaper morgue? Let's get closer to working this out."

"First I have to deal with something I've been putting off for too long. Should be back soon if all goes well," Kelly said. She grabbed her sweater off the hook near the door and turned back. "I'm taking my coffee with me. And oh, Noelia? If you see me sitting on the bench over there looking like I'm talking to myself…"

"Don't worry, dear, I'll just assume you're talking to the imaginary friend you have there. I really do think you should get out more. Maybe that sexy hunk Brett will help you?"

With a snort of disgust, Kelly flounced out from the store and headed across the road. She hated it when Noelia could see right through her. She was pretty sure her assistant had known that Brett sent delicious shivers of lust shimmering through her boss, long before Kelly herself was ready to accept it.

The restless spirit was still sitting there, although he looked paler than ever. *If this keeps up, he won't be visible at all.* That idea should have pleased her until she thought about having an invisible grumpy old ghost wandering around, possibly in her private space, never being able to see where he was. She shuddered.

"I was going to bring you a coffee but the last time I did that I ended up spilling it all over my shirt. Besides, ghosts can't drink coffee."

"Don't be cruel. Have you any idea what I'd give for a sip of coffee? Even that dishwater brew that comes from that ancient machine of yours...and, oh, my heavens, a sip of good French wine..."

"Well, maybe you could get out of my imagination and go somewhere where you can enjoy these delights." Kelly took a deep drink of her coffee and smacked her lips theatrically.

The ghost snorted. "At least you've figured out what I am. Now you need to learn who I am."

"Mostly, I need to know what the hell I have to do to get you to go away and bother someone else."

"There aren't many people who can see us."

"Us?" Kelly looked around the street and the park behind them in dismay. "There are more of you?" She imagined whole lineups of restless spirits waiting their turn for a chat, making demands she couldn't possibly fulfill...

As if he could read her mind—he was a ghost, he probably could—the old guy said, "Don't worry. I'm the only one here at the moment. You and I have a connection."

Confusion reigned. "You do realize I don't have a clue what you're talking about? What connection could we possibly have?"

A sound like a sob echoed rustily from the spirit. Kelly saw a tiny drop of moisture on the bench and wondered if it were possible for ghosts to cry. *And what could she do?* She could hardly pat him on the shoulder or offer a hug. Her hands would probably pass right through him.

And it was bad enough to appear to be talking to herself on this bench. Whatever would people think if they heard her making soothing sounds and saw her patting and hugging apparently thin air? Some people already whispered she was crazy—could it get any worse? She waited him out.

"I told you I did something awful. I made two people very unhappy, and I need to put it right before…before…whatever comes next. Find them for me, tell them I'm sorry…ask their forgiveness, and I'll be gone."

"Hey, wait a minute! Do you have any idea what you're…?" Kelly cried, but it was too late. The spirit was gone, and all her outburst had brought was worried looks from two women passing by on the other side of the street.

"That's the girl from the wedding shop," one of them said, ducking her head in Kelly's direction.

"Maybe it's all that stuff about the wedding dress that's cursed, driving her nuts," her friend replied. Neither woman made even the slightest attempt to keep their voices down.

"Well, wouldn't you be a little bit nuts if you'd supplied a wedding dress and three couples had broken up because of it? It's a curse, and she should do something about it."

What am I supposed to do? Kelly wanted to yell at them. But the women were right. Buying that wedding dress seemed to be a surefire way to ruin any dewy-eyed bride's dreams of happily ever after. Her thoughts went to the perky realtor, Daria Welcome, and her wedding plans.

And despite the fact that her own fiancé had waited until they were almost ready to walk up the aisle before he ended their relationship, Kelly still believed there should still be a happily ever after.

At least, for other women.

****

It had been a long and frustrating day. Kelly took a glass of wine out onto the deck at the rear of her home. Sullivan the cat followed her out and jumped up into her lap, rubbing his battle-scarred ears against her chin in a rare show of affection.

She absently stroked his soft gray fur. "Did you miss me today, Sullivan?" He pinned her with his impossibly green eyes. "I'm sorry. I have to go to work, otherwise there'd be no expensive kitty cat food for you." She bent her head and kissed his whiskered nose. The cat shook his head in disdain and hopped off her lap to go and settle underneath the birdfeeder. From there he watched longingly as some feathered stragglers swooped in for a late supper.

She couldn't help but think back to her conversation over dinner with Brett Atwell. She'd never been so open about her hopes and dreams with anyone until that evening. *How long had she been in town now?* she asked herself. It seemed like forever. The very first day she arrived, before she had even unpacked, she'd walked along Main Street and the public pier, munched on a snack from one of the food stalls there, and promised herself that if she ever was rich enough, she'd have a little boat of her own and spend time relaxing on the soothing water. Until then, she'd definitely take a tourist cruise several times during the summer, just to get the feel of it.

Yet she had never been on a tour cruise even once. Time spun by, seemingly out of control. There was always something that needed doing for the business, work on her house renovation, or paperwork connected with Wedding Bliss or taxes, or to her army days and the injured compensation benefits she was entitled to receive.

Here she was, in her own little house, her own business. All hers. In a beautiful bayside town where people came from miles and miles away just to spend a few days' or weeks' vacation. And she never took advantage of her surroundings. No playtime.

No playmate.

Brett. His image was so clear in her mind that for a moment, she wondered if he was actually there—she could almost reach out and touch him. How she wanted at that moment to put her arms around his neck, to feel the hard muscle beneath his shirt...and his hot mouth on hers. Memories of their very first meeting and their very first kiss filled her with heat and longing.

She wondered how Noelia coped, living alone, her husband long dead in that boating accident, her children flown on to their own life paths. Which led her to wonder again how her assistant made enough money to live a comfortable lifestyle even after putting her three sons through college. It certainly wasn't on the small amount Kelly was able to pay her for working at Wedding Bliss.

The middle-aged woman was always reticent about her personal life. She chatted proudly about her children and occasionally, usually on the anniversary of his death, she would talk about her husband. Kelly knew she also belonged to the Catholic Church in Marina Grove and helped out with the churchwomen's activities.

Was that enough to fill a life, much less pay for it? And wasn't Noelia lonely, or had the love she'd shared with her husband been enough to see her through the lonely years after his death?

Chapter Seven

Brett nodded a friendly hello to the young woman on the reception desk at the Holywell Home, the nursing facility where his aunt was recovering from her bout of pneumonia. She smiled and blushed a little as he told her she looked very pretty today.

"Pink is definitely your color," he teased. "How is Aunt Mary doing today?"

"Oh, pretty much the same as she was yesterday when you visited. Wanting to know when she's going home." The receptionist lowered her voice and leaned toward Brett. He caught the lush scent of roses in her perfume. "I have to say that she's been so much happier since you have been home and visiting. Mrs. Sasha Atwell Montgomery didn't come often—I think because they tended to have words each time she was here."

Brett clicked his tongue against his teeth. "Sasha and my Aunt Mary have never got along very well. Mary thinks my sister is flighty, and Sasha thinks Mary is a prude. I love them both, but they are two very different personalities."

"Yes, and your aunt is a different generation. Young women are different now than when your aunt was in her twenties." Sandy Lewis smiled conspiratorially. "Mind you, sometimes she has this hilarious sense of humor. One of the nurses told me yesterday that Mrs. Atwell was threatening to turn Dr. Frazer into a duck...because she thought he was a quack! Get it?"

Oh yes, Brett got it. He managed a weak smile, all the while wondering how Sandy would react if she knew his aunt really believed she could cast spells. Surely it was a harmless fantasy, he told himself.

Brett bade her goodbye and went off through the double doors that led to the elevators and his aunt's room on the second floor. He never quite knew what to expect these days. Mary had been a bit mercurial as long as he'd known her. Or maybe she was a little crazy, with her beliefs in witchcraft. As a child, he'd been impressed at the idea, but as he grew up, he'd become concerned. If his aunt really believed she was a witch, what did that say about her mental health? He wondered what she had been like as a young woman in love, before the disaster of her wedding had turned her into a virtual recluse. Had the shock of that betrayal affected her mind?

He decided to take the short flight of stairs rather than the elevator. He was happy to be back in Maine, but he knew he didn't get enough exercise and missed the hard, outdoor life of his non-profit organization work in some of the poorest parts of the world.

He wished he could get Red out of his mind. He wished he could reassure his aunt, who was still firmly convinced she wasn't long for this world. He wished his sister Sasha would grow up and act like a responsible adult.

Conversely, he wished he never had to leave the peace and beauty of Maine. A wish that was maybe tied in with his recent meeting with a certain red-haired beauty. On impulse earlier he had called into a local florist intending to send her a dozen red roses. He was thinking red roses for Red but common sense stopped him at the last moment. Red roses were the symbol of love, and it was way too early for such a declaration. He smiled as he considered how Red's eyes would spark at such over-the-top behavior.

Brett sighed. He wished life could be simpler.

Most of all he wished he could untangle the problems that had arisen, turn back the clock, and have him and Kelly meet at a party, a dance, the theatre, through friends…and begin a calm, uncomplicated relationship that could bloom…

Then he had a wonderful idea. After the talk they'd had at dinner, he'd learned one thing that Kelly would like far more than flowers…

****

Kelly thought that perhaps the only good thing that had happened to her that day was that there was no need to pore over back copies of the *Marina Grove Telegraph* in the rather dank, gloomy basement of the newspaper. The managing editor told her proudly that "the whole shebang, back to our genesis" was now available through the library archives.

So, trudge, trudge, heart down, off she went to the local library branch. The part where the files she needed were kept was in an elegant building that used to be the town hall, way back when, and it still boasted the original elegant woodwork and tall, deep windows of its Victorian heritage. The effect was one of dignity and scholarship, a calming atmosphere that she always enjoyed.

Area libraries had recently received funding to

transfer historic documents to computers, and a smiling librarian told Kelly that the year she was looking for, 1972, was now available digitally.

It took only a few clicks of the computer mouse to find the society pages in each issue starting in May of 1972, the date of the receipt for the Cursed Bridal Gown. She worked slowly and steadily through page after page until a photograph on the second week in July's issue stole her breath away.

A beautiful young woman, petite and slender, face radiant with dreams, stood on the steps of a church Kelly recognized as being in a Derry parish. She looked glorious in a beautiful floor length gown with a delicate lace veil, two small chubby-cheeked flower girls in attendance. A silver-haired man who the caption stated was Mary Atwell's father, Richard, stood proudly beside her.

In a second photograph, the weeping and disheveled bride, her face turned away from the camera, clutched onto her father and mother for support as they appeared again on the church steps.

The headline read: *Heiress Mary Atwell Left at the Altar!*

And the sub-heading: *No Sign of Missing Groom at Fairy Tale Wedding—Did Childhood Sweetheart Scarper?*

Tears pooled in Kelly's eyes, and her heart went out to this long-ago bride, seeing in her the ruined dreams and broken promises she'd known herself when Wayne ended their engagement.

At least he'd done it before their wedding day. The rat.

Dammit, if she found Mary Atwell's groom, she'd

probably punch him on the nose.

How satisfying it would have been to punch her own erstwhile groom when he'd broken their engagement, but she had known even then that wouldn't have mended the crack in her heart, shored up her battered self-esteem, or fixed her broken trust.

One thing was sure—Mary Atwell was wearing the Cursed Bridal Gown at that long-ago wedding. That distinctive French designer styling and sumptuous lace and silk fabric was unmistakable to a trained eye like Kelly's, and the reporter had waxed poetic in giving such a detailed description of the beautiful gown that Kelly had no doubts that this was the one she had bought at auction. Mary Atwell's gown. The gown Brett Atwell's aunt had worn for a wedding that was never to be. Was it simply that ill luck clung to the gown? Or was there a deeper, more sinister reason the gown had caused such heartache in other brides?

One look at that broken bride, and it seemed obvious why that gorgeous fifty-year-old wedding dress might be cursed. The next question would be to find Mary Atwell and see what could be done about the ill luck that dogged the gown before it wrecked the hopes and dreams of yet another couple. Despite what Daria Welcome insisted about not believing in hexes, Kelly wasn't at all sure disbelief took away their power.

The question in her mind was whether Mary Atwell's wedding turned into a disaster because of the gown, or whether she had cursed that wedding dress in her grief. If she had been the one to lay the curse, then Kelly thought she probably wouldn't like Brett's favorite aunt very much. Which was a pity because she liked Brett. *A lot.*

"She must be one powerful witch to lay a curse that would last half a century," she muttered to herself, and shivered in a sudden cold draft.

The only good thing she could think of was that at least she had established a connection that pointed to the reason the dress appeared to be so unlucky. She noted the name of the groom. Troy Matthews. Chewing on her bottom lip, she wondered if the Old Man on the Bench was actually the ghost of the long-lost groom. If Brett was Mary's blood relative, then that would explain the connection, the way the ghost disappeared whenever Brett appeared. This seemed such a cozy explanation, before she remembered that the ghost had claimed to have hurt *two* people. Assuming Mary Atwell wasn't into a ménage a trois, just who could the other person be?

She was so deeply engrossed in these thoughts that she jumped visibly when a hand came down gently on her shoulder.

"Oh, my goodness, I'm so sorry. I didn't mean to startle you," library staffer Rachel Riley cried, her green eyes wide. "I just brought over the copies you wanted printing, and I couldn't help but notice you were looking at that page about the Atwell wedding that never was."

"If this is about that wedding dress everyone says is cursed, Rachel…"

The librarian laughed. "Don't be silly—I really don't believe in all that mumbo-jumbo. But obviously some folks do."

Kelly glanced around, grateful to see there were no other readers in the records room. No one to hear and spread further speculation about the Cursed Bridal

Gown.

"Don't I know it. I'm sure some people have been avoiding Wedding Bliss while all this talk has been going on," she answered.

The librarian, a tall, serious-looking woman, slapped an open book down beside the keyboard on the computer desk. "I'm not talking about those silly women who think they see ghosts and goblins everywhere."

Who says you're silly just because you see ghosts? Kelly wanted to snarl, but discretion being the better part of valor, she just asked instead, "What do you mean?"

Rachel pushed her glasses up on her nose and pulled up a chair from another workstation. Tapping the book cover, she said, "Well, you know a couple of hundred years ago there was all this witch hunting and stuff going on?"

Kelly snorted. "Yes, but Marina Grove isn't exactly Salem's Lot."

"Of course not. But we did have a few women accused of witchcraft way back then. And guess whose ancestress was among them? Mary Atwell's great— several greats—grandmother." Rachel grinned at Kelly's startled expression.

"What? You're kidding me?"

"No, it's all here in this book. *East Coast Witches & Wizards.*" Rachel tapped the book again.

"That's an actual book? You mean, someone actually researched and wrote a book on this?"

"Oh, yes, and connected the dots right to the present-day descendants."

"But wouldn't a wealthy family like the Atwells

sue over something like this? I mean, who wants to be accused of being the descendant of a crazy witch, even now?"

Rachel laughed again. "Mary Atwell's grandmother, I think, or great grandmother, Gracie Hollowell, fancied herself as a movie queen, back in the day. She actually played on the glamorous side of being the descendent of a witch herself. She claimed to also have witchy powers in order to get publicity to help her career."

"And did it? Help her get famous, I mean?"

"Only in Maine, I guess. She finally gave up and married respectable and very wealthy Mr. Atwell. Wonder if Great Grandma several times removed passed her magical powers onto her great-whatever granddaughter who went and turned her missing groom into a toad?"

Kelly could think of no better fate for Mary Atwell's missing groom than to be transformed. Although that was perhaps maligning toads. "Can I check the book out? I mean, it's not in the reference section or anything, is it?"

Rachel went over to the librarian's station and hit a few keys on her computer. "Good heavens, m'dear, seems this book hasn't been out of the library for darn near forty years! Makes sense, I suppose, because I found it in a stack in the basement when we were clearing out. It was in such good condition, and there is a lot of interest in the area's history, so I put it back on the shelves. Hasn't seen much action, though…do you have your library card?"

Kelly dutifully handed over the little plastic card, thanked Rachel, and left the building with a stack of printouts and the book on witches.

****

She was researching available flowers from local florists for the Parker wedding on the computer in the back room of Wedding Bliss when she heard voices in the store. Noelia poked her head around the door with a great big grin on her face.

"You have company, honey," she said, ducking back into the main store before Kelly could ask who was there.

She got up and moved toward the connecting door, and the words "I'm really busy right now" died on her lips. Standing in the center of the store, looking ultra-masculine surrounded by all those pretty, lacy things, was Brett Atwell.

He looked tanned and fit, wearing a sleeveless tee that molded itself to his chest in a way Kelly would like to mold herself at that moment. The Sub-Saharan sun had brightened his already fair hair to a golden color, and his skin glowed. A white Aran sweater was slung casually around his shoulders.

"What…what do you want?" Her mouth went dry as she caught his look, an expression that flickered long enough to tell her she was what he wanted.

"I've come to whisk you away for a couple of hours—you can leave the store, can't you?"

"Well, no, I mean…"

"Sure, she can," Noelia spoke over Kelly's stuttered excuse, winning a death glare from her boss.

"Good, let's go before it gets too late. The weather can be pretty cool in the evenings." He hoisted a wicker hamper from the floor at his feet.

"We're going on a picnic?" Kelly's eyes narrowed.

"Just what you need: some sun, fun, and relaxation." Noelia handed Kelly her lightweight windcheater jacket. "Off you go now."

"But…"

"Come on, Kelly. It'll be fun, and we'll only be gone a couple of hours." Brett grabbed her arm with his free hand and towed her toward the door.

"But I'm not dressed for…"

"You look fine to me."

Outside, Brett held onto Kelly's arm as if he thought she'd disappear if he let go. He strode along the sidewalk toward the pier, his long legs covering the ground quickly. Kelly had to scurry to keep up. "So, what's the big secret? Where are we going?"

"You'll see in a moment," came the mysterious answer.

They arrived at the small marina area reserved for private pleasure craft, and a tall, dark-haired man in a seaman's jersey and sunglasses came out of the clapboard office to meet them.

"Is everything ready?" Brett asked, shaking the man's hand.

"Oh, yes, all shipshape," he replied with a grin.

"Kelly, this is my good friend Rob MacAvee. He's lending us his cabin cruiser for a couple of hours."

"How do you do, ma'am," Rob said, treating Kelly to a broad smile before striding away.

Her face must have registered her shock. Staring at all the beautiful craft that were moored, gently bobbing, at the pier, Kelly said, "A boat ride?"

"Didn't you say you'd been wanting to take a sail around the bay since you moved to Marina Grove? Well, that's what we're going to do." He grinned like a magician displaying a new trick.

Kelly swallowed and tears came to her eyes. *When was the last time someone had done something this sweet for her? Something that involved listening to her dreams and making them come true?*

Brett reached out to swipe away the tears from her cheeks. "I didn't mean to make you cry," he said, dropping a gentle kiss on her forehead.

"I'm not crying, I'm happy." Kelly sniffed.

Muttering something about never being able to understand women, Brett led the way along the dock to where a modest cabin cruiser, painted blue and white, sparkled in the sun.

"What sort of a boat is this? I mean, what are they used for?"

"Cabin cruisers are remarkably comfortable and safe for cruising, fishing, or just plain having fun, depending on the size and style. They vary from utilitarian to luxurious. This type is designed for several people or a family to sail in comfort, with a kitchen, bathroom, and other facilities."

Kelly studied the smallish vessel, excitement swelling within her. *Imagine Brett actually remembering her confiding how much she wanted to go out on the bay!*

"Ma'am?" Brett said, offering his hand to help her climb the short ladder onto the deck before handing up the picnic basket and climbing on board himself.

****

They sailed around, hugging the shoreline first. Brett enjoyed watching the variety of expressions that played on Kelly's face as she viewed Marina Grove from an angle she had never seen it before—out in the bay.

"Look! That's my cottage right there! I think I can even see Sullivan sitting in the kitchen window." Her face glowed with delight.

An expression he had helped put there. Brett dragged in a deep breath at the thought. If he got so much pleasure from giving Kelly this one small treat, what would it feel like to spend a lifetime bringing her happiness? *Don't go getting ahead of yourself, man,* he warned himself.

He reached into the duffel bag he had brought and handed her a pair of binoculars. "Here, you'll be able to see a lot more through these."

"I used these a lot in the military," Kelly said, and a sober expression flashed across her face before she raised the glasses to her eyes and studied the view. Brett wondered what painful memories had slipped across her mind to create such a deep, if momentary, sadness. His heart ached to help her heal.

After the shoreline tour, Brett anchored the cruiser out in the bay and brought out the picnic basket the housekeeper, Mrs. Patrowski, had prepared for them. As the vessel bobbed gently, they sat close together on the small, covered bench and ate a traditional fare of ham and fresh bread, cheese, potato salad, hard boiled eggs, and fruit.

And they talked about anything and everything, sharing past adventures, future hopes and dreams, and laughing together. At one point, Kelly took a linen napkin and wiped a smear of mayonnaise from Brett's mouth, then she leaned over and kissed him gently on the lips. He deepened the kiss, and they slid slowly down onto the deck where they lay together, entwined, looking up at the fluffy clouds scudding across the darkening sky.

He didn't think he had ever felt so peaceful, so complete, in his life.

"I think it's time to get back, even though I'm reluctant," Brett said. "We have to watch the evening tide." Even now the waves were swelling beneath the vessel as the tide began to flow. Marina Grove had taken on a fairyland appearance as dusk began to fall, and twinkling lights appeared in the streets and buildings.

They stood together at the wheel, Brett's arm around Kelly and his hand over hers as he taught her to stay on course toward land.

"I wish this could go on forever," Kelly said dreamily, looking up at him as she snuggled under his arm. He tightened his hold on her, wishing the same thing.

They tied up the cruiser at its berth and stood looking at each other, the moment of parting awkward. He wanted to ask her to stay with him that night, but was afraid it was too sudden, too early, and would frighten her away.

He settled for kissing her hard and long, putting his brand on her, before letting her go back to pick up her car at Wedding Bliss while he dropped the vessel keys off at the marina office.

****

Noelia had placed the closed sign on the door at Wedding Bliss and locked everything up. Kelly was relieved she wouldn't have to answer her friend's questions about the outing. She wanted to go home and sit quietly on her deck, savoring all the wonderful memories she and Brett had made that day. She still could hardly believe that he had taken to heart her comments about wishing she could go sailing—not only taken them in but acted on them in such a thoughtful way.

She picked up her purse, some files, and some notes she had made for clients, and then locked the store up again. Before she did so, she glanced out of the window.

There was no Old Man on the Bench.

The day was just getting better and better.

Chapter Eight

Noelia wore her black suit to work the next day, an instant tell for Kelly that her assistant had something very serious on her mind. Once they stopped for a morning coffee and cookies break, Noelia cleared her throat.

Here it comes, Kelly thought. "Please don't tell me you're leaving me, Noelia."

Noelia's dark eyebrows shot up. "Why ever would you think that?"

"It's the black suit, the sort of classy outfit to wear going for an interview for a serious job. I've always thought you were too smart to be my part-time assistant." Kelly crunched a chocolate whole-wheat cookie and avoided Noelia's gaze.

"Honey, I wouldn't dream of leaving you! I couldn't have the disaster you would get yourself into if you were on your own on my conscience."

"Thanks a lot." Kelly tried to look offended but couldn't help the smile of relief that curled her lips.

"Actually, I'm visiting a friend later today and wanted to look smart. Anyway, we do have to talk about something that's been troubling me. Please hear me out. Now that you know there is a connection between Mary Atwell and the Cursed Bridal Gown, you have to do something about it."

"What would you have me do? I mean, I'd love to

settle this. Our profits are getting slimmer by the day."

"My opinion? You have to be honest. First tell Brett what you've learned and what has happened to the women who've tried to wear that gown. See if he can get his aunt to take the curse back or hide it in her witch's coven or whatever. Then tell Daria Welcome she must give it back—tell her you'll get an even nicer one for her at no extra charge."

Kelly sighed in frustration. She wasn't happy at what she was hearing. "Actually, I've tried that with Daria. No dice. And I should take responsibility for all this because…?"

"Because you should never have sold that dress again in the first place. Now that you know its full history, you have a duty to protect other brides. Call Daria. Now!"

Kelly chewed on her bottom lip. She'd rather crawl ten miles through the desert in full combat kit than deal with either Brett or Daria about that dress. "You know how much better you are with people than I am. Why don't you call and talk to them?"

"You know I love you and I'd walk through fire for you. But there's not a snowball's chance in hell that I'm talking to these people about this. No. Never." Noelia's mouth set in a determined line.

"Not even if I promise you a new coffee maker?" Kelly was prepared to beg.

"Not even if it's gold plated and sings 'Come Back to Sorrento'." Noelia folded her arms over her black-clad chest, her expression stubborn. "You owe it to future brides who might want to wear that gown. Either destroy it or fix the problem. And if it's cursed, even destroying it might mean the curse affixes it to something else—you, for instance…"

Kelly shivered and reached for the last chocolate cookie. "Okay, you've guilted me into it. I'll make those calls right now."

"Oh, and Kelly?" Noelia swatted Kelly's hand away and snatched up the cookie for herself. "Just don't mention your little imaginary friend on the bench outside. Not everyone would be as understanding as I am. Some might think you're crazy." She took a triumphant bite of the sweet, enjoying Kelly's frown.

Ten minutes later Kelly was hiding out in the small rear room of the store, trying to work up the courage for a private conversation with Brett and then with Daria. "Think of the other women whose lives might be ruined if they choose that dress," she reminded herself, holding up Daria Welcome's card from the Rolodex. "Guess Daria is one of those brides."

She took a deep breath and dialed the number. It really didn't go well.

Daria said she was looking at a happy ever after that included the vintage wedding gown, and she made it abundantly clear to Kelly she had no plans to give that up.

"I'm sorry, I'm sure this old lady would like to have the dress back but hey, it's not like she needs it for her wedding now, is it?" The realtor was adamant. "You said it yourself; this gown is perfect for me. It could have been made for me—it doesn't even need alterations. Now I have this whole picture in my head of my wedding, and I can see myself walking down the aisle at St. Christopher's wearing the absolutely perfect dress, with Drake standing at the altar dazzled as he waits for me. No, there's just no way I can return it.

Tell the old dear I'm sorry."

Daria cut the telephone connection abruptly and left Kelly listening to dead air. She sighed. She hadn't really expected Daria to agree to give up the dress. She'd searched and found another, in her eyes equally gorgeous vintage dress, but the bride-to-be wouldn't even look at it.

Maybe if she hadn't been so chicken and had gone to meet her customer face to face rather than over the telephone and showed her the other gown she was offering; she might have been able to persuade her to do an exchange. Something in Daria's tone, however, made her think that possibility unlikely.

Feeling defeated, Kelly dialed the number on Brett's business card. Another difficult call to make, and one that should also perhaps have been made face-to-face. She knew it was cowardly, but she flinched from seeing the expression she was sure would appear on Brett's handsome face when she brought up the subject of The Cursed Gown. After all, how do you tell a guy that his favorite aunt is a weirdo who may have cursed a wedding dress and ruined the romantic plans of several other brides? *Yeah, that would go down really well.*

She liked him too much to want to see him lose interest in her face to face. She dialed the number he had given her and crossed her fingers. That didn't stop her pulse doing that funny little jump when she heard his voice.

"Gee, I was just thinking about you." He answered with warmth that turned her knees to jelly. Would that sexy tone still be there after she told him why she was calling?

"I was thinking about you, too. I think I do have the wedding gown you're looking for, but there's a problem with it."

"If you need to get it professionally cleaned or mended, then obviously I'll pay your costs and return whatever you paid my sister for the dress."

"This isn't something that can be fixed by a seamstress or a dry cleaner."

A seconds-too-long silence. Then, his voice, laced with a suspicion that caused Kelly's heart to plummet, growled, "Look, you have me over a barrel; you know how much I care for Aunt Mary. If you're after making a profit on the gown, just name your price. But I warn you, Kelly, I won't be blackmailed."

Tears pricked at her eyes at his suggestion that she wasn't on the level, but a hot flash of anger saved her from letting them fall. "It's nothing like that. I'm not that kind of person," she snapped. "It's just that the dress was purchased by a young woman who is getting married soon. She refuses to return the dress, even though I offered her an equally nice substitute. I'm afraid there's nothing more I can do. Tell your aunt I'm sorry." *And let's hope she doesn't decide to put a curse on me.*

She heard Brett draw in a deep breath. "Listen, why don't you give me the name and contact information for this woman. I am sure if I talk to her she'll see reason…"

"I can't do that. I have a duty of privacy to my clients." Kelly bit her bottom lip. Maybe if she did let Brett talk to Daria…? No, the bride-to-be had made it very clear there was no way she was giving up the gown.

"Perhaps you could arrange a meeting?"

"I'm sorry, Brett. There are other...issues at play here. Your aunt will probably forget all about her anxieties about the dress once she's home and back in good health."

"She's coming home the day after tomorrow, in good health, and she's not letting the subject drop." Something in his tone made Kelly sure that Brett was being given a very hard time by his aunt. Hard to imagine a big strong guy like that being harassed by an old lady. Strangely Kelly found the idea both amusing and endearing. "Just what aren't you telling me?"

He wasn't going to let this drop unless she really convinced him. Kelly closed her eyes tightly and blurted out the truth, glad she hadn't met up with him in person. "Brett, you're going to find this hard to process, but a lot of people think that wedding gown is...cursed. Your aunt is better off staying well away from it." *Well done, Kelly. So much for giving him a rational explanation.*

This time the silence went on for so long Kelly was sure she'd lost him somewhere in the ether. He spoke just as she was about to close the connection.

"Is this your idea of a joke? Or a way of trying to wriggle out of returning the gown? Because honestly, Red, I'm not laughing."

She pulled in a deep breath, glad he was at least giving her the opportunity to explain. And the use of that hated nickname gave her a little flicker of hope. Perhaps he wasn't too angry with her. Maybe there was a chance to make him see reason.

"That dress has been purchased by three couples. Each couple has fallen out and canceled their wedding plans. It's an awful coincidence, and I don't believe in coincidences. It seems everyone in town here believes there's a curse on the gown, and I'm coming to think that's the only possibility. You know what Sherlock Holmes said about discounting all other possibilities?"

This time the silence stretched out even longer. Finally, when he spoke his voice was a mixture of hard and sad. "Kelly, I've grown to really like you even though we've just met. I'd never have put you down as a scam artist…but when I hear this stuff I'm wondering, what's your angle?"

This time, it was Kelly who was silent. *How could he suggest that she was trying to trick him out of money she hadn't earned?* Finally, she cut the connection without answering him.

Her heart ached even though common sense said it was better to find out the guy was a jerk who couldn't have any faith in her now, rather than later when she might have given him a piece of her heart.

As if that hadn't already happened.

****

She sat with her feet up on the back veranda rail of her home, sipping a cold beer and wishing she had nothing to think about but the beauty of the gathering twilight throwing purple and deep blue shadows over the ocean. The book on local witches and their descendants sat on her lap, but she had a curious reluctance to open it. It was bad enough to have the Old Man on the Bench hovering in the back of her mind; she wasn't keen on cluttering her thoughts with a lot of nonsense about witches as well. And it was nonsense. Wasn't it? Certainly, Brett Atwell had made it clear that he thought so.

Occasionally a pleasure craft or a fishing boat passed by in the distance, hurrying to return to port before dark. Kelly watched them pass, and memories of the few hours she'd spent with Brett on the cabin cruiser flooded back into her mind. Her pulse raced and her skin felt hot, as if she were sitting under the hot sun instead of the cooling evening. Tears pricked at her eyes. Was Brett really a jerk, as she'd told herself after the fiasco of a telephone conversation? How would that meld with the thoughtful, sweet gesture of their picnic on board the boat? Would a true-life jerk remember a dream mentioned in passing and make it come true? She shook her head, watching Sullivan the cat snoring softly, sprawled out in one of the last sunbeams of the day.

Maybe she was being too hasty in judgment. After all, it must have been quite a shock for him to be told that his favorite, his only, aunt was maybe crazy as an outhouse rat and setting curses on inanimate objects.

Except that Mary Atwell couldn't be crazy if the curse were real.

The argument went around and round in her head until a dull headache settled on her temples.

If Brett reacted this badly to the suggestion of a cursed bridal gown, just how would he react if she told him that her so-called 'hallucinations' were actually real dead people talking to her?

Feeling truly depressed now, Kelly swigged the last of her beer and rose to go inside. She carefully placed the book in a closet and shut the door, as if she didn't like having it out in the open. Sullivan curled around her legs, giving his plaintive 'I'm starving' meow. She put a little extra kibble in his dish and then got out her list of things she wanted to do the next day to look over before going to bed.

The top of the list was something she should probably talk to Brett about. She was pretty sure that he would hit the roof if he knew she planned to visit his aunt and ask her directly about the curse. If she asked his permission, he'd certainly order her not to go.

Which really left only one choice.

She'd go and find Mary Atwell and hope that Brett didn't find out.

The idea of this petty defiance made her smile, and she was humming as she climbed the stairs to her cottage bedroom. Even the sudden hard rain blown against her window by a strong wind off the ocean did nothing to disturb her sleep that night. No restless spirits visited her dreams.

Chapter Nine

The night's storm had dissipated, and the autumn sun was peeking through clouds to illuminate a newly washed world when Kelly set off the next morning for the long drive to Derry. She hummed and sang along with the tunes on a soft rock station as she navigated the coast road, and her lip-syncing performance behind the wheel had a couple of other drivers waving to her as they passed. She couldn't help but smile; it was such a beautiful day, and she was actually taking some action at last!

Once she arrived, it didn't take her long to make her way to the auction house where she'd bought the Cursed Bridal Gown, and her good mood held despite the busy late morning traffic. It began to fray when Ron Drury, the auction house manager, proved reluctant to help her, citing client confidentiality. Hadn't she used the same when talking with Brett about Daria Welcome? Brett had told her his sister Sasha had put the gown up for auction, but she didn't know the woman's last name or address and had to launch a campaign of charm, along with a considerable amount of pleading and the unspoken threat of an incipient tearful session, to get Mr. Drury to give her the address of the party who had provided the auction item #43 (Vintage Wedding Gown).

That earlier sunny good mood was pretty much

gone as she stood under the covered portico of a stately mansion in Derry's outskirts, tired, hungry, and increasingly stressed. The mansion overlooked the ocean, and she took deep, calming breaths while she admired the breathtaking view. The double front doors were painted a bright Colonial blue, and one side was opened abruptly, and a middle-aged woman in an apron covering a staid black dress stood looking out. She treated Kelly and her elderly car with the same haughty expression.

Her look said the ten-year-old van just wasn't the usual class of vehicle to stand in the curved driveway. The same assessment seemed to extend itself to Kelly, for she said, "We don't buy from door-to-door sellers," and began to close the door.

Desperation made Kelly stick her foot in the door, wincing as the heavy oak slammed into her big toe. "I'm not selling anything. In fact, I bought something, and I need to meet with Ms. Sasha Atwell-Montgomery."

"She's out."

"Well, it was really Ms. Mary Atwell I was looking for." Kelly was sometimes disturbed at how easily lies seemed to spring to her lips.

"She's out, too." The pressure of the door on her foot was gradually increasing. If she didn't get this settled in the next couple of minutes she'd likely walk with a limp for the rest of her life.

"Look, I came a distance to see Ms. Atwell or Ms. Montgomery. Maybe I could just come in and wait."

The woman issued a long-suffering sigh. "I'm sorry, that will not be possible." She didn't sound at all sorry to Kelly's ears.

At that moment, a flirty red sports convertible breezed up the driveway and came to rest teasingly alongside Kelly's elderly vehicle. The van looked even more discouraged beside the other perky vehicle. Which was the same reaction Kelly had as the car's slender blonde driver hopped out. She was as flirty and perky as her car, and Kelly suddenly felt too tall, too chunky, too old, and just, well, just too everything.

"Hello—are you from the cleaning service?" Little Miss Perky chirruped as she climbed the steps armed with a couple of shopping bags with elegant store logos on them. They were from stores whose windows Kelly couldn't even afford to stand in front of let alone shop inside. That made the reference to the cleaning company even more offensive, and she drew herself up to her full height, which was a good two inches over the blonde.

Not that the other woman was intimidated. The entire Russian army probably couldn't stop this one in her tracks for long. "No, I'm from a store called Wedding Bliss in Marina Cove. The proprietor, actually, and…"

Sasha gave a little gasp. "You're the one that paid that outrageous price for Aunt Mary's scruffy old wedding gown? I hope my brother hasn't been hassling you too much about that silly thing! Mrs. Patrowski, I'll have my tea in the parlor."

Dismissed in a couple of sentences. Kelly frowned. The housekeeper frowned, too. At least they had something in common besides being ignored by Sasha, who sashayed into the house as if they weren't there. They both traipsed through the foyer after her.

"Brett's your brother? Yes, it would be fair to say

he's been bothering me." It was true. Thoughts of Brett had actually woven through Kelly's dreams, although she wasn't going to tell Sasha that.

Brett's sister gave a genteel snort, reminding Kelly of a purebred racehorse she'd once seen. "He's such an old stick-in-the-mud! Making such a fuss about that old dress. Honestly, as if Auntie Mary is ever going to want to wear it again!"

The housekeeper gave a disgusted sniff and walked away.

Kelly looked around the beautiful old house, with its richly appointed furnishings sparkling in the multi-colored rainbows cast by the sun through art nouveau stained glass. The place screamed old money. What would it be like to live in such a place? To grow up rich and secure? To take for granted all this comfort and beauty and the assurance of ancestors going back generations?

Sasha's next question interrupted her musings. "I hope you're not thinking to ask for your money back, because it's not going to happen." She cast a narrow-eyed glance at her visitor. Kelly cast a disparaging glance at the expensive shopping bags the other woman clutched. It was obvious that much of the money from the auction had already been spent. Anger riffled up and down her spine, but she swallowed it, remembering Noelia's 'catch more flies with honey than vinegar' mantra.

"I'm doing some research, and I wanted to talk to your aunt about her dress. Lots of people have admired it, by the way."

"Oh, Auntie Mary's recovering from pneumonia; she's in the Holywell Home—it is a nursing and retirement residence. Very upscale." Sasha's cheeks took on a guilty flush, and Kelly remembered that Brett had had some harsh words for his sister over abandoning their aunt to the care of strangers.

Kelly had to fight the big smile that wanted to crawl over her lips. She thought she'd have to really press Brett's sister, but it turned out she hadn't even had to ask for Mary Atwell's location. She put on a suitably serious expression and said, "I'm sorry to hear that. She's feeling better, I hope?"

Sasha didn't bother to hide her look of disappointment. "Yes, she is, and Brett's making this big fuss about her coming home tomorrow. It was supposed to be today, but the doctor who must sign her out was away until tomorrow."

"Well, that will be nice for you to have her back, won't it?" It was mean of her to tease the other woman, but as far as Kelly was concerned there probably wasn't enough mean in Sasha's life. She headed toward the front door.

"Hey," Sasha called after her. "You're not the one everyone's talking about? The one with the Cursed Bridal Gown? Myself, I know a sales gimmick when I hear one—you'd better not be putting that around about Auntie Mary's dress!"

Kelly turned and, with the sweetest smile she could muster, said, "Of course not, Sasha—a person would have to be really dumb to believe in that stuff, wouldn't they?" And then she made her escape.

****

Kelly congratulated herself on obtaining information that wasn't easily come by and decided she deserved a quiet lunch. Her growling stomach agreed.

She was starving and figured she could take a half hour or so to eat and get her strength up. If Mary Atwell was in a nursing home, she wasn't likely to be taking off on a hot date, so there was no real urgency to get to the Holywell Home and interview her.

She needed to watch her cash flow, so it looked like lunch under the Golden Arches. She stopped at one that had one of those children's play areas, and the place was swarming with little rug rats of all varieties. Still, the food was predictable, cheap, and quick, so she grabbed a newspaper off the rack and settled down with her tray at a table for two.

She couldn't help but notice the young mother at the next table who was discreetly breast-feeding a tiny baby. Kelly was an only child of parents who themselves were only children, so she hadn't had a lot of contact with babies and found herself unable to take her eyes from this tiny being. Who would have thought they came in such diminutive sizes?

She must have been staring because the young woman said, "Is this bothering you? I mean, this is the only chance I have for a few quiet minutes to feed Davey while Dixie is busy in the play area."

Embarrassed, Kelly apologized. "I'm sorry for staring—and no, it doesn't bother me at all. In fact, I think it's quite beautiful."

The other woman smiled. "Thank you. My name's Merry, by the way. And you probably wouldn't think it was so beautiful if you had to do it regularly at two a.m."

"Probably not, but you look happy enough."

"Oh, good heavens! Dixie!" Merry jumped to her feet, a look of panic on her face as she stared through the Plexiglas that separated the play area from the restaurant. Her tiny bundle of joy gave an outraged wail at being separated from his lunch.

Kelly followed her glance and saw a tiny girl, a miniature of her mom, tottering on the top of a climbing frame. As they watched in horror, the little girl lost her grip and fell to land on the cushioned floor. The specially designed flooring saved the tot from injury, but obviously her pride was hurt because moments later an ear-shattering howl filled the play area. Kelly's new friend struggled to straighten her clothes and grab her purse while holding the infant.

"You need to go to her," Kelly said. "Shall I hold the baby for a moment and watch your things?"

Undecided, the woman looked her over. The wailing grew in volume, people were starting to stare, and she made an executive mom decision. "Just for a moment—I'll be right back. Just promise me you're not a kidnapper!"

"No, not on Tuesdays, anyway." Kelly reached out her arms to receive the baby, who was bundled up in a soft blanket. The child rested in her arms, looking up at her with such a serious expression she found herself smiling broadly. And out of the blue, a longing filled her, a deep longing she'd never experienced before. At that moment, the idea of having a baby of her own seemed like the most important life goal she could have.

"How could I do it, though, sweetie? It takes two to tango, after all," she told those wide blue eyes. The tot, who couldn't have been more than ten weeks old, smiled and gurgled as if he hadn't a care in the world and thought that Kelly should feel the same way.

Unbidden, Brett Atwell's honest brown eyes and gentle touch came to mind. Kelly had to fight to tamp down a flood of warmth at the very idea of creating a wee person like the one in her arms with Brett.

The impact of these hither-to-unknown emotions was so strong that a wave of disappointment washed over her when the child's mother returned and gently reclaimed the baby. "This is Dixie," she said, as she introduced the chubby faced angel who looked as though the tragedy of a few minutes before was now a distant memory. She stuck her thumb in her mouth and clung to her mom's jeans but managed to smile around the digit when Kelly said hello.

"Thank you so much. Dixie and I appreciate your help. And I'm so glad you're not a kidnapper, although some days…" Merry rolled her eyes as she struggled to corral the tired toddler while balancing the baby, car seat carrier, coats, and children's meal box.

****

Holywell Home was a high-end convalescent home featuring luxury tempered with practicality. Kelly had to press a button to gain entry through the big glass-and-brass doors and then walk across a mile of expensive but easy-care low pile carpeting to a half-moon cherry wood desk that glowed softly in the discreet glow from ceiling pot lights.

The carpeting was a soothing moss green, the walls a soft beige. Three comfy looking loveseats braced a glowing gas fire with brass surround and cherry wood mantel. On the table were two piles of magazines, corners squared and looking pristine as if they'd never been flipped through.

Several large, fake, green plants were dotted about.

Two or three generic pictures, prints of old masters and a surprising Dali abstract, provided visual relief on the broad expanse of beige walls. Soft classical music spilled from speakers embedded in the walls and flowed over the subdued quiet.

The receptionist looked to be in her thirties, wearing a pink trouser suit and about fifty extra pounds. Her name tag said Sandy Lewis. She treated Kelly to a warm, impersonal smile and asked how she could be of help.

"Are the doors always locked like that? No one gets in or out without you knowing?" Kelly was genuinely interested.

The receptionist assumed a serious, concerned expression and leaned forward over the cherry wood counter. "Some of our guests are suffering from Alzheimer's or dementia," she confided. "We have to monitor the doors, like other nursing homes. Some places have had people go wandering away, and it has ended in tragedy."

Kelly, who since being wounded had suffered from slight claustrophobia, shuddered mentally but maintained her smile as she announced that she was here to visit with Aunt Mary Atwell. "I only heard recently that she had been ill, you know, after Brett returned from abroad."

"Hmm, there haven't been many visitors, and I'm sure Mrs. Atwell will be delighted." She tapped pink tipped fingernails on the keyboard, brow furrowing with concentration. "What was your name again?"

Kelly told her, and the brow furrow became more pronounced. "I'm sorry, but your name isn't on the visitor's list."

Kelly heaved a theatrical sigh and clicked her tongue against her front teeth. "Oh, Brett and Sasha said they would call you to let you know I'd be here, but you know how busy they are. I'm sure you'll hear from them soon."

"I really can't let anyone in to see Ms. Atwell unless you're on the list." The receptionist looked genuinely sorry, then crossed her arms over her chest and looked stern.

"Like I said, you should hear from them momentarily, and I really don't know what they'll say if they find I've come all this way and you couldn't let me see Aunt Mary. Could you give them a call? I have Brett's number here…"

"No, dear, I can't do that. Mr. Atwell calls regularly as clockwork at about three o'clock; why don't you go and have a coffee and come back in half an hour? We'll get you on the list then, and everything will be fine."

Kelly heaved a huge sigh of frustration, and she wasn't acting. "I guess if that's the best we can do…I certainly wouldn't want to upset Aunt Mary. But one thing—is there a bathroom close by? I'm recovering from a tummy bug and all this anxiety and travel, well, it seems to have stirred things up again."

"I don't think…"

"Listen, this is urgent. I could even have an accident…" Kelly screwed up her eyes in a well-played look of embarrassment as she wrapped her arms around her mid-section.

The receptionist's eyes went panic-wide. "Of course—go through the double doors and there's a toilet two doors along on your right…"

Kelly scampered off, looking for all the world like a woman with a dire emergency. Once through the doors and out of sight of the dutiful gatekeeper, she relaxed and wandered along with a puzzled expression like a visitor looking for a room. A pleasant-looking middle-aged woman in pink flower-patterned scrubs came out of one of the rooms, and Kelly asked for help. "I'm a bit lost, I'm afraid. I'm looking for Mary Atwell, but I seem to have got the room number wrong…"

"You want room 202. Go along the corridor, take the elevator to the next floor, turn right, third door on the left."

"How is Aunt Mary today? In one of her moods?" It was a guess, but apparently spot on.

"Between ourselves, she is a bit of a dragon, I'm afraid. I don't want to speak out of turn, but that woman isn't going to be happy until she's home again." The woman gave Kelly a meaningful look and strode off.

She found room 202 easily. So far, so good. A querulous voice answered her knock, and she slipped inside. She knew she didn't have too much time before the gorgon at the reception desk tattled on her to the Atwells and then hit the panic button. She'd only think that Kelly was in distress in the washroom for a while before twigging that she'd done the unthinkable—sneaked up uninvited to Mary's room.

"Ms. Atwell?"

"Who else would be in this room?" The woman in a fluffy pale blue dressing gown and matching slippers sat in a tall wing chair by the window. She was so petite her feet hung above the floor, but her expression was of the 'don't mess with me' variety. Kelly bet a lot of people didn't dare mess with her, which was probably why the thought of her aunt coming home and noticing all the missing objects she'd auctioned off left Sasha looking a bit green. Ms. Atwell didn't look like the kind of woman who would tolerate fools gladly.

Kelly took a deep breath. Before she could exhale, the woman snapped, "I hope you're not here to do another test, young lady. I've had it up to here with your tests. Won't someone just tell me what's wrong with me? My nephew insists there's nothing, but if that's true, then why am I still here having tests if I'm perfectly healthy?"

Kelly remembered Brett's comment that his aunt thought she was dying and that's why she wanted that wedding gown. To be buried in. A cold chill ran along her spine. Letting out a nervous breath, Kelly replied, "No, I'm not here to do tests."

"Good. You heard that my nephew will be taking me back home soon? Then I can see what a mess my niece has made of her life and my home while I've been cooped up in here."

Kelly experienced a momentary pang of sympathy for the feather-brained Ms. Sasha Atwell-Montgomery. "Then you've heard what happened?"

"Of course. I didn't expect anything better from that girl. Been a problem to her parents all her life, and now they're gone and she's a problem to me."

"I'm so glad you know because I needed ask you some questions about your wedding dress…"

Mary tilted her head to one aside, reminding Kelly of a hungry predatory bird. "What do you mean? You want to talk about my wedding gown? What's that got to do with that silly girl getting a divorce again?"

Ice formed in the bottom of Kelly's stomach as she

realized her mistake. Embarrassed, she realized she had jumped to the wrong conclusion. Mary knew nothing of the sale of her wedding dress. *Oops!* As she struggled to come up with a good explanation for her gaffe, another problem rose up before her eyes.

Standing right on the other side of Mary's bed was the Old Man on the Bench. Except he wasn't on the bench outside Wedding Bliss; he was right here in Mary Atwell's room.

"You're not supposed to be here!" she hissed.

"Who's not supposed to be here?" Mary threw a puzzled glance around the room.

"I shouldn't be here? You're the one who shouldn't be here!" a familiar voice boomed.

In her shock at seeing the ghost, she hadn't heard the door open. Kelly whipped around to see a furious Brett Atwell standing in the entryway, an angry flush of red across his cheekbones.

Oh, my goodness, now I've really done it!

Of course, she couldn't explain that her remark was really aimed at the restless spirit who even now was fading from view. That would obviously go down like a lead balloon. Did that nasty old man smirk as he was fading away or was that just her imagination?

She was still struggling for a reply that wouldn't make her look like a lunatic when Brett's aunt spoke up.

"This girl wants to talk about my wedding gown, Brett. What does it have to do with her? And have you brought that dress with you? I don't see…" The high quavering voice trailed off as the old lady's sharp intelligence kicked in. "Something's happened to my dress, hasn't it? Has that silly girl Sasha done something with it?"

Brett pinched the bridge of his nose between his thumb and forefinger, signaling a budding headache. "Yes, Auntie, there is a problem with the wedding dress, but nothing that we can't solve. Trust me, you'll get your gown back—not that you'll need it. There won't be a funeral anytime soon. There's nothing wrong with you, Auntie. You're over the pneumonia and healthy as an ox."

Mary refused to be sidetracked. "Get my dress back? Where is it? What has that stupid girl done? Does this girl have my dress? Is she a thief?"

"No, she's not a thief. Can you excuse us a moment while I talk to Kelly?" In two quick strides, Brett crossed the room, and his fingers closed over Kelly's wrist in an iron grip. Ignoring her shocked squeak of protest, he dragged her effortlessly toward the door. For a brief moment, she wanted to throw herself on the old lady's mercy and beg to be allowed to stay. But the way Brett's aunt was looking at her, she thought the woman would have no compunction in throwing her to the wolves.

Or wolf. Brett's upper lip was curled back in a very feral snarl. Kelly wrenched her hand from his grip and began to walk away down the corridor, putting on her best 'I don't give a damn' look. The same look she used to turn on her fellow officers in the military when the men would tease her.

It didn't work on Brett. He closed his aunt's door behind them and quickly caught up with her, moving them both a little way down the hallway; she knew he wanted a chance to bawl her out without the old lady hearing. Kelly's chin tilted higher.

"Look, I didn't know your aunt hadn't been told that the gown was sold. How could I?"

"Didn't I specifically tell you to stay away from her? Didn't I tell you that she's fragile and doesn't need the stress of your little games? Cursed gown, indeed!" He spat out the furious words. His hand was on the wall next to Kelly's head, and he was leaning in much too close. She swallowed hard and wondered if he was feeling the same heat she felt.

Apparently, his feeling was the heat of anger. "I was actually going to try to find you and apologize for being so mistrusting earlier. I have to confess I've found dealing with this situation very stressful. Sasha is so deceitful, and I guess I was tarring you with the same brush. Then I get a call from the home here and find you've lied your way into my aunt's room, when I explicitly told you not to bother her..."

His words trailed off, and he stood for a few long moments staring directly into her eyes. She gazed back, afraid the feelings in her heart might just be reflected in her own eyes. Brett's look softened, the pupils smoky with sudden desire as his eyes moved to her lips. His mouth followed, catching hers in a kiss as intense as it was short-lived.

Suddenly he pulled back, scrubbing his hands over his face. "Kelly Andrews, half the time I don't know what to do with you—whether to kiss you or yell at you!"

And with that he turned and walked away, leaving her shell-shocked but smiling.

But Kelly knew what she wanted at that moment.

Kiss me. Kiss me, please. Kiss me again.

Chapter Ten

Kelly didn't know what had shaken her the most—the ghost's appearance in Mary's room, Brett's heated kiss, or her own breathless, needy reaction. Either way, she had to find a calm sanctuary to regain her equilibrium. A glance at her watch showed that it was after five o'clock and her assistant would have shut up the shop and gone home for the day.

It was Noelia's calm common sense that she needed, and she took the short detour toward her assistant's home almost without conscious thought. Noelia Russo's little house stood on the edge of town. Neat and well-cared for, the dignified Cape Cod with its blue siding and fresh white paint reflected its owner's character. The house was small, but the gardens surrounding it were the envy of every other gardener in Marina Grove. Noelia had a special way with plants as well as people, and it seemed that everything she planted flourished under her care.

The older woman was a very private person, and Kelly had only visited her home once before, when Noelia had held a small graduation party for her younger son. She'd been impressed then by the simplicity of the home and the quiet calm that pervaded it.

It was that quiet and calm that beckoned her as she returned from her confrontation with Brett over her visit to Mary Atwell. She brought with her a bottle of red wine recommended by the woman behind the counter in a convenience store. She hoped Noelia would be happy to share it with her and perhaps dispense some of her good advice.

She was admiring the flowerbeds alongside the crazy-paving garden path when a voice caught her attention.

"Oh, yes, yes…my darling, love me now!"

The words, spoken by Noelia but so very un-Noelia like, froze Kelly in her tracks.

"Kiss me, now…oh, keep doing that! You know just how to pleasure me…"

Realization dawned that her assistant had a visitor and wasn't likely to want her company. Kelly started to back down the path.

"Ahhhh! Don't stop now! Your touch is magic…I need…"

Kelly covered her ears, not wanting to hear what Noelia needed. She'd heard enough. Obviously, the old adage that still waters run deep had a lot of truth to it. Noelia, her sweet, competent assistant, middle-aged widow, mother of three, a member of the Marina Grove Book Club, and an active churchwoman, was enjoying red hot afternoon sex!

A blush flamed across Kelly's cheeks. Darn it, she was jealous. She couldn't remember how long it had been since she'd enjoyed mediocre sex, let alone the hot kind that Noelia was obviously enjoying. Depression swamped her as she realized that the last bedtime frolics she had were with Wayne, the fiancé who'd dumped her five years ago. And that had been mediocre sex, too, compared to the erotic sounds coming through that open upper window.

Still backing away from the house and hoping not to be noticed, Kelly didn't realize she'd gone off the path until she sprawled backward over a large granite boulder with the words 'You're Welcome—Come Right In!' painted in colorful letters on the side. She grabbed at a three-foot-tall metal windmill to try to halt her fall, pulling the garden ornament out of the ground so that it clattered onto the boulder with enough noise to alert the whole neighborhood. Certainly, enough noise to distract even the hottest lovers. Kelly winced and wished the ground would open up and swallow her as the window on the upper floor was pushed right open and Noelia called, "Kelly? Is that you? What are you doing lying in my hostas?"

Before Kelly had a chance to think up a suitable answer, the window had slammed shut, and within moments Noelia was standing over her. Her expression was worried as she held out her hand to help Kelly back to her feet. "Whatever happened? I thought that boulder was safe enough, being far from the path and everything…"

"I was, er, just passing and I thought I'd call in and say hello…" By some minor miracle, the bottle of wine had survived the tumble, and Kelly raised it as if it would confirm her words.

Noelia's eyebrows went up as she glanced at the bottle. "Have you been drinking one of that bottle's companions? Is that why you fell over? Are you drunk?"

Kelly certainly wished she were. "I can hear, er, see that you're busy. Maybe we can talk later…"

"Not at all—whatever gave you the idea I'm busy?

Come on inside."

"But I heard you…you and your visitor…" Now she was beginning to feel foolish. Just what was the etiquette to follow when you had unwittingly barged in on a friend in *flagrante delecto*? Suddenly she noticed that Noelia was fully and neatly dressed. How had she managed that and to run outside in just a few seconds? A strange idea was beginning to take shape inside her head.

"You must be mistaken." Noelia sounded strained. And was that a faint blush rising on her cheeks? "Maybe you heard the radio program I was listening to…"

The deepening bright pink flush that had spread up from Noelia's neck to paint her cheeks was a real giveaway. "Oh, no, that certainly wasn't a radio program. It was a really hot love scene. And you're alone…"

A visual memory of herself opening a box and taking out copies of spicy romance novels by a Mimi L'Amour, Marina Cove's reclusive writer of sexy romances…

A customer had come into the store as they were unpacking, and she had immediately bought the two most recent books. Kelly had joked that they should try and reveal the identity of the mysterious author and ask if she'd do a book signing…

…and Noelia had been adamant that such an event simply wouldn't be suitable in Wedding Bliss…

"It's you, isn't it? I've walked in on the creation of the latest novel, oh, my God, you're Mimi L'Amour!"

"Shhh! Someone might hear you." Noelia had blushed a scarlet befitting the pen name. She put her arm around Kelly's shoulder and almost dragged her into the house. She pushed Kelly into one of the big, comfortable wing chairs in front of the window.

"You have it all wrong. If you must know, I've been doing some part-time work. Apparently, I have a great voice, and I get lots of work from a company that produces audio books. That's why I was...you know, with Mimi L'Amour's...And don't you dare laugh. It's darned hard, talking dirty out loud into a microphone, even if you're alone."

With a last baleful glare, Noelia Russo snatched the wine bottle and rushed off into her kitchen, her face still flushed, leaving behind a completely incredulous Kelly.

She returned moments later with two filled wine glasses and a plate of the English chocolate digestive cookies she was addicted to.

"I think I need a drink as badly as you do," she said, taking the wing chair opposite Kelly and handing her one of the glasses.

"You know that my husband, Andre, was killed in a fishing boat accident? The insurance money I got from my husband's death ran out fast, what with three kids in school, a mortgage, and all the other bills. I did all sorts of jobs. There was a period when I was working at a convenience store, waitressing at a café, and cleaning offices, all at the same time. But it never seemed enough, and I was so darned tired all the time. I remember thinking that, for all the time I spent with them, my kids might as well have lost both parents."

Tears clouded Noelia's eyes as she spoke. Kelly leaned forward to top up both their wine glasses while she waited for the other woman to continue her tale.

"Oh, and I did a lot of crying, too—grieving and

self-pity. But one day I woke up and said, God, if I'm going to survive this, I need something more. I was pretty peeved at God at the time and didn't expect any kind of God Breeze to help me out. But I got one. On my way home from my afternoon waitressing job the next day, I passed this bookstore and thought, well, I can go in and pretend to be a customer, sit in one of those nice comfy chairs and just...just be. So I did, but I can't say that I felt any better. There was a woman doing a book signing, and I watched her for a while. She greeted customers, spoke to everyone she could buttonhole, and signed quite a few books.

"My feet hurt so much, but I didn't actually want to go home. I was putting off the moment when I'd have to tell the three boys that I couldn't enroll them in hockey that year. No money." Noelia took a deep draught of her wine, her eyes seemingly focused on some far away memory.

"Anyway, there was a quiet time and I got talking to this writer. She was a single mom with two children, so we had a lot in common. She said I had the sexiest voice she'd ever heard and asked had I ever considered doing audiobooks?" Her face took on a dreamy expression.

"My Andre used to say he could listen to my voice forever. It was so seductive, he used to say..."

Too much information. Kelly wasn't sure she believed the story or not, but had to admit that Noelia had a deep, rolling, seductive voice that men would find indeed sexy.

Noelia said she'd always liked history and had taken her degree in Nineteenth-Century studies. The author she met had told her how difficult it was to get someone with just the right voice, someone who understood the romance of history, to read aloud her historical novels. "She offered to put a word in for me with the company who produced her audiobooks and said I could probably make some decent money if I was willing to put in the work.

"Well, I applied, got the job, and that's the reason you heard what you did this afternoon." Noelia's voice was firm, but Kelly was still suspicious.

"Are you sure you're not really Mimi? Honest, I won't tell anyone."

Noelia snorted. "Of course I'm not! Do I look like someone who would write sizzling sexy books?"

Kelly's eyes narrowed. Certainly, plump and matronly Noelia didn't look like a sexy author, but the words she'd heard from the window while she was in the garden… She was right to be skeptical. The identity of the famous writer was a mystery and a major topic of conversation in Marina Grove. There would be a real triumph for the person who could reveal her true identity. Kelly shook herself. It was Noelia's secret, whatever the truth was, and she was entitled to her privacy.

But still…Noelia as Mimi L'Amour? No wonder she was able to sell so many sets of sexy honeymoon wear. Kelly caught her assistant's eye. Noelia looked back, unflinching, the picture of innocence. She sighed. Maybe she would never know the truth.

Noelia broke the silence. "So, spill. I've told you my secret, now you have to tell me yours in exchange."

"What makes you think I have a secret?" Kelly kept her voice light.

Noelia placed raised her fist and lifted a finger at

each point. "Hmmm, now, let's see. Acting funny, jumping at shadows, talking to invisible old men on street benches, collapsing at the feet of hot hunks? No, wait, the last item isn't strange at all. I bet a lot of girls would like to throw themselves at the feet of that hunky Brett."

"I did not throw—" Kelly blushed when she saw Noelia's mischievous smile. "Okay, I do like Brett. In fact, I really, really like him. But somehow we're not connecting. I think it's maybe because…"

And she went on to tell Noelia all about her secret. About her head injury, about seeing people who weren't there, and how the doctors had written that off as hallucinations and told her they would go away in time. About realizing that she really was seeing restless spirits, had actually talked to some of them. And finally, about the old man on the bench and her suspicions that somehow his appearance was connected to that cursed wedding gown.

And how all of this meant she couldn't let a relationship with Brett develop.

"He'll think I'm a candidate for the psych ward," she murmured.

"If you were a total geeky genius, or if you had two left feet or some other oddity, he'd accept it as part of you, right? In the case of the genius part, he'd probably be proud of it. If he wasn't, then he wouldn't be worth wasting time over. The same goes for this. Whether you're talking to dead people—and as my Grannie used to say, there are more things in heaven and earth than this world dreams of—if you are talking to ghosts, then he should accept that as part of you, too. If he can't accept the whole package, then you're better off walking away."

Kelly sighed. "Where did you learn so much?"

"The School of Hard Knocks, honey. Will you tell him?"

Kelly sank her teeth into her upper lip. "I can't, not yet. Maybe never."

Chapter Eleven

Brett yawned and checked his watch again. It was awful. Way beyond awful, sitting in his car, waiting outside Kelly's edge-of-town home for her to return. As if the waiting wasn't bad enough, the rain was beating down on his windscreen, heavy enough to flow in miniature waves across the glass.

But he was determined to stay until he could capture Kelly's attention. Hard as it was to apologize, it was even harder to imagine a life without the red-haired beauty. How had she got under his skin in so short a time? He sighed. He wasn't a man used to sitting and waiting, although his job as an engineer and negotiator with the non-profit charity often demanded patience and diplomacy which strained his need for action. But this was different—this was waiting for a woman he'd treated badly and left upset and alone.

He'd been forced to explain about how the wedding dress had come to be in Kelly's possession, and his aunt had taken the news of Sasha's little auction very well. She'd declared that she would believe anything that stupid girl did, and then she grilled him about Kelly. He'd tried to keep a disinterested tone to his voice, but he could tell by Mary's secret little smile that she knew Kelly was more than just a businessperson he was dealing with. *Too smart for her own good, that aunt of mine!*

As the hours passed and he waited outside Kelly's cottage, his imagination taunted him with all kinds of terrible scenarios. Who could blame the woman if she took solace elsewhere after the way they'd parted company at the Holywell Home, with her close to tears and him so angry? What if she'd been so upset that she'd crashed her car on the lonely coast road? He shivered as a hundred dreadful scenarios flitted through his mind even as he told himself that a woman who could face down the Taliban wasn't going to be thrown into emotional turmoil by anger or a kiss.

Those kisses! The first one in her store, and then oh, my! That kiss on the cruise boat… He could feel it even now, the sweetness of her in his mouth, the heat that had spread throughout his body… He slammed a fist on the steering wheel. *What a mess!* No doubt about it, he'd overreacted when she'd shown up at the Holywell Home. His Aunt Mary had been surprised at his virtually dragging Kelly out of the room.

"That was so impolite, young man," she'd declared when he returned. "You were brought up better than that. And she seemed a nice young woman, even if a little mixed up."

"Kelly Andrews bought your wedding gown at an auction, and she says she won't give it back."

"Umph." Mary sniffed in disgust. "We'll see about that."

Brett had paced around the nursing home room. "Really, Auntie, I want you to stay away from her. You need to look after your health and get your strength back. Kelly has some strange ideas…"

Mary scowled at him. "What kind of strange ideas? Does she howl at the full moon or refuse to eat meat or dairy products?"

"Not eating meat isn't a strange idea." He hardly thought someone who believed she was a witch could judge anyone else's ideas 'strange'.

"If you say so, dear." Mary smiled. She was teasing him, and he fell for it every time.

"If you must know, Auntie, Kelly believes your wedding dress is cursed." He thought that would make Mary see reason about wanting to meet with Kelly again. Instead, the older woman started to laugh. She was still laughing, tears streaming down her pale cheeks, as Brett said goodbye, promising to pick her up late tomorrow afternoon, and escaped from her room.

His aunt had to be the most exasperating woman on the face of the planet.

And Kelly Andrews was probably a close second for that title.

Yes, he really needed to understand that Aunt Mary wasn't the fragile flower that everyone thought she was. Just because she'd been jilted fifty years ago and had what his grandparents claimed was a nervous breakdown, that didn't mean she couldn't cope with life now.

Or with a visit from one of the cutest redheads he'd ever had the pleasure of kissing.

He had to find Kelly and put things right with her.

He tried her cell number again, and again there was no answer. He was worried enough, guilty enough, that he'd called round earlier to the store in the forlorn hope that she was maybe working off some emotions by checking inventory or some such drudgery. The place was in darkness although the sexy wedding night lingerie backlit and displayed in the window mocked him.

Brett kept the radio tuned to the local channel, listening carefully to the news and dreading to hear that there'd been a traffic accident. He'd even phoned his buddy, Deputy Ryan Lockwood, and casually asked him how his shift was going. Ryan had snapped that he wasn't even on duty that evening but as far as he knew all was quiet and he intended to take advantage of that. In the background, he could hear a woman's voice calling Ryan. The sensuality of the sound made Brett feel lonelier than ever. Unbidden, the thought that maybe Kelly had found solace in another man's arms, another man's bed, crept into his consciousness. He banged the steering wheel with his fist, a motion he immediately regretted as his knuckles stung and....

Wait...that was weird—he sat up suddenly in his car seat. Lights were coming on in Kelly's house when up until now it had been dark. He was out of his car in an instant and up the garden path to hammer on the door. He used his fist, wincing as his bruised knuckles complained, but too worked up to use the delicate looking brass door knocker. No answer. "Kelly! It's Brett. Open the door. Please."

There was no response other than the muttering of waves on the ocean behind the cottage. All the lights went off, one by one, but no one answered his knock. Puzzled, he considered the lights. The sequence of them being switched on and off was erratic. Whoever was doing that would have had to run from room to room in order to create that pattern of on/off, even though the space was small.

"There must be an electrical fault. I'll tell her to get an electrician in to check it out before her house burns down," he muttered to himself.

The lingering thought that Kelly might have returned home without him seeing her and was refusing to open the door to him was depressing. He returned to his vigil in the car, watching the night slowly fade into anemic gray dawn. He decided that he'd give her another hour, until full daylight. Then he'd start calling everyone and anyone he could think of who might know Kelly's whereabouts. If that went nowhere, well, he'd phone hospitals and then...

Kelly came sauntering up to her front door, looking like a woman who'd had very little sleep. But she was smiling and humming to herself, lost in a world of her own. That smile—it looked like it hid a secret that both excited and pleased her. In fact, she looked like a satisfied woman.

Wherever she'd been, whoever she'd been with, it had sure made her happy.

And that made him jealous as hell.

****

The sun was rising as Kelly finally arrived back at her own home, hopping over the puddles in her pathway from the previous heavy rain. Her body felt sluggish and hung-over despite having slept for a couple of hours in Noelia's spare bed, but she smiled to herself as she remembered suspecting that Noelia, her friend and assistant, was Mimi L'Amour, Marina Grove's own bestselling sexy writer. Whatever had she been thinking? That wine must have been stronger than she thought.

The older woman wouldn't let her leave after they'd killed that bottle of wine, even after downing several strong cups of coffee.

"There's no way you're going out of here, tired and with alcohol still in your system," Noelia had declared. "Driving home in the dark like that, and in teeming rain, well, it's asking for an accident. And how could I ever forgive myself if my best friend killed herself on the road after I let her go home when I knew she wasn't fit to drive?"

Her best friend? The words made Kelly feel warm all over. She couldn't remember when she'd last had a best friend, if ever. She just wasn't a girly sort of girl. But she liked the idea, nonetheless. After the night of shared confidences, they'd better stay friends because they knew all about each other's secrets. So she was humming some half-forgotten tune as she dodged some tardy raindrops toward the heavy wooden cottage door.

She was too muzzy to notice the car parked at the curb or to hear the footsteps behind her, and she jumped about a foot in the air when a hand landed on her shoulder. She whirled around to see Brett standing close behind her, a grim expression on his face.

"I've been waiting all night for you—where've you been?"

Such a domineering attitude brought out the instant bitch in her. "Who do you think you are? My mother? I was out. With a friend. I stayed over." She got immense satisfaction out of the glare he gave her. *Was he trying to figure out whether this was a male friend or a female friend?*

She pushed open her door and went inside, startled to see that he had followed her in.

"Whatever it is you want, Brett, make it snappy. I'm tired and I have to shower, dress, and get to work."

"Maybe you shouldn't party all night before a

workday," he snapped.

Kelly glared. "I'm a big girl now. I can do as I like."

He gave her that look, the one that went from head to toes and then back to linger on her mouth. "Yes, I can see you're all grown up, Red." And before she knew what was happening she was in his embrace, lips locked together in a kiss that was hot enough for one of Mimi L'Amour's novels. His lips were hard, masculine, demanding, posing an unspoken question that set her heart thumping. Strong hands on her back drew her close, closer, and she melted into him, clinging as he deepened the kiss. She opened her mouth to answer his demand, and the taste of him flooded her senses.

When he finally let her go, she was heart-poundingly bereft. He grinned a very satisfied male grin, reading her reaction as if he knew, at that moment, she would be his without protest. Cheeks flaming, Kelly placed her hands flat on the hard wall of his chest and pushed away. She tried to glare, but the only expression she could summon up was a smile. She turned and scurried upstairs, muttering that she had to change her clothes for work. She half expected that he would follow her to finish what they'd started; she wasn't sure how she would react if he did, except that she was both disappointed and relieved when he remained downstairs.

In the bathroom, she splashed cold water onto her burning cheeks, noting the hectic light in her eyes and her swollen, well-kissed lips. She was afraid she'd spontaneously combust if he reached for her again. He literally took her breath away, setting her heart racing and filling her with a passion she'd never felt before.

And she wanted more.

She gave herself a talking to as she smoothed face cream into her reddened cheeks. She wasn't the kind of girl to act on lust alone—although that was very tempting. Things were moving too fast—or perhaps not fast enough. It had been so long since she'd wanted someone who wanted her back with such intensity. Maybe never. Deep inside she knew she wanted more, and for her heart's sake she had to slow things down.

Leaning over the banister rail, she called downstairs that she wouldn't be long and why didn't he make coffee while he waited. Then she slipped into her bedroom to change into fresher clothes.

She came to a screeching halt just inside her bedroom door. Sullivan the cat was in his usual post on her bed, but instead of dozing he was in battle position, hissing and growling...at the Old Man from the Bench, who was sitting in the chair under the window beside her bed. Kelly shivered as cold fingers of terror whipped along her spine, followed by white hot anger.

"What are you doing here?" she yelped, picking up and cuddling her terrified cat. Her worst nightmare had come true. Ghosts could appear anywhere, even in her most private retreat.

"Well, I thought it was better than following you to the bathroom."

Her pulse was slowing to normal, but Kelly swallowed hard to hold back the knot of frustration that had curled in her throat. After all, he was right. A ghostly appearance in the bathroom would have been much worse. The scary thought was that there was really nothing to stop him appearing anywhere at any time.

"It's time we set some ground rules. You are not to show up here, especially when I have a visitor."

Surprisingly, ghosts can blush. Or at least go a pinker shade of gray. "I'm sorry. I wasn't thinking. I thought the bedroom would be the perfect place for privacy. I didn't realize you were planning to have a one-nighter."

"Shut up! Don't say another word. None of this is your business."

"Well, get rid of the guy and..."

The early morning bliss that had come with Brett's kiss seemed to evaporate before her eyes. "Darn it all, just stay right here while I explain."

She didn't get a chance to explain anything. When Kelly got back downstairs, out of breath and still flushed with annoyance, she found Brett pulling on his jacket. "Uh, where are you going?"

"I don't want to be a gooseberry, and it seems you already have company." His face was tight with anger, his voice cold enough to make her shiver. "I heard your conversation upstairs."

"No, I don't...what do you mean? How could you...?"

"Obviously you're not aware that the vent in the room upstairs delivers every sound from there into the kitchen. Maybe you need to get a heating engineer in to fix that before you make a fool of anybody else. You sure made a fool out of me."

"Brett, wait, I can explain..." But he was gone, the door closing behind him with a very final sounding slam.

Kelly collapsed onto the hall chair, her head in her hands. The very first guy she had met in years who really interested her—lord knew, there was a spark between them like wildfire—and a ghost had to ruin everything. Perhaps it was as well Brett had left. After all, how could she explain that she was talking to a dead guy in the bedroom? Yeah, that would sure bump up the romantic atmosphere.

Come to think of it, what guy would want to take a relationship to the bedroom level if a ghost might appear at any moment and peer over his shoulder?

****

Kelly was in a terrible mood when she arrived at Wedding Bliss. She stamped around the store fixing displays that didn't need fixing and snapped at Noelia when she asked her a simple question. Finally, Noelia sat Kelly down on one of the Victorian armchairs, telling her to sit and take deep breaths while she went to fetch coffee.

When they were both sitting comfortably, coffee mugs in hand, Noelia asked Kelly to tell her what had happened.

"I had a real screw up with Brett. He's got to be the most unreasonable man on the planet," Kelly snarled, but her eyes were filled with tears.

"He always seemed rather a kitty cat to me. A gorgeous, sweet, sexy kitty cat. And the way he looks at you…wow! It's a wonder you don't both spontaneously combust."

"He looks at me as though I'm something that crawled out from under a rock. He thinks I'm sleeping around because I had a man hidden in the bedroom when he came to visit this morning, after he'd been sitting outside my place all night, worrying about where I was…"

"Ohhh, this is getting interesting. So, put Brett on hold for a moment and tell me about the guy in your bedroom." Noelia smirked. "Who is he, and where did you find him? Are there anymore where he came from?"

Kelly gave her a nasty look. "There was no guy, or there was but not someone you'd be interested in."

"Honey, when the only romance in your life is the stuff you have to read aloud into a recording program, you can get very interested in the strangest strangers." Noelia winked over her coffee cup and helped herself to a second chocolate cookie.

"Yeah, well, even a sexy author wouldn't get a kick out of this one. The Old Man from the Bench. You know, the restless spirit? Well, he was seated on a chair in my bedroom, large as life. Only still dead. Scared the hell out of me. And out of poor Sullivan. The worst thing was, Brett and I were getting on so well together and I'd slipped upstairs to change..." She scowled at Noelia's raised eyebrow. "And I ended up having this conversation telling Mr. Ghost to take a hike and not come back, but it seems the heating vent that runs up to my bedroom is somehow connected to the one in the kitchen. Brett heard my side of the conversation, added two and two, got five, and skedaddled."

Noelia munched quietly for a moment, then she sighed. "Kelly, I swear you have the most interesting life of anybody I know. Interesting like that old Chinese curse of 'may you live in interesting times.' I honestly don't know how you get yourself into these things, but you need to get yourself out of them."

Kelly groaned. "I'm trying. It's just that since that shrapnel hit my head, it's like I'm a magnet to all sorts of weird spirits. And I can't seem to shut it down, although that cute paramedic told me that I should get an x-ray. He said it's possible there's a tiny sliver of metal or bone sticking into my brain and causing the 'hallucinations,' as he called them."

"Then you have your answer. Go get the x-ray done."

"There's only one problem, Noelia. These aren't hallucinations. These are real dead people."

Even Noelia had no answer for that one.

Chapter Twelve

It was a good thing traffic was light as Brett drove to the Holywell Home to pick up Mary and bring her home. He had a hard time concentrating on the road as his thoughts kept dancing themselves to Kelly Andrews and that morning's disastrous revelations.

She had sure fooled him! Disappointment lodged like a stone in his chest. How could he have been so mistaken about her? Maybe his initial reaction had been correct. His first instinct when he met Kelly Andrews—after that burning desire to sweep her off her feet and kiss her silly—had been to stay away from her. That long, curly, red hair signaled danger to his hormone levels. But the more time he spent with her, the more he wanted her. *On every level known to man.*

Then all that nonsense about the wedding gown being cursed. *Please.* He'd been furious when he had found her sneaking around the nursing home against his express orders. What had she been thinking? Aunt Mary was eccentric enough, what with all that witchcraft stuff, without being encouraged by a fellow weirdo like Kelly.

He sighed. There *was* something different about her. He'd been coming to the conclusion it was a nice difference, up until the moment he realized she was stringing him along while another guy waited upstairs in her bedroom. He'd have found it hard to believe of

her if he hadn't heard her telling the other guy to wait
for her. Heard it with his own ears. It certainly wasn't
her cat that she was talking to. Oh, no. And if some guy
was lurking there, waiting for her to come home, it
explained why the lights were going on and off in her
house. And he'd thought she needed an electrician!
What she needed was a good spanking…

Oh, no, he shouldn't let his thoughts go there…but
somehow he couldn't help himself. Ever since he met
the wedding shop owner, his thoughts—and other
parts—had been attracted to Kelly.

Thank goodness he'd found out before it was too
late. To think he'd been waiting most of the night to see
her just to apologize for his behavior at the retirement
home while Kelly had been…doing whatever she had
been doing that put that little satisfied smile on her
lips… Brett's mouth tightened into a hard line as he
remembered the scolding he'd received from Mary
about being rude to the young woman. Rude, indeed!

As if it wasn't bad enough that he couldn't get
Kelly out of his mind—or stop wanting her in his bed—
now Mary wouldn't stop demanding to meet with 'that
interesting young woman' again. She was insisting he
invite Kelly for tea at the Atwell home. Brett sighed. He
knew Aunt Mary was eccentric, but she was also a
butterfly, flitting from thought to thought. Maybe his
aunt would forget all about her wish to see Kelly again
once she was immersed in the routine of life at home
again. Brett crossed his fingers on the steering wheel.
As kids, he and Sasha believed she was a witch. It
wasn't just a kid thing—it was because she had told
them so. Well, as an adult he didn't believe in that
witchy nonsense, and he certainly didn't believe in

curses, or that his aunt, an eccentric lady but no witch, could possibly have cursed anything.

He'd reached the upscale Holywell Care Home and turned into the car park. Through the glass of the double entryway doors, he could see Aunt Mary standing with her suitcase in the reception area. She straightened her shoulders and waved as she spotted Brett's car. *She looks like some waif out of a Dickens' play,* he thought, and was instantly ashamed of himself.

The last thing an emotionally fragile lady recovering from a serious bout of pneumonia needed was to have her weird thoughts solidified, confirmed, and played on by someone like Kelly Andrews. It was bad enough that his own sister, Sasha, was taking advantage of their aunt being away to sell items from the Atwell family home to raise a little pocket money.

Although, he'd seen the sales slips from the auction, and you certainly couldn't call it a little money. He'd also seen what Kelly Andrews had paid for his aunt's wedding dress. It was no wonder she wasn't willing to give it up after paying all that money to purchase it. What was she charging the bride who had bought it, given the amount she'd already invested in it? He toyed with the idea of trying to find out from her assistant who the bride to be was and seeing if he could bargain directly, offer her whatever price she wanted to get the wedding dress back for his aunt. Usually money spoke very convincingly.

Kelly would probably kill him. The idea of her finding out, her sea-blue eyes sparking and that copper-gold hair glowing like fire…

He shook himself out of these thoughts. He had to protect Aunt Mary from Kelly. And protect himself.

Because if she got too near either of them, they might never recover.

****

"So you see, Daria. That's why the dress needs to go back to its original owner. I have another dress equally as lovely, but if you don't like it, I know that I can find you one every bit as beautiful, probably an even more expensive gown, but I won't charge you anymore because this is all a mistake." Kelly knew she was gabbling, but she had to make one last attempt, short of falling down on her knees and begging, to get Daria Welcome to let her take the dress back.

In the end, the realtor remained unmovable. No amount of pleading, not even the emotional blackmail—somewhat exaggerated—that this was the original owner's dying request, moved her. Seated in the comfortably appointed reception area at the Captain's House B & B, where they'd agreed to meet, Daria sipped coffee from a fine china cup and shook her head after every plea Kelly made.

"You know, I wasn't one of those little girls who dreamed of her wedding day," she told Kelly. "I was always out competing with the boys at football and hockey and whatever, one of the gang. After school and college, I got into my career and stayed competitive and never gave a thought to the old happily ever after. Thought it was a myth, really.

"Then I met Drake, and suddenly I was daydreaming about white lace and flowers and wedding bells and all the trimmings. That's why it is so important to me that my wedding day and my wedding dress be perfect. I don't intend to ever do it again!"

So that was that. Kelly trooped dejectedly out,

shivering and averting her gaze as she passed by the study where three men had died in a violent confrontation. The last thing she needed right now was another angry restless spirit tagging along with her. The miserably persistent ghost on the street bench was more than enough for her.

****

Her phone rang as she got into her car, but when she saw Brett's name on the screen, she considered throwing the instrument on the floormat and pretending she hadn't seen it. No doubt he had another litany of complaints and recriminations. *Better get it over with.* Taking a deep breath, Kelly agreed to meet with Brett for coffee, her feelings somewhat mixed as she remembered the way they had parted after the 'kiss-and-ghost' event at her home. Nonetheless, when she saw him waiting for her, her lips began to tingle with the memory of his mouth, and her cheeks flushed with embarrassment, although Brett didn't seem to react at all as she seated herself across from him. They met at the same diner where they had enjoyed a meal before, but this time the relaxed getting-to-know-you feel was missing and the conversation a tense contrast.

"What's going on, Kelly? This morning your assistant, Noelia, called me, and we had the weirdest chat. She claims you see dead people. Ghosts. Restless spirits." Brett looked shell-shocked and angry. His expression she'd come to know, that one raised eyebrow and the hard glint in his eyes, managed to convey the incredulity he was obviously feeling. Kelly's hackles rose.

"I do."

"Didn't the paramedic tell you that you might be

hallucinating from the brain injury? That's a far cry from calling in Ghost Hunters Anonymous."

Kelly glared. She didn't like his sarcasm at all and had a childish desire to squirt him with ketchup from the dispenser on the table. *Grow up, Kelly.* "I started to tell you after...after that incident when you walked me home and I collapsed. It was shock at seeing an old man who's been haunting me at the shop. He shouldn't have been at my home, and every time I see him and try to pretend I don't, I get this awful pain..."

Silence, which Kelly filled by imagining all the ways she could wreak revenge on Noelia, a fantasy which gave way to thoughts of how she could wipe the smug expression off Brett's face as he commented, "Oh, that's okay then. For a moment, I thought your assistant was crazy. Obviously, it's not her, it's you."

Kelly pulled in a deep breath, trying not to like the way his eyes traveled over her breasts in her low-cut sweater and the tremor that ran over her as she watched him. She shouldn't be reacting this way when she should be punching him on the nose for being so—so priggish. "Noelia had no business talking to you about anything like that."

"You could have told me yourself." Brett fiddled with the lobster-shaped salt and pepper shakers, his long, strong fingers distracting Kelly from her annoyance.

She reached across the table and moved the condiments out of his reach. When she was sure she had his full attention she replied, "I did try...would you have believed me if I'd told you I see and talk to restless spirits?

"Probably not." He didn't meet her gaze.

"Then there's your answer." A little worm of disappointment lodged in her chest. She'd hoped when Brett called and asked to get together for coffee that he was looking for more than just to ridicule her. Like maybe friendship, or hot sex, or preferably both. Her hopes were fading away fast.

"I do remember what that medic said, that you were hallucinating because of the head wound. It's a problem that could maybe be fixed, and then you won't have these weird visions anymore."

"Sure, I just have something sticking in my brain, and all they have to do is saw into my skull, take it out, and abracadabra, I'm normal?"

"Yep. Something like that."

"Like hell."

His eyes widened in amazement. "You won't even try?"

"I went to the hospital today, and they did the x-ray. I talked to the doc afterward, and he said he could see some scar tissue but no metal or bone fragments. In fact, he thought everything looked just fine and there was no reason for the hallucinations except perhaps post-traumatic stress disorder."

"Okay, then."

"That's all you have to say? *Okay, then?*" Her voice was shrill, and people were looking at them. No doubt this would be the subject of coffee klatch gossip all over the town, too, right alongside the talk of the Cursed Wedding Gown. Kelly sighed and tried to keep her voice calm.

Brett seemed completely unaware of the curious glances they were getting. "No, I've lots more to say, but it will have to wait. Aunt Mary has asked to see you. After your last visit, I filled her in about the missing gown. She's back at home now, and she is insisting I bring you along to talk to her about it. Against my better judgment, I should add."

Kelly's heart beat a little faster. Could what she'd read in that book about Aunt Mary being descended from witches be true? There was a scary thought. But if she could get Mary to lift the curse, she'd save Daria Welcome's future nuptials and marriage and Wedding Bliss's reputation. And she was getting to spend an afternoon with Brett as a bonus, assuming he would have to at least be pleasant while in his aunt's presence. She smiled at the frustration that would cause him, and vowed to make the most of that discomfort... As an added benefit, she wasn't going to have to try to think up a way to sneak back into Holywell Home now that she was an invited guest at the Atwell Mansion. She was pretty sure she would be persona non grata at the nursing home anyway after her last visit. At least with the receptionist in the pink suit, who'd given her the stink eye look as she was escorted out by a security guard.

"Just remember, Aunt Mary is used to being alone and being her own person. She's still recovering from the pneumonia, and I'm afraid she's a little fragile. She can get a little...difficult...at times. And she's not at her best at the moment. Being in the nursing home drove her nuts."

"Would you like to be stuck in there when you're not an invalid?" she asked.

Brett was silent for a few moments. He avoided her eyes as he went on to say, "There are some things that you should know about Aunt Mary. She has lived alone for a long time and is a bit set in her ways and, well, some would say she has some strange ideas."

"Oh, sure. I've heard she comes from a long line of witches." Kelly laughed out loud at the surprise on his face. "Come on, Brett—surely you didn't think I wouldn't do a little research, considering all the trouble that wedding gown has caused me? I also know your aunt was jilted, left at the altar. I think she cursed the wedding dress, and that's why no other bride has been able to wear it." Kelly bit her lip, watching his face for signs of his thoughts. She hadn't intended to blurt that out, not in the crowded café.

"Next thing, you'll be wanting an exorcism on a lump of silk and lace." Brett's face darkened. "I don't want you to encourage her in all this stuff, Kelly. She retreated from society after she was abandoned by that…that…I'm too much of a gentleman to describe the jerk. She never heard from him again, you know, not even an apology or a postcard from some foreign tropical paradise."

"She was so hurt that she adopted her mother's claims of being a witch as some sort of protective cloak." Kelly's eyes filled with tears as she thought of that lonely bride so long ago, clutching onto the idea that she had supernatural powers in order to feel safe from the world of hurt that had fallen on her. It was a feeling she could relate to herself. "You know, the woman who bought the dress believes that strong emotions leave an imprint on their surroundings, a kind of emotional atmosphere, if you like, that people sense. And there's no doubt that dress has a sad history woven into it."

Brett didn't say anything.

"I was engaged once, years ago. Wayne, my fiancé, never liked my military career; he said it stressed him out wondering all the time whether I was safe or not, and we'd argued about whether I'd stay in the military or find some other line of work. We'd set a date for our wedding, just after my last tour of duty in Afghanistan was supposed to end. It ended early with me wounded and in the hospital, and then the rehab center back in the States. Wayne didn't visit me often, but he was living so far away…"

Brett surprised her by reaching over and clasping her hand. His fingers felt warm on her chilled hand, his touch comforting, intimate, as though they were in a private bubble in the middle of the crowded diner. "I was determined to get well so that I could keep our wedding date because all the arrangements were made. The therapists told me it was good to have a goal to aim for, and mine was being well enough to walk down the aisle. I was so focused on that, I guess, that I missed the warning signs. Until…until the letter came." Kelly paused, biting her lip. The pain of that memory had faded somewhat, but the humiliation still ate at her. "Wayne wrote a brief letter, saying he could no longer cope with the choices I made and thought it best for both of us if we called it quits."

"You must have been devastated." The compassion in Brett's tone, the softening of the hard line of his mouth, were nearly her undoing.

Determined not to give way to the feelings of inferiority and rejection that had engulfed her from time to time after Wayne had walked away, she gave a grim smile. "Actually, I was too busy trying to get back to normal to dwell on being hurt. Head injuries can cause all kinds of crazy things to happen, and at that moment I was so glad to just be alive that it didn't hit me hard until I left the rehab center.

"Since then, I've wondered whether I subconsciously knew that marrying Wayne wasn't the right thing to do. The rejection hurt at the time, though. A lot. So I think I have some idea of how your aunt must have felt. She must really have loved this guy if she never married? She's been gun-shy about relationships ever since?"

Brett nodded. "What about you, Kelly?" He held her blue gaze with his dark one. "Are you afraid of relationships and where they might lead?"

She struggled to breathe around the surprise emotions that had suddenly clogged her throat. How would he react if she were to tell him she wouldn't be afraid of a relationship with him? And was that true? Fear of his reaction and knowing how different they were held her back. *Better not to jump without a safety net,* she told herself, pulling her hand from his. "I think that is something only time—and the right guy—can answer."

"Well, I think Wayne must have been crazy to let you go." And he threw some coins on the table and strode off, looking tall and handsome and leaving Kelly wondering if she'd actually heard his final words right.

****

Brett had a meeting with the Chamber of Commerce in Marina Grove to make a pitch for a donation toward the building of a school in Ghana, so Kelly agreed to meet him afterward at Wedding Bliss for the drive to see Mary Atwell in Derry. That left her just enough time to eat lunch and chew out her assistant.

Noelia must have sensed her boss's mood when she walked into the store because she made herself look extra busy arranging white elbow-length gloves and pearl necklace and bracelet sets in a glass case, looking up only to say, "Whatever it was, I didn't do it."

Either extra sensory perception or a guilty conscience, Kelly thought. "Yes, you did. You blabbed about my little eccentricity. Brett called you, didn't he?"

"Er, no, actually, I called him. And seeing ghosts isn't what most people would call a little eccentricity. I told him what was happening with you. He seemed to take it well."

"Sure he did. He thought a quick poke around inside my brain by a surgeon and the problem would all be solved. But the docs at the hospital say that's not my problem, so it's not going to happen. And when I want you to intercede on my behalf, I'll ask you."

"So you're mad at me? Well, let me tell you, girl, I know a lot about romance, and I know that sometimes it takes a third party to give people a little push…"

"I'll give you a little push under a sixteen-wheeler if you don't stop."

"That's the thanks I get for trying to give you a little fun with a guy you're attracted to like mad?"

"Who said I'm attracted to Brett Atwell?"

"Every hormone in your body stands up and sings the Hallelujah Chorus every time he's around. Anyway, he did call you, didn't he?"

"Yes, he did. And he's taking me to see his Aunt Mary."

"There, then. Isn't that good?"

"Just keep your fingers crossed. And watch the store this afternoon while I'm gone?"

"Sure thing." Noelia turned back to her display work, a smile hovering on her lips.

"And Noelia—stop looking so smug. I can see you. Remember, you only read the books out loud. Even Marina Cove's famous author, Mimi L'Amour, couldn't second guess Cupid, you know." Kelly slammed the door behind her.

Chapter Thirteen

"So, you're the one who has my favorite nephew in a tizzy these days." Mary Atwell gazed at Kelly over her half-moon eyeglasses as if she were examining some new species of life. The older woman was holding court in her small private parlor in the Atwell mansion, with Kelly and Brett seated before her like supplicants on a burgundy velvet loveseat opposite his aunt's recliner.

"I am not in a tizzy, Auntie," Brett snapped. "And I'm your only nephew."

Kelly enjoyed watching the faint pink flush rising from beneath his finely starched shirt collar up into his cheeks and joining the slight blond stubble that was gathering there. How amazing was it to watch a big, strong man bullied by his tiny relative? She tried to hide her grin.

Mary treated Brett to an amused raised eyebrow then turned her attention back to Kelly. The scrutiny concluded, she closed the book on her lap and nodded to herself. Dressed in a lavender twin set and double strand of pearls, Mary looked every inch more like a debutante from the 1950s than a woman from the hippie, love beads, free love generation. She certainly didn't look like anyone's idea of a witch, with her snow-white hair beautifully coiffed—there must have been time for a beauty parlor visit—and her calm patrician features. "Well, m'dear, I can't say I blame Brett for being intrigued." Another look over those half-moon glasses. "You look like a gal with a bit more substance to her than the bimbos he usually finds himself with."

Kelly grinned as she heard Brett's outraged snort. It amused her that this diminutive lady could get her tall, blond, and handsome nephew in a state of spluttering speechlessness with a few well-chosen words.

And it pleased her more than she'd admit that the older lady thought she compared favorably to the other women Brett had dated.

Except they weren't exactly dating, were they? More like fencing with each other, dancing around just out of reach, trying to avoid getting wounded. "Well, I think Wayne must have been crazy to let you go." Had he really said that, or had she misheard? Kelly realized the room was silent except for the soft ticking of a grandfather clock on the far window wall and shook herself out of her reverie.

"Ms. Atwell, I believe Brett has told you how I came to purchase your wedding gown. I am so sorry there has been such a misunderstanding about it, but I'm afraid I have bad news. The young woman who purchased it from me just loves the gown and is not willing to return it. I explained the situation to her, but she is very taken with the dress and wants her wedding day to be perfect.

"What worries me is that three other couples have returned that dress. There's a silly rumor that it's cursed. I know you'll find that ridiculous, perhaps even offensive. But I do have a liking for the young woman who wants to wear it, and I don't want to see her heart broken over some silly dress. I was wondering..." Kelly stopped and chewed her lip. Would Brett's aunt have hysterics if she made the request she wanted to make?

"Go on, my dear. Spit it out." Mary's voice indicated that she had guessed what Kelly wanted but was going to make her speak the words out loud.

Kelly took a deep breath, one hand smoothing the fabric of her best dress slacks. "Let's just suppose for now that there is such a thing as a curse, and you had cursed that dress while you were so upset about the ruined wedding. If you had cursed it, could you lift the curse?"

She heard Brett snort derisively.

"Brett, dear," Mary said firmly, "would you please go and get us some coffee and ask Mrs. Patrowski if she has any of that nice chocolate banana bread? After all, we can't have an all-girls discussion with a big lump like you hovering over us," she added, making Brett blush again. His mouth thinned to a tight line, thinner still when he saw Kelly grin, but he rose to do his aunt's bidding.

Kelly fixed her gaze on Brett, trying to telegraph a plea not to leave her alone at Mary's mercy. All her senses warned her that this was no guileless old lady but a formidable woman. After all, someone who could put a curse on an inanimate object and have that curse still be strong enough years later to wreck several relationships, well, she was probably not someone to cross.

Maybe she'd turn Kelly into a toad if she said the wrong thing. Brett either didn't catch her unspoken plea or ignored it out of spite. The door closed firmly behind him.

As if she could read her visitor's mind, Mary said, "Does the idea of magic frighten you?"

"I really don't believe in magic." She didn't add that she did believe in ghosts. And, lately, curses. Some things were better kept private.

"Well, you should." Mary looked quite smug. "I did curse that gown, using a curse from a book inherited from my mother, who got it from her mother."

Despite herself, Kelly felt a little shiver of unease run like ice water down her spine.

"You really think…"

"It's not what I think, Kelly, it's what I know. And I know that Troy and I had a solid relationship—and a passionate one—otherwise I wouldn't have wanted to marry him. So, I wasn't jilted, as you put it, because there was something wrong between us."

"But that was before the curse. So why did he not turn up for the wedding? There has to have been a reason." Kelly gulped. She wasn't all at all sure it was safe to challenge the other woman.

Mary's eyes, so like Brett's, had turned a rusty brown, the color of dead autumn leaves and just as emotionless. A tiny wisp of lace handkerchief in her hands was being slowly twisted and tortured by these thin, surprisingly strong fingers.

Kelly braced herself, prepared to beat it out of the room if lightning bolts of magic started flying. Then she took a deep breath and reminded herself she had faced enemy fire in the desert, and if she could handle that, she could handle Brett's little old Aunt Mary.

She straightened her shoulders and stared right

back into the depths of Mary's chilly, dark gaze.

The older woman seemed to pull herself back from somewhere far away—a place Kelly was sure she herself didn't want to go—and she managed a gentle smile as if shaking herself from some distant memory. She leaned forward and patted Kelly's hand.

Her touch was icy cold. "Now, dear, let's get to why I wanted to see you."

"I was hoping it was because you'd decided you didn't want the dress back and were going to lift the curse."

With eyebrows raised in that peculiarly smug manner, Mary replied, "You are one of the gifted, aren't you? Oh, don't try to deny it." She raised her hand as if to quell any objections.

Objections Kelly was far too stunned to raise. It was one thing to think that maybe a head wound had led to her seeing ghosts and talking to dead people, but it was quite another to find yourself being put into a category of the sisterhood of witches. She was not at all sure that she liked this idea.

"Ms. Atwell…" she began, but the other woman was just getting into her stride.

"Now, dear, don't try to deny it. I knew the moment I saw you at the Holywell Home that you were one of the gifted. What is your specific gift? Can you read the future? Are you able to read minds? Can you translate the tarot? Or…or maybe you can talk to the dead?" Mary Atwell could not conceal the flash of feverish excitement that flamed in her eyes and flushed her thin face as she looked closely into Kelly's eyes. "That's it, isn't it? I knew there was a reason why all this is happening. You have come to help me find Troy, haven't you?" She leaned forward and grasped Kelly's hands in her own cold fingers. Kelly shivered. Mary's hands felt as fragile as the bones of a small bird, but she had a grip of iron.

She pushed to her feet, feeling that she had to escape from this room as her imagination ran riot. The very air seemed oppressive, filled with magic and witchery. "Ms. Atwell, I don't know what you expect from me, but I am afraid you are sadly mistaken." She was lying, but the weight of what the other woman was asking lay across her shoulders like a mantle of ice.

The door to the room opened as Brett came in carrying a tray of coffee things. At that same moment, across the room, the Old Man on the Bench materialized, a wavering almost-not-there vision that set Kelly's world whirling around her. Her vision blurred as the pain began to throb under the wound on her temple.

She heard Brett exclaim from an impossibly long way away, "Good Lord, Kelly, what has happened? You're white as snow. Aunt Mary, what did you say to her?"

"Nothing to get her this upset. I just asked if she could communicate with the dead, if that was her gift." Mary sniffed to show how offended she was.

"You said what?" There was no mistaking the shock in Brett's voice, but whether it was that he truly thought his aunt was off the wall or if he thought she had simply violated the rules of good hospitality, it was hard for Kelly to tell. She couldn't take her eyes off the wavering, ghostly figure in front of her.

The pathetic, loathsome jerk seemed to be going into some sort of dance motion, his whole body swaying as his thin, claw-like hands reached out toward the chair where Mary Atwell sat as if to grasp her in his embrace.

"No! Leave her alone!" Kelly screamed as she sprang backward toward the door. She knew with sickening certainty that she had brought the ghost here, that he was in some way attached to her because she could recognize him. She swallowed the hard ball of fear that had lodged in her throat. What would happen if the apparition from beyond the veil succeeded in touching a very live Mary Atwell? In horror movies, it would mean her death…and that seemed to make perfect sense to Kelly at that moment…

It was a pretty sure bet that Brett would never forgive her if she was the one who let a ghost lead his favorite aunt into the Afterworld. Come to think of it, she'd find it hard to forgive herself. The only way to save Mary was to leave and hope she was right that the ghost would have to follow. She turned and pushed past Brett to rush from the room on legs rubbery with panic and stumbled through the anteroom and the short hallway toward the big double doors. Freedom beckoned outside, and she had to reach it before disaster struck.

She dimly heard Brett calling her name, but his deep voice couldn't still her panic. Outside, she bent over at the waist, gasping air into her aching lungs as she struggled for breath. Brett caught up with her, his face pale as he managed to capture her and pull her tightly against him into the protective circle of his arms. "Jeez, Kelly, I don't know what my aunt was trying to do, but whatever it was, you're in shock, you're trembling." He hugged her even closer to him. "I never would have brought you if I'd known this would happen."

Kelly snuggled into his warmth, breathing in the scent of him, grateful to have a flesh and blood man to lean on. Brett's solid presence emanated the safety she so badly needed, anchoring her to the real world. She kept her eyes tightly closed, afraid if she opened them she'd see the Old Man on the Bench gazing down at her from Mary Atwell's parlor window. A chill breeze swirled past her then, and she knew she had lured the ghost away and Mary was safe. At least, for now.

"Take me home, Brett...I...I need to get out of here."

****

The pain in her temple had subsided, but it took most of the drive back from Derry to Marina Grove before Kelly stopped shaking. Brett turned the car heater on full even though it was a mild evening. His warm, strong hand lay on Kelly's thigh as he drove, and every few moments he shot her a worried glance.

Finally, they pulled into the parking spot in front of her house. He turned off the ignition, left the heater running, and pulled her toward him.

Kelly had to bite her lip to stop from howling and sobbing into the strong sanctuary of his chest. She hadn't cried since, well, since a Taliban bomb changed her life. *Not even when she got that Dear Jane letter from Wayne.*

This whole restless spirit gig was starting to wear on her. The moments of sheer terror she had felt when she saw the ghost reaching out as if to embrace Mary Atwell...even now, the idea of that shimmering essence pulling a living, breathing woman into its arms was enough to set off another round of shivering. Nausea rose in her throat, but she swallowed it back.

When she finally relaxed in Brett's arms, he dropped a gentle kiss on the top of her head and then asked, "So, are you going to tell me what really happened at my aunt's house tonight?"

Kelly swallowed hard around the warring emotions that had set up shop in her throat.

"Only if you promise not to go off at the deep end again."

Taking his silence as assent, she went on. "You know how Noelia told you I can see dead people?"

She couldn't see his nod in the darkness of the vehicle, but she could feel his chin gently brush against her hair. "I know you don't believe in this whole spirit thing, that you think they really are just hallucinations and that I'm a little—or a lot—crazy. But do you think you could keep an open mind and hear me out?"

He was silent for so long, she thought she'd lost him. It was asking a lot for someone, especially someone as grounded as Brett Atwell, to believe in ghosts and other strange goings on.

Brett seemed to spend an eternity staring out into the gathering gloom of the evening as it fell on Kelly's cottage and the churning sea beyond. But when he finally spoke, his reply came as a surprise. "You know, I work for a non-profit charity overseas in some of the most primitive areas of the world. Areas that are deeply rooted in superstition and what to us are weird beliefs. I learned not to dismiss them out of hand because of some of the things I've witnessed. I guess what I'm thinking is, if strange phenomena can occur there, perhaps I'm wrong to think they couldn't occur here.

Especially when I grew up with a weird aunt like Mary, who had us convinced as kids that she really could cast magic spells. I just didn't expect to find something like this, right here in good old Maine in the U.S.A."

The smile in his voice brought one to Kelly's heart and slowed her shaking. And she told him everything.

Chapter Fourteen

Kelly had finished her story and was enjoying a quiet moment with her head cuddled against Brett's chest when her mobile phone trilled. She had chosen the Wedding March as an appropriate tune for incoming calls, and she could see Brett's amused smile in the light from the screen as she pressed the answer key.

Noelia's panicked voice came through loud and clear. "You'd better get to the store, fast." The shrill scream that came down the line galvanized Brett into action. He had the ignition turned on and the car in motion before Kelly had even managed to assimilate the words.

What was happening? Was Noelia facing an armed robber? Her stomach clenched with fear for her assistant. She couldn't actually imagine what a robber would want from her store unless he'd been inflamed with lust at the sexy display of wedding lingerie she'd placed artistically in the store window. Or perhaps it was someone desperate to get one of those delightful stocking topper garters that looked so cute in the display…

She made two panicked attempts to call Noelia back, but each went straight to voice mail. By the time Brett drew up in front of the store, Kelly was beside herself with anxiety. They arrived to find all the store lights blazing through the window and glass panel of the door. Brett and Kelly stood momentarily transfixed on the sidewalk, gazing through the window as they watched boxes, gloves, hats, veils, and all kinds of bridal paraphernalia whirl around the room as if in the grip of some angry storm. A richly brocaded gown with a long train danced amid the confusion, all by itself with its empty sleeves swaying madly.

The sight of Noelia staggering past the window with a cream lace teddy wrapped around her head shook them both from their shocked paralysis into action.

The store door was locked. Kelly fumbled with the key, wasting precious seconds until Brett took the key from her trembling hand, unlocked the door, and, sheltering her behind him, strode into the store.

It was like walking into a tornado. A tornado made up of lace and pearls and silky wedding garments. Kelly broke away from Brett's protective arm and immediately ducked as six copies of Mimi L'Amour's sexy new romance novel flew at her head like crazed pigeons. She ran to Noelia and put her arms around the frightened woman, all the while yelling at the entity she was sure was causing this turmoil to stop at once.

Apparently, Noelia thought Kelly was talking to her and shrugged her boss off. Her hair stood out around her head in sweaty gray-blonde tufts, and her face was crimson with panic as she struggled to maintain her footing in the whirlwind of bridal stock. Standing with her hands on her hips, she glared at Kelly and yelled, "What do you think I'm doing? It's not me! It's that curse!"

And at that moment a bridal purse hit her in the face and Noelia went down as if cold cocked.

Kelly gritted her teeth. "Look, old man, I know what this is about. It's about Mary Atwell, isn't it? It's that cursed wedding dress that brought you to my door? Whatever you want, I'll try and help, but you have to stop this now."

Kelly stood her ground, and slowly the whirlwind of circling bridal goods slowed. Items began to drop to the floor as if released from a centrifugal force. All except one, a box with the numbers nine-nine in large letters on all sides, which hovered in front of Brett before losing impetus and falling among all the other items.

Brett was on his knees beside Noelia, helping her to stand, when the sudden stillness fell over the store. "We should call the police," he said, standing and taking in the carnage of bridal items strewn everywhere.

"No, whatever you do, do *not* call the police. That would make us look like fools. Can you imagine? *'Officer, I know who the perpetrator is—he's a restless spirit trying to get a message across.'* Oh, yeah, I'm sure that would go down a treat with Marina Grove's finest."

Noelia snorted. "I suppose this was one of your spirit friends having a tantrum, eh?" She scowled at Kelly as she brushed dust and lint off her clothes and untangled a pair of white stockings from around her neck. "If this is going to become a regular occurrence, I'm afraid you'll have to count me out. You couldn't pay me enough to deal with this sort of thing. And why can't he just tell you what he wants? Why does he need the dramatics?"

Kelly had a fair idea why the dead guy was angry.

She'd robbed him of contact with Mary when she'd broken their connection by running out of the Atwell mansion. There had to be something more, though. The old man had seemed fairly sane and definitely not dangerous until tonight.

"I guess I'll have to ask him what's going on next time he chooses to appear."

"Well, please let me know when that is. I want to be miles away when it happens." Sniffing to hide the tears that had gathered in her eyes, Noelia grabbed her jacket and purse and stalked from the shop without another word. She slammed the door closed behind her with such force that the silver bells that hung over it jangled and danced madly.

"And she didn't even offer to help me clean this up."

Brett put his arms around her. "Either you and Noelia have some kind of super special effects skills, or I have to accept that there's something in this crazy idea that you have your own pet ghost." His face was pale under the tan, and his voice sounded shaken.

Kelly looked sadly around the room at the devastation, and her heart sank. "We could be here all night."

"We?" Brett asked, one eyebrow raised. "You're counting me in on this, Red?"

Oh, yes. She was beginning to count Brett Atwell in for a lot of things in her life. Right now, she had a great idea for a joint activity that didn't involve rearranging bridal paraphernalia. "This stuff can wait until morning. I will get here early and get it sorted out. Meanwhile, unless you have somewhere you want to be in a hurry, then I have a suggestion…"

She was pretty sure Brett blushed, just a little, that fair skin, when she stood on tiptoe to whisper in his ear. Then he wrapped her in his arms and delivered another of those killer kisses.

"I don't think we should do this in front of Wedding Bliss's window for all the town to see," Kelly said, unable to keep the smile off her face. "I thought we'd perhaps go back to my cottage?"

She was dismayed when Brett hesitated, frowning. Had he changed his mind about her in the last few minutes? Had she misread the electricity that had been sizzling between them since the moment they met? Disappointment and embarrassment zinged all the way down to her toes.

"It's okay. I'm a big girl. I can take it if you're not interested..." Kelly knew her expression was anything but that of a big girl; she felt like an idiot and knew that must be reflected in her face.

Whatever way she looked, the expression made Brett smile. "It's not that I don't want you. Hell, I've wanted you since the moment I first saw you, with your feathers all ruffled and making threats... It's just that, well, you'll think this is odd for someone who's only just coming to terms with the idea that there might, just might, be such a thing as a haunting..."

Kelly placed her hand against his stubbly cheek. "Hello, you're talking to a woman who sees dead people. Can't get much odder than that."

"Frankly, I can't wait to get you into bed. I'd rather go to my place and—well, I mean, even if it's only an invitation for coffee—I'm not being presumptuous or anything." He looked sheepish, and Kelly wanted to laugh and scream and yell *Please! Please be presumptuous!* but she just treated him to a smile that would have done the Mona Lisa proud.

"Won't your aunt, your sister, and the housekeeper be there?"

Brett gave her an uncomfortable little shrug. "I have a small apartment of my own, over the coach house. It's private and, well, I'd rather not have a ghost popping up while we're...er..."

She squeezed his hand. "It's okay, Big Strong Guy. I don't even mind you being presumptuous. But I thought you didn't believe in ghosts...?"

"After the display we've just seen, I guess there's not much option than to believe in *something*. And you saw this *apparition* outside your cottage the other night. And from what you said, he was actually inside, in your bedroom...I guess I'd rather not be around where he might just wander by. Getting caught in the throes of passion by a nosy restless spirit could cause a man serious dysfunction."

Kelly laughed out loud—she couldn't help it. "Well, we certainly wouldn't want that, would we?"

****

As it happened, there was definitely no dysfunction for either of them that night.

Kelly was shy at first. It had been some time since she'd made love to a man, and that man had rejected her with a curt note almost on the eve of their wedding day. Then there was the little matter of a few scars that showed in white raised lines on her body—scattershot shrapnel wounds, a parting gift from the Taliban.

She need not have worried. From the very beginning, Brett was patient and loving. And very, very sexy. He made it clear with his actions, his tender touches, his kisses, and his murmured words that he found her beautiful in every way. Kelly grew in confidence as he loved her, and she loved him back as he brought her to a climax so intensely shattering she thought she'd fly apart.

And then he gently put her back together again and finally entered her willing body, sliding smoothly inside her until he was fully sheathed. When he paused above her, resting on his elbows and looking deep into her eyes, Kelly was breathless at the wonder of it all.

****

Her lazy tangle of red hair spread across his pillow was every bit as erotic as his imagination had suggested. *She* was every bit as erotic as his imagination had suggested. He had to school himself to take it slow, to enjoy every creamy curve, every tiny cry, every sigh, and every touch.

The scars that stood out whitely on her skin were beautiful to him. They spoke of her courage, her strength, her compassion in trying to save the life of another soldier at the risk of her own. He marveled at the idea of such fragile femininity harboring such courage, and he wanted to give her everything.

He captured her lips with his own as she pressed against him, then he worked his way down again to her breasts, sucking on one, then the other. His fingers found her hidden center, caressing until he felt the pulsing there and she threw back her head and moaned in pleasure.

Then he covered her with his body and hotly entered her welcoming flesh, stroking her body and thrusting into her with the combination of strength and tenderness that she evoked in him until he felt her pleasure build again and finally anticipating the approach of their summit of sensuality, he joined his release with hers.

Later, much later, they fell asleep in each other's arms, naked and sated.

****

Dawn was slowly seeping in through the bamboo blinds on Brett's bedroom window when Kelly suddenly sat bolt upright in bed—or as upright as she could with Brett's arm still resting possessively over her belly.

"It wasn't Mary he was reaching for!" She blurted out the words aloud without thinking, and Brett groaned as her voice dragged him from a deep, satisfied sleep.

"What are you talking about, Red? In fact, why talk at all? Just come here and…"

"No, there's no time! Don't you see? He wasn't reaching for Mary at all. It was the photograph on the table by her chair."

"And why would he do that?"

"Because he's her long-lost lover? He's the ghost of Troy Matthews."

Brett sat up now too. "Okay, I'm wide awake now. What's on your mind?"

"First off, don't call me Red or something nasty might happen to you. You were warned." She tried to frown at his grin, but the attempt turned into a satisfied smile on her well-kissed lips. "Don't you see? He's trying to make amends for the hurt he caused her. He wants her to forgive him before he passes over to whatever comes next."

Brett snorted. "Then he might as well just toddle off to his own little spot in Hell. I don't see Mary forgiving him anytime soon, not if she hasn't got around to that way of thinking in the past fifty years or more."

Kelly shrugged that off. "I ran from your aunt's house because I could see the Old Man on the Bench. The dead guy. I told you I thought he was reaching out toward Mary, and I thought…well, I thought he was trying to embrace her and…"

Brett scowled. "You thought that the dead guy was amorous and trying to take Aunt Mary with him into wherever it is he's doing time?"

Kelly swallowed hard. "That's what I thought yesterday. I thought the ghost is somehow attached to me, so if I left, he'd have to leave, too, and Mary would be safe."

Brett reached up and pulled her back down onto the rumpled sheets. "You're one brave lady, Kelly Andrews." He kissed her long and hot, and then released her. "So, what does all this mean?"

Kelly chewed on her top lip. "I have to go back to Mary's and take a closer look at that photograph. It might help the pieces come together."

Even though it was still early, and even though Kelly had intended to get into Wedding Bliss to clear up the mess that the ghost's temper tantrum had left behind, she knew she had to do this first. Brett's apartment was over what used to be a carriage house for the old Atwell mansion, so it was really just a matter of walking a few steps to the house and ringing the doorbell. Before she could put her finger on the buzzer, Brett caught her hand in his. Kissing her on the nose, he held up a key.

"The bell sounds like the trumpet of doom. There's

really no need to wake up the entire household. It's still really early. In fact, it's far too early to be out of that warm bed." He inserted the key in the lock and then paused to kiss her thoroughly again before turning the handle and pushing the door open.

Kelly took a deep breath while the kiss sizzled through her and ordered herself to focus on the job at hand rather than the delightful idea of taking Brett up on his suggestion that they simply go back to his tousled bed.

She thought her sanity might be in danger if she didn't solve this mystery and send that old dead guy on his way to whatever comes next. She said as much to Brett, who raised one eyebrow in that sexy way of his with the unspoken message: *How sane is focusing on a years-old curse and a restless spirit?*

Once inside, Kelly led the way through the big square foyer and into the small parlor where she had met Mary Atwell the previous day. Brett followed, keeping an eye out for anything of the other-worldly variety. Kelly caught his eye and teased, "So now who's a believer?"

"After last night's little display in Wedding Bliss? I was convinced by those dancing lacy panties..."

Kelly punched his arm. "Typical male reaction."

She picked up the photograph in its heavy silver frame and studied the four people there. It was easy to spot Mary Atwell; despite the passing of years, she looked very much the same.

"Probably because she hasn't changed her hairstyle in all this time, and her clothes still have an early sixties look," Brett said when she commented.

She perched on the arm of the chair that Mary had

occupied the previous night. Now that she was back in the room, she was even more convinced that the ghost had been trying to call attention to this photograph rather than drag poor Mary off to the Other Side.

The reason had to be because the ghost was in this picture and he wanted her to recognize him. She ran her index finger over the handsome, fine-boned face of the man sitting next to Mary in the photo. There was no doubt in her mind that this was the Old Man on the Bench, despite the years that had passed. Everything began to fall into place. The dress, that cursed wedding gown, had led this miserable apparition to her door, or rather, to her street bench, because *he* was the cause of the curse. He was the missing groom, the one who'd stood a fragile young Mary Atwell up at the altar.

He was the loathsome, selfish, cold-hearted jerk who'd walked away and left a bride with no comeback other than to spend the rest of her life in lonely seclusion, shielding herself with the belief that she'd inherited the power of the black arts from a long line of witchy ancestresses.

Not to forget the revenge of cursing her wedding gown…a curse that was echoing years later and wrecking the lives not just of several other brides, but of Kelly herself. *Enough!* She fisted her hands. If only the ghost were solid enough, she'd punch him.

"Brett? Look at this man. This is the dead guy, I'm sure!"

"So this is Troy Matthews? The man who broke Mary's heart?"

Kelly sighed. "You know what this means. Of course, if I'm seeing him, then he's dead."

A small cry alerted them to someone else in the

room. They both swung around to see Mary Atwell, in fuzzy pink robe and slippers, standing in the doorway looking grief-stricken.

"You mean—you've seen my Troy? Is he a ghost? He really is dead?"

Brett was at his aunt's side in two quick strides, guiding the older woman to a chair.

"Auntie, the man left you literally at the altar, and in all these years he's never had the decency to even check if you were all right."

Tears seeped from Mary's eyes at the anger in his voice. She blew her nose into another of her stash of tiny, lace-edged handkerchiefs. "Don't be angry with him, Brett darling. Something happened, I know it did. I could just never bring myself to believe he was dead. At first, I just hated him for what happened. As time went by, I realized I still loved him, no matter what. And I found myself hoping that wherever he was, he was at least happy. You'd think, when we loved each other deeply, that I would have known if he had departed this world."

"Maybe he's trying to make up for everything now, Mary," Kelly suggested, casting a quick warning look at Brett as she handed the photograph over to his aunt.

Mary smiled a watery smile as she looked down at the four young people frozen in happier times within that frame. She tenderly stroked her finger over the photograph, smiling sadly. "Oh, Troy, have you really come back to tell me what happened?"

Kelly's own eyes filled as she saw the woman was wearing a diamond ring on her left-hand ring finger. Was it the engagement token Troy had given her so long ago?

She refocused as Brett placed his hand on her arm. "Listen, this has gone far enough. Kelly, I know that you are finding this a strain. But that is nothing to what you're putting my aunt through by encouraging her with all these questions. I think it would be a good idea if I took you home."

"Kelly? If you believe that the spirit you are seeing is my Troy, then that means he's dead?" The tears were now coursing down Mary's cheeks.

"Well, the ghost I see is an old man now…" Kelly groped for a kinder way to explain what she thought.

Mary tapped the picture thoughtfully. "If the ghost is an old man, then he only recently left us…"

Kelly knelt beside the older woman's chair, holding onto those thin, birdlike hands. Instead of the alarming iciness she had felt previously, Mary's hands just felt like the cool fingers of a fragile older woman. "I am so sorry," she whispered. "I should have seen this a little sooner. All the clues were there. Believe it or not, I woke up with this photograph in my mind."

"Maybe it was my poor dear Troy, whispering to you in your sleep."

"Well, something like that." Kelly caught Brett's eye and flushed, knowing he was remembering their own whispered endearments last night. Mary looked from her to Brett, a small knowing smile fluttering across her lips.

Kelly's blush deepened. *That hot sex must be written all over our faces!* Remembering the visitation of the previous night, she glanced nervously toward the end of the room, half expecting the ghost to reappear. This time there was only empty air. With an odd feeling of loss, Kelly realized that she had fulfilled her mission;

she had brought closure to a grieving bride and carried out the wishes of her dead lover who should now be able to find his rest.

"I know I will be grateful to you for this once the initial shock has worn off. I did hope that there would be some answers to the questions I have asked so many times over the years, wondering why he did what he did. If he has gone on to the next plane, then I suppose I will have to wait until I see him there and everything else becomes clear."

Mary wiped her eyes again with that wisp of a handkerchief. Brett bent and put his arms around her, and she looked up at him with a tearful smile. "I should thank you, too, Brett, for caring enough to find my wedding gown and so start the chain of events that brought Kelly and her gift to me. But now I think it's time you took this lovely young lady home."

They reluctantly left her there, a sixty-something woman lost in reminiscence of her youthful love affair, her fingers absentmindedly stroking the silver framed memories.

****

They were back on the road to Marina Grove when an awful thought slammed into Kelly's brain. "Brett! Turn the car around. We have to go back right now."

Tires screamed on the tarmac as Brett stamped on the brakes and pulled hastily into the hard shoulder, responding to the urgent note in her voice. "What's wrong, Red? Have you forgotten something?"

She was too abstracted to even threaten him about the use of the nickname. "Yes, I've forgotten my common sense. I need to check something…but don't ask me about it yet."

With a good-natured shrug, he did a U-turn. Fortunately, it was still early, and the traffic was light. "I'm happy to go back, actually; I was pretty worried about Aunt Mary, and I think I'll ask the housekeeper to check up on her during the day. And I need to check at the post office."

Kelly frowned. "Can't it wait? I mean, I really need to get back and talk to your aunt. Then I've got to get back to Wedding Bliss and clean up the mess from the old ghost's tantrum last night before Noelia comes in at lunchtime. If she ever comes back to the store, that is. She was understandably very, very frightened by that little show last night."

"Won't take a minute." Brett was soon pulling into a parking spot in front of the post office. He got out of the car without another word and strode inside while Kelly fretted and watched the minutes on the car dashboard clock mount up.

Left alone in the car, she thought about the swaying shoulders and waving hands of the apparition. The ghost looked as if he were miming a message in some awful game of charades, but was he really reaching out to clasp his abandoned bride? It was a reasonable assumption if the relationship between the two of them had been as strong as Mary claimed. And yet it made much more sense that he was trying to give them a clue hidden in the photograph...

Stuck in her mind was the fleeting glimpse of Mary Atwell as they were leaving her a short time ago. In her mind's eye she could see the other woman, her face a mask of sadness, her thumb caressing one of the faces in the photograph.

The wrong face.

Kelly burned with the need to hurry and take a closer look at that photograph.

"That was a lot more than a minute," she snapped when Brett finally reappeared.

"Don't be so impatient, Red. I think it may well have been worth the stop." He pushed a pale blue envelope into his inside jacket pocket. It was torn open, so he'd obviously taken the time to read its contents. She was desperate to ask him more, but she was darned if she was going to appear to be prying into his private affairs. After all, she couldn't imagine how Brett's mail could possibly be anything but a private matter to him.

"Just watch the road, Atwell!"

"I told you…" But they were already turning into the circular driveway in front of the Atwell home, so she let him away this time. Brett would pay for his constant use of that hated nickname another time. She smiled secretively at thoughts of just how she'd make him pay…

Brett had barely stopped the car before she threw herself out of the passenger seat and hurried toward the big front doors. Anxiety about Mary Atwell's story was gnawing at her incessantly now She chewed her bottom lip, worrying the tender flesh as she struggled with an idea that was taking root. Only one *living* person could give her a straight answer to that puzzle. That darned Old Man on the Bench was playing with her—she knew he wouldn't, or maybe couldn't, come out and tell her what she needed to know. Only Mary Atwell could do that.

"Did you know that thing you do with your teeth on your bottom lip is incredibly sexy?" Brett caught up with her on the doorstep and nuzzled her ear, getting a sharp look from Mrs. Patrowski when the housekeeper opened the door. Hiding a smile, Kelly reached for his hand, reveling in the warm intimacy between them.

He smiled back, the kind of exclusive, secret smile of lovers. Kelly's pulse jumped, and she held his hand tighter.

Brett led her through the door, and she made her way directly to the small parlor where she had met Mary earlier. As she guessed, the older woman was there, looking shrunken in her chair as she gazed sadly at the photograph she still held in her hands. Her eyes were bright with tears still unshed.

She looked startled to see her nephew and Kelly back so soon, but she managed a gracious smile and invited them to sit down. "I'll ask Mrs. Patrowski to bring us some coffee—or would you prefer tea at this hour?" she asked, reaching for a small bell on the table near her elbow.

Kelly accepted, to be polite, even when every fiber of her body wanted to ask Mary just one simple question. She curbed her impatience until the housekeeper had wheeled in a small cart with coffee things and a variety of pastries.

When the housekeeper had left the room and everyone was settled with coffee, Mary spoke dreamily. "I was just enjoying a bittersweet trip down Memory Lane." She looked down at the photograph in her lap." I have such wonderful memories of the times Troy and I shared, and our friends. Oh, we didn't get into the whole hippie thing that was going on in the sixties. We didn't need psychedelic drugs to enjoy each other's company or to know what was real."

Kelly rose and went to kneel beside Mary's chair.

"I am so sorry if the things I told you—that the ghost I was seeing was Troy—made you sad."

Tears welled in her eyes. "There was a time when I wished him alive and I could confront him. Then I took comfort from imagining all the nasty things I'd say, to try to hurt him as badly as he'd hurt me. I even fantasized that he was dead, that I'd someday find a note, or see a reference, or something like that, that would tell me he'd died a hero in Vietnam…anything to ease the pain that ate away at me. Because I still love him, Kelly. I just needed to know what happened. No one would talk to me about it. They all thought I was too fragile, too hurt. Now it's too late."

"I think maybe…did you ever look him up on the internet?" Kelly asked, ignoring the snort of laughter from Brett.

Mary looked at her, wide-eyed. "Are you joking, my dear? I've never even touched one of those computer things, although I have heard a lot about them. No, not for me. I'm too old…"

"My eighty-year-old grannie uses one. She loves it. You should try it sometime," Kelly replied.

"Maybe, but I don't know…you say your grannie knows how to use one?"

"Yes, she says it's her window on the world. She is diabetic and can't get out much, so she stays in touch by email and social media."

"Well, who'd have thought it?"

"You're probably wondering why we came back so soon after leaving?" Kelly prompted.

"I certainly am," muttered Brett. Kelly shot him a quelling glance.

"Actually, I thought either you'd forgotten

something or that Brett was worried about me. He's a real worrywart, you know."

The worrywart blushed, and Kelly grinned at him. She was constantly amused by the way his fair skin colored so easily under his tan. Who'd have thought that a man's blush could be so sexy? "Is he now? That's good to know. Ms. Atwell, I have a question that I should have asked before." A dreadful idea was prickling to life inside her brain. She knew she couldn't put this off much longer, so she drew in a deep breath and asked, "Who are the people in that photograph?"

Mary lovingly stroked her fingers along the faces of the four people there. "The woman in the cloche hat is Elizabeth, my best friend, and the other man is Peter Arnt, who was Troy's best friend and would have been his best man." Tears filled her eyes as she looked backward at the past. Mary was the picture of grief.

Brett looked on, frowning as if he was about to intercede.

Before he could, Kelly asked, "Is that Troy sitting right beside you?"

Mary drew in a deep breath as if the air had all been sucked out of the room. She directed a puzzled glance at Kelly. "This is my Troy, right here, standing behind me. The man sitting next to me is Elizabeth's beau, Peter. Poor Elizabeth, she tried to stay friends with me after the fiasco of a wedding, but it was hard. Then she went to live in France and married Peter there. I didn't want to see anyone, you see." She dragged out a deep sigh. "I heard the poor dear died of breast cancer a few years ago, long before her time."

Kelly rose to her feet, the anguish in her voice causing Brett to put his hand on her shoulder. "Oh, dear—it looks like I've got hold of the wrong end of the stick somehow. The ghost I'm seeing is that of Peter. I am so sorry…"

Mary looked up, a brilliant smile lighting her face. "Why would you be sorry, dear? Surely that means that Troy might still be alive?"

Chapter Fifteen

"I think I know the answer to this puzzle, or at least part of it, now that we know who Kelly's restless spirit is." Brett's voice fell into the uneasy silence of the room as he pulled out the blue airmail envelope from his pocket with a flourish. Mary and Kelly turned to look at him, their faces questioning.

"Kelly, remember when we were in the store and the whirlwind of items came to a halt? Do you remember anything odd that happened?"

"Oh, my heavens, Brett—anything odd? Nothing, except that every item in my store, from gowns to suspenders, was flying around all by itself!"

Mary raised a puzzled eyebrow but wisely didn't say anything. Kelly assumed she'd acclimated herself to weird happenings in her witchy studies.

"Think carefully. All the items fell to the floor except one after you yelled at the…presence…to stop."

She visualized the store the previous night when chaos had reigned. Noelia, hit by a marauding pearl bridal bag and slumping to the floor; a whole slew of embroidered gloves, empty fingers waggling, flying by like migrating geese; a few pairs of white lacy honeymoon thongs dancing madly… "The box! Everything suddenly fell to the floor except a box that hovered right in front of you!" She was so pleased to get the answer she wriggled in her seat.

"What was on the box?"

Darn it, another test question. She thought for a moment. "Nine-nine! The box said nine-nine or ninety-nine."

Brett gave her an indulgent smile, like a teacher with a star pupil. "Yes, box ninety-nine. The post office box number I've kept on for when I'm out of the country, even though I get office mail delivered to Mary's house when I'm home…"

Mary grasped his meaning first. "Yes, and when the ghost showed you the box, you figured it out and remembered you might have mail and…"

"…we stopped at the post office and you picked up that letter?" Kelly finished.

Brett enveloped them both in that indulgent smile. "Yes. I wasn't really expecting anything except fliers in that box, so I hadn't bothered checking it except for when I first arrived back in the country a couple of weeks ago. Been kind of busy." He winked at Kelly, who blushed.

The two women exchanged mystified looks. "Remember, I'm coming late to this party, so explain," Mary told Brett.

Kelly admired Brett's well-trained technique of giving the long story of the ghost's tantrum in Wedding Bliss in just a few succinct sentences. She could imagine him making such presentations to corporations and government officers and to foreign government committees as he put the case for the projects his non-profit organization was proposing to implement. A little frisson of pride ran through her thoughts.

"What a naughty thing for this ghost to do. I have to say, though, that it would be very like Peter Arnt;

you've no idea of the times he got us all in trouble when we were children, playing practical jokes on people who didn't share his sense of humor." Mary smiled at the memory. "So, I'm up to speed. Now go on and tell us what's in the letter. I can see Kelly is like me, just dying to hear it."

Kelly wasn't sure that, in this context, she liked the expression 'just dying', but she decided to keep quiet. However, she couldn't help but look over her shoulder a few times, wondering if the mysterious Peter Arnt's restless spirit was prowling.

Brett told them the gist of the mysterious letter: that it had been written about six weeks or so ago and signed by Peter Arnt in France. "He says he's ill and doesn't have much time but wants to put the record right. It's rather a long letter, and you can read it yourself, Aunt Mary, but here're the basics for Kelly. You remember that Troy was still at Harvard, finishing his last year? The wedding was the day after he sat finals?"

"Yes, he was supposed to drive over to Derry early the next morning. We'd deliberately set an afternoon time for the wedding to give him time to get here. And we broke with tradition and didn't bother with a rehearsal dinner the night before. We were so eager to get married," Mary finished wistfully. Kelly reached out and patted her hand.

"So, in a bit of a wild mood after finals were over, Peter and some friends took Troy out for a stag party. They pub crawled, and after a few drinks too many, for laughs started to spray paint a wall. Someone must have reported them because they heard a police siren in the distance and ran off."

"That doesn't sound at all like Troy, but it certainly fits for Peter." Mary's voice dripped disapproval.

"When the group of them finally stopped running, laughing so hard at their prank and outwitting the police, Peter noticed that Troy wasn't with them. He assumed he'd run in a different direction and would meet up with them later. They were all pretty drunk." Brett looked up from the letter he was reading. "Seems Troy didn't show up at the apartment they shared, so Peter assumed he'd taken off to drive overnight to Derry for the wedding. Early the next day, armed with what he describes as the world's worst hangover, Peter drove the three hundred miles or so to Derry, stopped at his parents' house to change into what he called a 'monkey suit'—I think he means tie and coattails—and arrived at the church to wait for Troy. Who, as we know, never arrived?

"He talks a lot, rather self-indulgently, about how shocked he was and how he worried that Troy may have been driving drunk and got in an accident. He took off back to his folks' house from the church and started calling hospitals along the route but couldn't find any trace of Troy. He told Troy's father what had happened, and his father said he'd deal with it. The next day, with still no sign of Troy, Peter flew to France for a job interview. Later, Elizabeth joined him. They were married in France, and their parents and friends flew over there for the ceremony. Sadly, his father and mother died a few years later."

Mary nodded. "I remember now. They actually died within a few days of each other. Romantic in a depressing sort of way. I remember his father was so strict, a very dour and somewhat frightening man. I believe Peter was what we called 'a late life baby'. His parents had given up hope of having a family, and they were overjoyed when Peter came along. His father was so determined that Peter would be an upstanding citizen and not get into trouble but be very successful, that they were quite hard on him, which didn't do because he was such a free spirit. It was winter, and there were no formal funeral services. They held a memorial service at the church later, for both Mr. and Mrs. Arnt. I didn't go because I was afraid Peter would be there," Mary told them.

"Well, apparently he did go, and he looked for you. Someone told him they thought you'd left Derry because you hadn't been seen around town for a long time."

Mary nodded. "I didn't go out hardly at all, didn't go to social events, passed up on college, lost touch with all my friends. My parents thought I was too fragile to strike out on my own at university or to get a job. I've wondered since if they were really right."

"He goes on to say that Elizabeth's parents came to visit in France, and later to live there. Peter and Elizabeth never came home together. She was pregnant and couldn't come back to Derry for his parents' memorials, and he only stayed a few days."

Silence held sway in the small parlor until Mary broke it. "We still don't have the answer to the question of what happened to Troy? Still don't know if he's dead or alive?"

"I have an address here, in Paris, France, so I'm going to go and call and see if I can contact any of Peter's family there. They might know something more." Brett left the room, only to return some minutes later looking grim.

"I spoke to Peter's son, Auntie. I'm afraid Peter died three weeks ago. He'd been ill for some time. He said Peter never recovered from Elizabeth's premature death, and what had happened with Troy all those years ago had weighed heavily on him. The son, Peter Junior, said he hoped his father had found some answers now."

"You didn't tell him..." Mary questioned.

"That his father is a ghost stalking a pretty redhead around a little Maine town? No, even I am a little more discreet than that."

"Okay, then. So, what's next?" Kelly took her cell phone from her jacket pocket.

"Who are you calling on that newfangled thing?" Mary asked, eyeing the phone with suspicion. "I read somewhere that they damage your brain or something."

Kelly couldn't resist an eye roll. "Gee, Mary, when all this is over we're really going to have to get you caught up on the 21st century. You'll love it, I promise. Meanwhile, I'm calling to make sure that Noelia, my assistant, has recovered from her ordeal last night. I'm selfishly hoping she'll come into the store and help me clean up. Then I'm going to go and see a ghost about a missing groom."

Chapter Sixteen

It didn't take Kelly long to track him down.

He was exactly where she expected him to be, on the street bench opposite Wedding Bliss, his back to the pretty little park that occupied the square. He sat with his head in his hands, and as Kelly approached him, he looked up and she was appalled at the misery on his face. Peter Arnt's ghost looked even paler than the last time she'd seen him. It was as if he was fading away before her eyes.

"Hello, Peter," she said as she plunked herself down beside him.

He managed a dim smile. "So you've found out that much, at least."

"Yes, Mary's nephew got your letter. Why did you send it to him and not to Mary?"

"I just imagined her opening a letter from me, what you might call a blast from the past, and the shock making her ill. I researched and discovered she had a nephew, a responsible sounding young fellow who did charity work in poor nations, so I thought he'd be better able to care for her and break the news. You must remember I was alive when I wrote that letter. Things just happened faster than I expected."

"Don't they always." A sudden wave of sorrow for the man whose life had been filled with loss washed over Kelly and she really wanted to hug him but knew that was impossible. There was one question she had to have the answer to, even if it added to his distress. "Why didn't you just tell me the truth right from the start? Why put us through this guessing game?"

He looked her in the eye, a grin twitching at his lips. "Those are the rules, my dear. There are rules of etiquette, if you want to call them that, that we must obey. But I don't have much time left...I'm fading. I did so want to put things right before I cross to the Other Side."

Kelly reached out intending to pat his shoulder then snatched her hand back quickly before it went right through him. There was another comfort she could offer. "Do you know where Troy is?"

That grim, ghostly smile again. "No, that would be against the rules if I told you."

"Damn the rules...sorry. Do you at least know if Troy is still alive?"

Peter the Ghost gave a grim smile. "Oh, yes. I checked with the Powers That Be. They gave me that much. He is still alive—or was a little while ago. What's happened since I checked up..." Peter shrugged. "I didn't...did not want to have to face him on the Other Side without at least trying to make this right."

"In that case, you can rest assured that we'll find him."

The Old Man on the Bench smiled a little brighter. "Please, when you do, would you tell him I'm sorry from the bottom of my heart? And would you ask Mary if she can find it in her heart to forgive me? And Troy?"

Nodding, Kelly stood to leave. "Will you still be here when I get back?"

Kelly's heart went out to the despairing ghost. He

looked so sad as he replied, "I'll try to be. But I don't have much time before I have to report in."

****

Kelly was exhausted. After the deliciously sleepless night with Brett, she'd awoken early. Talking to Mary about the photograph, finding the letter in Brett's mailbox, going back to talk further with Brett's aunt, then rushing back to Marina Grove to talk to the Old Man on the Bench, she felt as though she'd already put in a full day's work, and it wasn't even nine o'clock.

Now she stood on the sidewalk outside Wedding Bliss, dreading the task ahead of her. Would Noelia show up to help her clean up the mess left behind by the ghost's tantrum or had she meant what she said about wanting no part of these events? The street was already starting to get busy with people on their way to work, and even a few late tourists. Even this late in the season, Marina Grove was a favorite recreation area. The street where Wedding Bliss stood boasted several antique stores, a couple of dignified 'junque' stores, a smart restaurant, a travel agency, and a delicious artisan bakery and ice cream outlet.

Kelly had been drawn to the area's eclectic style even before she'd noticed the small shop that was for rent and the idea of Wedding Bliss, the one-stop wedding paraphernalia and planning store, had been born. Of all the things she had ever done in her life, she was sure that moving to the seaside town and starting her own business there was one she would never regret.

She was screwing up her courage to open the store and face the mess when she saw a familiar figure exiting a car parked nearby.

"Noelia?" She walked quickly down the sidewalk toward her friend and assistant, not sure if Noelia would meet her with her usual good-natured response or if she was still angry and frightened after her naughty ghost encounter.

To her relief, Noelia smiled and hugged her. "I am so sorry I lost it last evening. To be honest, I was so scared I nearly peed my pants, and I was sure I'd have nightmares after it. But I slept like a baby, and when I woke up, I just felt bad for taking it out on you. I'm sure you didn't invite that mean spirit into your life to cause trouble."

Kelly swallowed with relief. "Oh, Noelia, you have no idea. I was so frightened, too, and when that purse hit you and you went down...it was so awful.... I would never forgive myself if you got hurt because of me."

"Not your fault, girl. And some of the images in my brain from that night are quite funny. Like the garter belts dancing across the room by themselves..."

"And do you remember all those lacy bridal thongs flying around Brett's head?"

"Oh, my goodness, yes—his face was a picture!"

In moments, the two of them were clinging to each other, laughing hard. *There is nothing like a bit of humor to dissipate tension,* thought Kelly.

With concentrated effort and elbow grease, they soon had Wedding Bliss back to normal, with the window displays attractively updated and the store shelves and settings tidy and inviting.

****

Brett had wanted to accompany Kelly when she was planning to meet with Peter the Ghost, but she had insisted that he meet up with her after work instead. "He won't hurt me," she'd told him with more confidence than she actually felt after witnessing the angry power that had caused chaos in her store.

Now she joined him and Mary for coffee at the Marina Grove Cafe and was touched by the relief in his eyes as she slipped into a booth beside him. Brett gave her a quick kiss which brought a big smile to the face of the waitress who approached to take their order, but a quick look of disapproval from Mary Atwell. *Kissing in public? Really!* the woman's face seemed to say.

In fact, Mary kept looking around her at what she perceived as an alien world—one that she had opted out of so many years ago. Kelly thought the rich recluse had possibly never been in a 'greasy spoon' cafeteria before, and the woman's reaction made her smile.

They decided to order a comfort meal of fish and chips, and once their food had arrived Kelly quickly brought everyone up to speed on what she'd learned from Peter the Friendly Ghost. She'd changed the nickname she had for him after realizing he was genuinely contrite for what he'd done and was trying to put things right within the 'rules' that appeared to have been laid down by a higher authority.

"What are we going to do now?"

Kelly voiced the question while dipping a large, fresh french fry into ketchup. Brett watched with a gleam in his eye as she raised the fried potato to her mouth, the mouth he had so recently kissed, and she struggled not to laugh aloud. Mary, who was delicately using a knife and fork, raised a curious eyebrow. Kelly sighed and bit back the *lighten up, honey* comment she wanted to snap at the older woman.

"According to Peter, Troy is still alive." She held up a warning hand to Mary. "I'm not sure we can really rely on that information. It's not as though he has a hotline to the Great Beyond right now. Anything could have happened since he made his own inquiries into Troy's status."

Brett gaped. "You know, you make all this stuff sound so...so *normal*! You accept that this ghost is real, that he's Peter, that he has inquired about Troy's whereabouts, and has been assured he's not yet in the Hereafter, and...good lord, I'm still struggling to accept that there is any such thing as ghosts yet."

"Poor Brett." Kelly leaned over and patted the cheek of the man who sat beside her. "This is all too much for you to take in, isn't it? But, you know, you're actually taking it all very well." She smiled as that slight blush crept up over his cheeks. She really, really wanted to kiss that pink stubbly cheek but was only too aware of Mary's censorious stare on the other side of the table.

Still, when Brett's hand slipped onto her leg, hidden beneath the table, she couldn't fight back the smile it sparked. Catching Mary's suspicious gaze, she swallowed hard. The waitress brought them coffees then, inquiring if everything was all right and if they wanted dessert.

Kelly did—she craved anxiety defeating chocolate and knew that the restaurant did a fine line in chocolate related goodies. With a huge effort, she controlled herself, refused dessert, and, after stirring cream into her brew, asked, "And again, what do we do next?"

Mary sipped her coffee then blotted her lips on a paper napkin, her movements so cute and ladylike that

Kelly couldn't stop a smile. Something about the woman was visibly changing, softening, almost by the hour as they worked toward solving the mystery of her missing groom.

"Well, dear, I think we need to go and find one of those computers and use that—what did you call it? Noodle? Strudel?"

"Google?"

"Yes, that's it. We should use that Google to see if we can find out anything about Troy."

"I don't have the internet, Auntie. I wasn't expecting to be home long, so I didn't get it hooked up. I have email on my phone, and I've been using the library facilities for anything requiring a larger screen." Brett looked at Kelly. "I bet Wedding Bliss has a computer and internet, though," he added.

"That's your business, is it? Wedding Bliss. What a cute name." Mary turned to look expectantly at Kelly, who sighed.

"Of course, we have the internet. Fast connection, too. And yes, we can go to the store and use it. Brett and I will call you if we find anything, and in the meantime…"

"Oh, no, no, you don't." Mary stood and pulled herself up to her full five-foot three inches to glower at them. "I'm coming with you. Don't even think of trying to leave me out now, or I'll cast a spell that will turn the two of you into frogs."

Kelly turned to Brett. "Well, in that case, I guess Aunt Mary isn't leaving us with much of a choice. Either we bring her with us, or we start new careers as amphibians."

Brett checked the time on the large-faced clock

over the serving counter. "It's late. Why don't we all meet up tomorrow early and use Kelly's computer? If that's okay?"

Kelly agreed that it was and reluctantly turned down Brett's invitation to return to Derry with them. "I'm getting behind with some of the wedding arrangements I need to do. I'm planning a long evening snuggling with my computer at home."

Brett agreed, adding that he had some work to do as well. "I'm going to miss you lots, Red," he murmured into her hair.

"I hate to break you guys up." Mary broke into their quiet moment. "I really want to go home and get some sleep so I'll be fresh for tomorrow. I don't want to meet Troy all these years later looking haggard."

They agreed that the best course of action was to start early the next morning. Brett offered to drive Kelly home before he and Mary returned to the Atwell Mansion.

****

"What a sweet little house," Mary cooed when they parked in front of Kelly's cottage.

"It's an old fisherman's cottage that I'm renovating," Kelly told her.

"All by yourself? Oh, the things you young women get into these days."

Brett, his back to Mary, rolled his eyes, and Kelly struggled not to laugh. Brett walked her safely to her door, and his goodnight kiss was so filled with desire that it made her knees go weak and banished all coherent thought as she clung to him.

When she was able to speak, she said, "Why don't you drop Mary back home and then come over for a nightcap…? Or…something?"

When he hesitated, she teased, "You're not still scared that the ghost might appear and ruin your play, are you?"

Brett shook his head. "Honey, I doubt that anything could spoil things when I'm with you. But I need to get back to Derry, and you've got work to do for your business. We've an early start tomorrow, and Mary is in a high state of nerves. I'm uncomfortable not being there with her. And neither of us will get any sleep if I stay with you." The desire that gleamed from his eyes spoke volumes.

Kelly nodded and, ignoring Mary watching from Brett's SUV, kissed him passionately. Heat ran from her chest to her belly as their mouths met, her body remembering how good the sex was between the two of them. Pressed tightly against him, in his arms, Kelly felt the evidence that he, too, remembered.

They finally pulled apart, and Brett reluctantly left her to drive Mary home.

Feeling bereft at his leaving, Kelly wondered if a time would come when they didn't need to part. On her shoulder sat a mischievous imp who whispered, "Why didn't he ask you to stay over at his place?"

She mentally swatted the doubting creature away, breathed deeply, and stepped through her own front door. Without even flicking on the light, she saw Peter the Friendly Ghost comfortably ensconced on her living room sofa and looking as relaxed as if he owned the place. Sullivan the cat was sitting on a windowsill, the fur ruffed up all along his back as he glared at their uninvited visitor. Kelly had read in novels that ghosts gave out 'an eerie glow', but she'd never witnessed it so strongly herself until now. *Get a few of these restless spirits together in one space and you'd save a pile of money on electricity bills.*

"I was wondering when you'd get back—it's really not seemly for a young woman to be dallying with a young man on the doorstep in public view." He had moved to a sitting position, a stern expression on his face.

"Who do you think you are, my dad?" she snapped, and was immediately sorry, for the ghost suddenly radiated a gray wave of sorrow.

"No, my little girl drowned in a friend's swimming pool when she was seven. Sometimes I've thought it was penance for how I ruined other people's lives. But I do have a son, a wonderful young man."

"I'm sure God wouldn't have let that terrible thing happen to your daughter just to punish you, however much you may have deserved it." Despite herself, she couldn't help feeling sorry for the man, er, ghost.

He heaved a massive sigh. "Thank you for that. But if I were your father, I wouldn't allow such loose behavior."

"Good thing you're not, then, isn't it?"

They glared at each other across the room. Kelly caved first. "I'm almost thirty years old. I'm not a child. And we're trying to figure out a solution to your problems so that maybe you can go on to whatever's next and leave me alone."

The ghost nodded. "I'm grateful, although it seems you are all pretty dumb. It's taken ages for us to get to this point."

She fisted her hands. If she punched him, her fist would go right through and into the hard-backed seat.

That wouldn't be very satisfying and would probably hurt. "You know, you could have been a bit more helpful. Why the need for lurking around? And that stunt of throwing all my stock about in Wedding Bliss and terrifying my poor assistant, Noelia? Couldn't you just have had a conversation with me like we're doing now?"

The restless spirit sniggered. "What fun would that have been?"

"Fun? You think all this is fun? I heard from Mary how much you liked practical jokes." She ground her teeth. "You know, I finally made the connection between you and the cursed wedding gown, then to Mary Atwell, but for the longest time, I thought you were Troy, her missing groom. Your sense of 'fun' made Mary cry, thinking Troy was a ghost."

He started to fade, his expression one of guilty sorrow. "My stupid sense of humor and practical jokes started all this trouble. Seems I can't stop… Tell Mary I love her still and I'm truly sorry. Tell Troy…I never meant for…"

And he was gone, leaving the sentence unfinished. Exhausted from the emotions of the day and from the encounter with Peter Arnt's spirit, Kelly stumbled upstairs. Wedding Bliss work could wait until she'd had some shuteye. She barely stopped to clean her teeth before falling into bed and into mercifully dreamless sleep, Sullivan snoring contentedly at her side.

****

Brett wasn't so lucky. Back in Derry, he'd decided to sleep in one of the mansion's ten bedrooms so that he could be on hand if his aunt needed anything. She still hadn't fully regained her vitality after the pneumonia.

The night ticked by, but he tossed and turned as sleep eluded him.

Finally, he acknowledged the problem in just one word: *Red.* Kelly Andrews was driving him crazy. She reminded him of one of the long-stemmed roses his mother had loved to decorate their home with—the slender body, the thick crop of shining red hair. *The sharp thorns.*

The idea of Kelly's prickliness made him smile then groan with frustration. He didn't think he'd ever sleep again unless she was there in his bed, her flaming red hair spread across his pillow, her soft, creamy body pressed against his. He was hard just imagining her there with him.

He had to face the fact that it wasn't just his body that longed for Kelly—it was his heart. What a marvelous, terrifying, beautiful thought.

There had been other women in his life, in his bed. Sure, some had been beautiful, most had been intelligent, and all had been desirable. He'd even thought himself in love once or twice. But he had never met another woman who moved him, who made him laugh, who intrigued him, as much as Kelly Andrews. He craved her not just for that beautiful body, but for the whole woman she was.

Was it possible to actually be in love with someone you'd met barely half a dozen times? His rational mind pooh-poohed the idea of love at first sight. But his emotions joined his hormones in shouting, *Yes! Yes!*

Chapter Seventeen

Brett, Mary, and Kelly had agreed to meet at Wedding Bliss by nine-thirty the next morning to start their online search for the elusive Troy Matthews. Kelly arrived way too early for their meeting and spent some time going over the plans for three upcoming weddings, including the one they were arranging for Daria Welcome.

Noelia arrived early, too, and peered over Kelly's shoulder. "You're an early bird, must be all this autumn sunshine that's inspiring us both."

Kelly explained that she was trying to make some headway with the tasks needed to be done before she met up with Mary Atwell and Brett. "We're going to see if we can bring up any news about the elusive missing groom on Google," she told her assistant. Noelia laughed out loud when Kelly told her about Mary's misnaming of Google as Strudel or Noodle, but her mood she quickly sobered.

"Let's hope this is all solved soon, or Daria may not get to wear that dress walking down the aisle," Noelia had observed darkly.

"Don't be a pessimist," Kelly replied, although in her heart she knew they had not set themselves an easy task.

They'd just finished catching up when Brett knocked on the door. Kelly saw Mary standing on the sidewalk to look in the store window.

She held back, worrying her bottom lip with her teeth. She wasn't sure how Mary Atwell would deal with being surrounded by all the wedding paraphernalia. At least the cursed gown was in Daria Welcome's closet and not at the store. Still, she took a moment to step outside and ask the older woman how she felt about all these reminders of a wedding that had never happened.

To her surprise, Mary smiled and told her that she'd been living with the pain of being jilted for so many years and doubted seeing a few wedding knickknacks could possibly bother her. Besides, she added, she wasn't going to let anything get her down now that there was a glimmer of hope that her questions might soon be answered.

Certainly, Brett's aunt looked more friendly and relaxed than Kelly had ever seen her. She couldn't help a frisson of anxiety, however. What if they couldn't find any further information about Mary's errant groom? Or what if he had died since Peter's last check-in or perhaps had a mental breakdown and never recovered? She wondered how Mary would deal with such a stark reality.

On closer inspection, though, she thought Mary had lost about a decade since the previous evening. When she commented on it, Mary replied, "I feel younger, you know. Somehow being near to finding out what happened, why Troy didn't come to the wedding and had never contacted me again, well, it makes me feel better about it all. In fact, I'm not sure now why I didn't do something like this long ago." She reached out and squeezed Kelly's hand.

"You know, my dear, you've been instrumental in taking a huge burden off my mind. Even if we find out Troy is dead after all, at least there'll probably be clues as to why he disappeared."

Reassured, Kelly led the way through the store and to the rear room where the computer set-up waited, its power lights blinking in readiness. She introduced Mary to Noelia, who spent a few minutes showing the older woman around the store and proudly showing off some of their special articles before Mary followed the others into the computer room.

"You certainly do have good taste," she said. "I think it must be fun to be a bride these days."

"If you could be a fly on the wall here when some of these brides are pouring out their anxieties, you wouldn't think so," Noelia told her. "No matter how sure a couple is that they love each other, there are still the same old insecurities and tensions about how the wedding will go. Will Uncle Bill drink too much? Will the mother of the bride and the mother of the groom get into a fight? Will grandma take offense at not being seated at the bridal table?"

"Oh, I do remember all that," said Mary. "My grandmother had hated Troy's grandmother ever since some boy she liked had asked the other one to a deb dance. They hadn't spoken civilly in years. I had to make my mother promise to keep them apart. And one of my bridesmaids got into a snit and threatened to drop out of the wedding because I'd chosen lemon yellow brocade for their gowns and she said it didn't suit her coloring…ha, but it's all a long time ago, and it didn't matter anyway, in the end."

"You poor dear," Noelia said with real feeling.

"You just go and sit down with the young ones and I'll bring us some nice chamomile tea and maybe see if there are some chocolate digestive cookies left." Noelia's recipe for all ills—tea and English chocolate digestive biscuits.

Kelly had quickly explained to Noelia that the ghost was not the missing groom but, in fact, his best friend. Or ex-best friend, Noelia corrected. "Obviously, he's the rat who had something to do with the wedding not going ahead, and I doubt the groom would still consider him his best friend. And rightly so."

"How do you reckon that?" Brett asked.

"The miserable beast seems to like keeping people in suspense and playing tricks on them. I mean, he could easily have confided in Kelly, explained what was happening, who he was, and what he wanted. But he's kept her dangling all this time, as if his wishes were some hilarious treasure hunt."

"Apparently there are rules that govern haunting," Kelly said dryly.

Mary drew in a sharp breath. "It's true that Peter liked to play practical jokes, but surely he wouldn't have been mean enough to deliberately ruin our wedding day. Although getting Troy drunk…"

A sudden, shrill, whistling sound pierced the silence, startling them all. "Is that…?" Mary asked, looking around nervously.

"The ghost?" Noelia asked sweetly. "Oh, no. That's just our old-fashioned kettle letting us know it's on the boil and ready to make instant coffee or tea for us." She aimed a meaningful glance at Kelly.

"You drink instant coffee?" both Atwells exclaimed at once, looking incredulous.

Kelly flushed with embarrassment, but before she could stutter an excuse Noelia chimed in. "Yes, we do, because some dumb ghost broke our glass carafe on the very ancient coffee maker we used to have, and we had that because the *boss* of this store is too mean to spring for a modern coffee maker."

Kelly flushed a deeper crimson. "It's just not been in the budget, but remember what I said? That we'd get one…"

"Yeah, well, until then, it's instant. But we do have cream."

"So, let's get to it, shall we? This your computer? Not as ancient as your coffee maker, I'm glad to see." Brett rubbed his hands together in anticipation of finally solving the decades-old mystery of his aunt's missing groom.

Noelia agreed to take care of whatever customers ventured into Wedding Bliss so, armed with steaming mugs of strong coffee and a plate of chocolate biscuits, Mary, Troy, and Kelly gathered around the store computer in the back room and accessed the internet. Kelly asked Mary to write down some of the things she knew about Troy.

"What sort of things?" she asked.

"Start with his age, birth date, where he was born, parents' names, and siblings, that sort of thing. And things he liked, hobbies, anything like that. These could be leads in tracking him down."

Mary looked doubtful. "After all these years? I mean, he used to love frozen bananas covered in chocolate, he jogged six miles every morning, and he collected superhero comic books. But he'll be in his sixties now. I think it's unlikely he'll have the same interests. After all, I used to be his main interest, and that obviously changed…"

"Don't be bitter—you're not the only bride to be left at the altar, you know." Kelly softened the words with a smile, but she could see that Mary felt the sting, so she added, "My fiancé chickened out just a couple of weeks before the wedding. Believe me, I now realize it was the best thing that ever happened."

"Don't you ever wonder what might have been?" Mary pulled up an old wooden chair from the corner of the room, deliberately avoiding Kelly's eyes.

Kelly sighed. "No, I don't believe in regrets like that. No one can build a life on might-have-beens."

Mary surprised her by plopping her bottom down on the chair beside her and leaning over to pat her cheek. "I know how much you must have been hurt. But you're a wise woman, too. You're not spending the best part of your life pining away for a man who obviously wasn't good enough for you, especially when there are such better choices around." Her eyes slid toward Brett, who was tapping his fingers on the mouse pad while watching the computer's search engine load. Kelly's redhead complexion blushed deep scarlet. How much did Mary know or guess about her relationship with Brett?

Mary sighed again. "That's what I did, wasted the best part of my life, and it took you seeking me out— and that nephew of mine—to pull the blinkers from my eyes."

"Group hug!" Brett declared with a grin, wrapping his arms around Kelly and Mary. "If all this warm and fuzzy stuff goes on much longer, I may forget I'm a big strong guy and cry like a girl."

The moment lightened, they turned to the computer, laughing.

At first their task looked daunting. "Who'd have thought there could be so many Troy Matthews in Maine with a birthday in March?" Kelly groaned as Google spat out a seemingly endless list.

Mary patted her hand over the computer mouse. "Don't get discouraged, dear. After all, we're not even sure Troy is in Maine. There are forty-nine other states as well, you know."

"And then there are the other 192 countries in the United Nations, not to mention the rest of the world..." Brett added mischievously.

"Thanks, guys. Ever heard the term 'Job's Comforter'?"

"Isn't that the guy in the Bible who...well, didn't get that much comforting?"

"Got it in one. Now, can we come up with some filters for these results?"

"Sure," Mary said. "Only, er, what are filters?"

Kelly resisted the urge to beat her head against the computer screen while Brett explained the mechanics of a computer search to his aunt.

"What about his war service?" Mary asked. "I'm pretty sure Troy would have gone to Vietnam if he was drafted."

"But so would many others," Brett pointed out.

"Yes, but it cuts down on the number of Troy Matthews we have to look at—by army service, age, etc." Mary looked down at her lap and added quietly, "There might also be records if he...if he didn't come back."

Kelly used Mary's list to filter for age, place of

birth, parents' names, military service….and let out a groan of frustration that startled the other two out of their Computer 101 conversation.

"I think this is Mission Impossible," she told them. "It's going to take years to check out all these Troy Matthews results."

"Are there no matches at all?"

"That's the problem. There are plenty of matches, and the only way to really weed them out is to start getting phone numbers, if we can find them, and start calling…"

At that moment, Noelia came in carrying a tray of sandwiches from the nearby Sweets 'n' Savories Café. "Thought you might need some refreshments, ladies and gentleman." She grinned. Peering at the screen over Kelly's shoulder, she murmured, "There sure are a lot of Troy Matthews."

"Too many. I feel defeated," said Kelly.

Noelia handed around the sandwiches and poured hot water onto instant coffee. "Do you remember that children's show thing? You know, 'one of these things is not like the other one'?"

Eye rolls all around, but Noelia ignored them. "You had to look at the objects and decide what made one of them different. You've got lots of results that look the same there, so what's different about our Troy Matthews?"

"Yeah, we have a gazillion of them to go through to find that one that's different. If he's even here." Kelly's voice was bleak.

"Don't despair—let Auntie Noelia help."

"She's your aunt?" Mary asked, looking from Kelly's tall, red-haired, slim figure to Noelia's short, gray-blonde, and comfortable one, with an eyebrow raised.

Kelly rolled her eyes again.

"Just a figure of speech, Auntie," Brett broke in.

"Well, now we've got that out of the way. Listen to my brilliant idea. This Troy comes from a pretty well-off family, right?" Noelia continued.

Mary nodded. "Oh yes. They claimed they could trace their ancestry back to the Mayflower. I believe their relative was a cook or janitor on board…" she added waspishly.

"So, we have a seafaring cook or janitor whose family has gone up in the world through a few generations. Wouldn't a scion of a family like that go to an Ivy League university? And don't they keep good records of their alumni and the years they graduated? As well as alumni associations…?"

Stunned silence followed. Kelly gave a whoop and threw her arms around Noelia. "I've always said you were brilliant—I just never knew how much!"

Noelia looked smug. "While you're feeling grateful, how about a new coffee maker?"

"Let's just see if you're right." Kelly turned a questioning glance on Mary. Her heart kicked up a notch when the older woman answered, "Oh, yes, generations of Matthews went to Harvard Law."

This time Kelly let Brett take over the computer as she finished her meal and drank coffee. Mary was so quiet she asked her if something was wrong. "Don't be too disheartened, we'll find Troy," she said.

"I was always afraid that I'd find out that all the time I'd been hating him and loving him and grieving, that he was dead." Tears stood out in Mary's eyes.

Kelly gave her a quick hug. Then she swapped places with Brett. He had already opened the Harvard Law School site and was working on lists of their alumni students from the relevant time period. After glancing at several, she gave a little victory cry.

Turning the screen slightly so that Mary could see, she asked, "Do you think this could be Troy, forty-some years on?"

Mary put on her reading glasses and peered at a small photo that appeared alongside the details of one Troy Joseph Matthews of Bar Harbor, Maine. "Oh, dear lord, yes, it surely just could be. He's got less hair, more wrinkles—haven't we all—and he didn't wear glasses, but yes, it could be him." She clutched her hand to her chest, and tears sprang into her eyes. But a mischievous smile danced on her lips and she added, "Still got that sparkle in his eye, though. My, Troy, you're still an attractive man!"

Brett and Kelly met each other's gaze and did a synchronized eye roll. Catching them, Mary sniffed and said, "What? Just because I'm old doesn't mean I don't have...feelings."

Chastened, Brett moved back to the computer. Several key taps later, he sighed. "It says he served in Vietnam and he's kept in touch with his alumni, but I can't find an address, and he's not listed in the phone directory."

"Ah, sometimes keeping up with friends can bring benefits. Just give me a few minutes. I still have some connections in the military." Kelly pulled her phone from her purse.

****

They almost needed a shoehorn to pry Mary away

from the online information, scanty as it was, about Troy Matthews. It appeared he'd finished law school, done service in Vietnam, been wounded, and returned to Maine. There he had spent some time in rehab, then attended college and become a Certified Public Accountant with a company in Bar Harbor.

"Golly, I can't imagine Troy as an accountant. All the ones I've ever met are staid and stuffy. And he did study to be a lawyer."

Brett and Kelly locked gazes above his aunt's head.

"Aunt Mary, have you considered the idea that you might not like the, er, mature version of your long-ago love?" Brett tried to be tactful. Kelly didn't know whether to cry or laugh at the attempt.

"What your nephew is trying to say, in his own special roundabout way, is maybe you'll be disappointed if we actually find this guy and he's a real boring old jerk and you don't fancy him anymore. Like looking at the photo of the class stud in the school yearbook, then meeting him at a school reunion years later, all beer belly, bald, and gone to seed, and wondering what the hell your crush had been about."

Mary was silent for a few minutes as she thought about that. Finally, she heaved a sigh and said, "Right now, however, I'd just like to look him in the eye and find out just why he dumped me like a...a..."

"That's okay, Auntie, we get the picture. Anyhow, now that Kelly's managed to get an address from some of her friends in the veterans' volunteer group, we should schedule a visit. Bar Harbor is a bit of a drive from here, so I suggest we leave it until tomorrow when we're all fresh and we won't be hammering on the poor guy's door after he's in bed."

"I don't want to phone in advance; I'd rather just call in on him, surprise him, and see how he reacts. See if he even recognizes me, remembers me, now." Mary's voice had a sad, wistful note that wrenched at Kelly's heartstrings.

Chapter Eighteen

Brett and Mary arrived at Wedding Bliss a little later than planned the next morning. Kelly watched curiously from the window of Wedding Bliss as Brett moved to the passenger seat and helped Mary out onto the sidewalk. The older woman was carrying a large, gift-wrapped box.

"I wonder whatever that's about," she murmured to Noelia, who had come to stand beside her.

"I haven't got a clue, but I do love presents. Wonder who it's for?" Noelia opened the door to let Mary and Brett in.

"You were so good to us yesterday, Noelia," Mary said. "And we thought a little gift was in order."

Mary made a great show of presenting the gift to Noelia Russo. Noelia glanced at Kelly, who patted her shoulder. "I know how much you love presents," she said. "Go ahead—you open it."

Noelia began to eagerly rip off the wrappings, then blushed and looked at her audience. "I'm sorry for tearing into it, but I don't often get presents."

"Go ahead, dear, and I hope you enjoy it," Mary told her.

The last sheet of giftwrap fell to the floor to reveal a box containing a gleaming state-of-the-art coffee maker, complete with bells and whistles. Noelia screeched with joy, hugged Mary, and carried the box into the back room to set it up, humming to herself. Mary went with her to enjoy watching her put the machine together, so Kelly took the chance to hug Brett. He gathered her into his arms for a lingering, hot kiss. "I'm glad you stayed with me last night, Red. I love falling asleep with you and waking up to find you still there."

His words made Kelly's pulse leap. "I feel the same, Brett—and I especially like the bit that comes before falling asleep with you." She enjoyed the darkening of his eyes in response to her mischievous whisper.

"You think that's only a 'bit'? I thought it would have deserved a somewhat more lavish description," he growled in her ear, his breath tickling the sensitive skin.

They were still laughing, parting reluctantly as a pleased looking Noelia returned with Mary. "It works! It's wonderful!" she told Kelly, and then shooed them all out of the store. "Go away, people, I want to play with my new toy while you go groom hunting."

The drive to Bar Harbor took the better part of two hours. They took Brett's SUV, with Mary sitting in the back so that Kelly could sit beside the driver and read the street map when they arrived. As well, she basked in hot memories of the night they spent together in Troy's apartment over the carriage house in Derry, and the promise he'd made that they would have a repeat performance.

It was agreed that they would try to locate Troy's home without calling ahead, as Mary had requested. "What if the poor guy answers the door in his boxers? Or worse, his grubby tighty-whiteys and sporting a beer belly and a mighty hangover?" Kelly whispered to Brett as they drove along.

"Then it would be interesting—I've never seen a grown man in his boxers before," Mary piped up from the back. "Most guys wore those jockey things back then. Or none at all."

Kelly and Brett exchanged indulgent grins, with Brett looking embarrassed at his aunt's revelations.

"And I thought she was such a prude," he whispered to Kelly.

"I heard that, young man. I'm not deaf, you know," Mary teased.

Kelly grinned, enjoying Brett's discomfort. He glanced at her and said, "Teasing is something I've never experienced much before with Aunt Mary."

"Don't wreck her good mood," Kelly whispered back.

"How often do I have to tell you two, I've got perfectly good hearing?"

Mary had started out in high spirits, assuring Kelly that she would be happy no matter what the outcome. At least a decades-old mystery would be solved.

Half an hour into the journey and she was snoring softly in the back seat. Kelly envied her, but at least now she could raise the question with Brett that had been bothering her since they discovered Troy's location.

Now that they knew where the man might be and that he was alive, there was a question everyone had danced around that was becoming all the more urgent, but somehow it had never been asked.

Nudging him to get his attention, Kelly asked Brett in a low voice, "We haven't talked about this, but what happens if a little wifey opens the door with a big, welcoming smile, not knowing it's her hubby's ex who's standing there, searching for him?"

Brett was silent for a moment, concentrating on overtaking a battered truck that was dawdling along in his lane. "I don't think we can predict what anyone's reaction would be. And anyway, there was no mention of his married status on the university alumni website. Did your friend in the veterans' association mention anything?"

Kelly worried her bottom lip for a moment before admitting, "You know, I never even thought to ask…I suppose I was so invested in finding the man who'd left Mary literally standing at the altar that it never occurred to me there might be another woman in his life."

Brett kept his eyes on the road, but his hand slipped across the seat to stroke Kelly's thigh. "It's been a lot of years. The man has surely had some romantic moments in his life. He wouldn't be a guy if he hadn't." Kelly could hear the smile in his voice. She wanted to grab his hand and hang on for dear life—or, if Mary hadn't been in the rear seat, make him pull off into the next country road and show her what he meant by 'romantic moments'.

Instead, she asked, "How do you think your aunt would be able to cope if the jerk's married with six kids and a passel of grandkids?"

"Don't talk about me like I'm not there, Kelly. I'm not a helpless old lady, you know." an irritated voice piped up from the backseat. The jilted bride was awake again. "To be honest, if he's got a wife, kids, and grandkids, I'd be really happy for him. At least one of us has had a life. I'd be delighted and compliment him. Then I'd kill the mud-sucking bottom pond dweller!"

Brett and Kelly looked at each other in amazement. Kelly was afraid to look in the rearview mirror in case she caught Mary's eyes. They both struggled, but the shared mental picture of five-foot three-inch Mary doing real damage to a boxer-clad man whose bio pitched him at six-foot-two made laughter impossible to stifle. Brett was laughing so hard he signaled and pulled onto the hard shoulder.

"Aunt Mary, you'll be the death of me," he wheezed when he could catch his breath again.

She glared at him through the rearview mirror.

"I'm finding that I'm a lot tougher than anyone has ever given me credit for."

****

The house at the address Kelly had obtained from her friend at the veterans' association was a modest single-story home with an attached garage. A very ordinary home in a very ordinary part of the town tucked away from the main tourist drag.

A tiny front lawn was neatly clipped, and an ornamental cherry tree swayed and rustled in the soft, sea-scented breeze that filtered over the short distance from the seafront. Over and above the obvious care was a patina of recent neglect. Pansies had browned and died in a box on the cement stoop, and the paintwork of the house and garage looked tired.

A large, fluffy ginger cat sat on the stoop. He was plump and confident as only a much-loved pet can be. Kelly thought that was proof at least that someone with a heart lived there. Unless, of course, he belonged to a neighbor.

"There's no car in the drive," Mary whispered.

Was Brett's aunt having second thoughts and

looking for an excuse to call the whole affair off? "The garage door is shut tight. Troy's car could be in there," Kelly replied. "So who wants to go and ring the bell?"

They stood in the driveway, each glancing at the other and looking away. Mary became fascinated with her shoes, and Kelly studied the road as Brett stared at his front headlights. Finally, Brett said, "I'll go. The man might think twice before he slams the door in another guy's face."

Kelly sighed dramatically at his tone of voice. "I think this is a situation that needs a little less testosterone and a little more finesse. Besides, a man is less likely to feel threatened if a woman is on his doorstep. I'll go and knock on the door."

"Unless she's red-haired," Brett muttered under his breath, but Kelly heard him anyway and gave him a look.

It shouldn't be so difficult to march up the three cement steps and knock on that dull green painted door, thought Kelly, except that so much seemed to be riding on what lay beyond. She took a deep breath, wishing she were anywhere but where she stood at that instant, and grasped the brass door knocker. Three loud raps reverberated through the home. A minute passed. Two minutes. Nothing.

She rapped again and then noticed the doorbell, so she held that down and listened to its chiming notes weaving through seemingly empty air to fade away unanswered.

Brett and Mary stood on the driveway watching her with mixed expressions. Mary's face radiated hope and anxiety, but Brett's expression was more of concern for the aunt who had taken him in as a grieving teenager.

Kelly sighed. Just how had she got tangled up in all this? Then she remembered the one window looking out onto the street. If she stretched just a little on tiptoe and held onto the edge of the wall, perhaps she could see into the room beyond. She took a deep breath and balanced herself, clinging to the clapboard with her fingertips as she peered in through the window, only to lose her grip and fall off the step in shock at a large pair of bright eyes glaring back out at her.

"Oh, jeez, Kelly, are you okay?"

Sure, she was okay. Nothing like an inelegant face plant into dead pansies right in front of the hunk you really would like to impress. She accepted Brett's hand to help her to her feet then shrugged his fingers away as he tried to pick dead petals from her hair. "I can do that," she snapped. "It was just another damned cat, the twin of the one on the stoop. But for a moment I thought…oh, never mind."

The 'twin' cat sauntered up to her, weaving between her legs and looking up with what Kelly was sure was a smile on its face. And she was equally sure that its twin inside the house was falling about laughing at the dumb human, too.

"A right pair of comedians," she muttered under her breath.

"What?" Brett looked concerned as if her words signaled a concussion.

"Nothing. It was just a cat. There's no one home so I think…" She looked over his shoulder, and the words she was about to say stuck in her throat.

Hobbling along the driveway next door heading for the sidewalk was the oldest woman she'd ever seen. She looked as though a blast of wind would blow her and her walker over. She wore a long flowing dress and a bonnet—a bonnet?—and could easily have stepped out of one of the pioneer history books. Her wrinkled face reminded Kelly of those dried apple dolls they used to make in school, but it was set in determined lines and her dark, wrinkle-bedded eyes were set firmly on the newcomers.

"You looking for Mr. Matthews?" she croaked in a voice that sounded unused. "If so, you're too late—the funeral's today. Try the cemetery."

Mary gasped a sob, and Brett put his arms around her. Kelly was caught between comforting Mary and rushing off down the driveway to pump the elderly neighbor for information. She left Mary to her nephew and followed the woman, but even as she moved toward the sidewalk a Prius pulled up and a gray-haired man got out and helped the woman into the vehicle. Kelly called to the couple, but they drove away.

"Guess they're both deaf. Do you think the old guy was her son?"

"Well, he looked too young to be her boyfriend," Mary said tartly, and Kelly blushed, realizing that the "old" man was probably little older than Mary's sixty-five years. *Oops.*

Mary's lip was quivering, and she burst into tears. "All these years he was living right here, we were just a couple of hours apart. And now…now I've found him, and he's gone. Just a few days too late."

Kelly put her arms around her. She appealed with her eyes to Brett for any ideas to comfort his aunt, but he looked as dejected as she felt. He pulled out a big, snowy-white handkerchief and held it out to Kelly, who used it to staunch the tears that were falling in black mascara-stained drops down Mary's cheeks.

Then all three whirled around at the sound of screeching tires and grinding gears as the car that had picked up the old lady came reversing back down the street as though the devil himself was after them.

They stopped at the entrance to Troy's driveway, narrowly missing Brett's precious SUV. Kelly noted with amusement that he winced and shuddered at his vehicle's narrow escape.

The old, apple-sculptured woman wound down her window, poked her head out, and yelled, "If you wanna go to the funeral, follow us."

It required no discussion. They ran to Brett's car, Mary with surprising speed as she scrambled inside. Kelly leaped into the front seat beside Brett as the car moved off the sidewalk.

"Hang on. I need to fasten my seat belt. Remember this is the eighty percent risk seat."

****

They followed the Prius through the town streets, past shoppers and idlers, tourists, and vendors. It seemed to Kelly quite strange that life was able to go on so callously when major tragedies were unfolding in the world in parallel with the lesser tragedies unfolding right there in Brett's car. She asked herself how she would feel had Wayne simply walked away without a word and then she had found him years later, motivated by love, only to discover that it was too late, that he was already dead?

It was hard to follow that train of thought. There'd been moments after she had read Wayne's quick 'It's not me, it's you' note that she'd wished him in the path of a speeding bus.

Now? Now, her feelings were empty. That was the best word. Her heart held no feelings one way or another for Wayne.

How could you measure the depth of feelings like Mary's, going from pain and sorrow to anger to undying longing over the space of half a century?

She shook herself out of these thoughts as Brett maneuvered their vehicle behind the couple's car and a long line of vehicles heading into the cemetery through a fancy black wrought iron gateway. Already a crowd had gathered around the spot where an open grave was marked with floral tributes. It seemed the deceased Troy Matthews had been a popular fellow.

"Oh, no, I wish I could have brought a wreath, some flowers..." Mary mourned.

"It's enough that you are here," Kelly comforted. "I'm sure that will mean a lot." Or at least it would if the ghost of Troy Matthews were hanging around to see. Kelly gulped back that thought. The last thing in the world she wanted to see right now was another restless spirit. The thought that maybe a graveyard was a perfect hangout for them made her shudder and momentarily close her eyes.

Chapter Nineteen

They joined the mourners walking toward the gravesite. Many were very elderly, very well-dressed people, some using walkers to get around the grassy area toward the gravesite, a couple using expensive electric wheelchairs to bump across the grass. The weather had turned cold and damp in contrast to the unusually warm fall weather they'd been experiencing, and people were huddled into coats and scarves.

The undertaker's men were having some difficulty pushing a gurney containing the flower-covered casket across the wet lawns to the final resting place of Troy Matthews, the errant bridegroom. The thought that the man had once again left a heartbroken Mary standing at the church flipped through Kelly's mind. "If he does appear as a spirit, I'll give him what for," she vowed.

As the service began, the funeral was graced by faltering sunlight after a rain shower that left sparkling drops in the grass and the branches of shrubbery.

" 'Happy is the corpse the rain rains on,' " Mary muttered, and when Kelly gave her a sharp look, she added, "It's an old saying. It also says, 'Happy is the bride the sun shines on.' If only we weren't so late…if I'd only thought of searching for him before now, we might have had a little time together…" Mary mused sadly.

Kelly was tempted to roll her eyes. This was the

woman who'd secluded herself for years and cursed her wedding gown after the non-event wedding, causing other brides all sorts of problems when the dress was sold. Now she was weeping and wailing...*just a minute, what was that?*

Dear God—is that a ghost? Had her nasty thoughts actually conjured him up?

"Er, Mary, did Troy have a brother?"

"No, dear. That's something we had in common, being only children..." Mary's gaze followed Kelly's toward the small crowd standing next to the minister. There stood a balding man clutching his Bible as if it were a lifeline, and next to him was Troy Matthews. Alive or dead, Kelly hadn't discerned yet. Mary went pale and swayed alarmingly. Brett grabbed her and held her upright, although he, too, lost color as he followed their gaze toward where Troy Matthews, in the flesh or spirit, stood alongside the yawning grave.

Their attention must have telegraphed itself to him because the man looked up from the sober-faced conversation he was having with the minister. At first, his glance was simply curious as he reacted to seeing strangers at the funeral. Then his eyes returned to Mary, and his face drained of color to a shade whiter than that of a Hallowe'en ghost mask.

With a mixture of longing, shock, and sorrow, his gaze fastened on Mary Atwell as if by sheer force of his will he could hold her in place as the graveside service began. Kelly wondered what degree of strength it took for him to remain standing in the chief mourner's place while everything in him had to be clamoring to know whether the woman he was seeing was truly the person he thought or simply an illusion conjured up by his own grief.

He looked away as the minister droned on about the upstanding member of the community, the brave soldier and family man they were about to bury.

The man who was Troy Matthews Senior, recently deceased.

****

"I don't understand any of this. I don't understand what's happening. How can my Troy be standing there if he's dead?" Mary struggled to hold back a sob, her mouth covered with Brett's mascara-stained handkerchief. She turned to Kelly. "Am I seeing a ghost? Is your gift contagious?"

"He's standing there because he's alive and well and looking rather chipper despite the occasion," Brett snapped.

"I think this is his father's funeral. Although judging by how pale he went when he saw you, I think he thinks you're the ghost." Kelly put her arm around the older woman and glared over at the man who'd caused so much heartache.

"I think I need to sit down. My legs..." Mary's voice faltered. "I can't believe we thought he was dead, now he's alive?"

"Yeah, risen like Lazarus. Honestly, Aunt Mary, I think we should just get out of here. Obviously, the guy isn't fit to breathe the same air as you..."

"Oh, Brett...please don't be like that. After all these years, I want to see him, talk to him. I really want to know what happened."

Brett harrumphed his disapproval, but he put his hand on her arm and led her to a wrought iron bench set some distance away from the funeral crowd. "You know, Aunt Mary, if all this is too much for you, perhaps we should just go home and maybe try and sort this out another day. I don't want you getting ill again."

"Maybe you're right. It's obviously it's not a good time for Troy," Mary replied.

Kelly snorted. "Why on earth are you worrying about what's a good time for that jerk who walked away from you and left you standing there in a beautiful French designer dress you later cursed? Now that you know he's alive and kicking, don't you just want to slap him silly? I'd say that's well overdue."

Mary looked up at Kelly, her eyes wide. And then she started to laugh. And laugh, like she couldn't stop. Immediately, heads turned among the crowd at the fringes of the funeral, mourners no doubt wondering at the identity of the elegantly dressed older lady who was now laughing like a hyena at a frat party.

"This isn't very appropriate behavior," Brett hissed, causing Kelly to start laughing, too. She and Mary put their arms around each other and laughed until the tears ran down their cheeks.

"Really, you two—pull yourselves together. It looks like we have company."

They followed Brett's gaze to see that the graveside service was over, the crowds were leaving, the gravediggers were starting to fill in that gaping hole—and a white-faced errant groom was striding in their direction. Kelly noted that the man walked with a slight limp, something he seemed to be trying to hide.

"Oh, my, he's still a handsome, sexy devil," Mary murmured.

"Aunt Mary!" Brett's scandalized tone sent Kelly back into peals of laughter.

"Stop thinking of her as your aunt and see her as a lonely woman who has just seen the man she once loved—still loves—and be happy for her," she whispered in his ear. "I think it may be time we made ourselves scarce." Kelly pulled on his arm.

"I'm not leaving Aunt Mary with that man. Who knows what…?"

"Brett, Mary's a grownup. I think she can handle this herself. When she was jilted, everyone rushed around to shelter her. She didn't get the chance to handle anything. No, I think she needs to handle this herself. My biggest worry is that she might seriously hurt the man right here in public. Not that he wouldn't deserve that."

****

They stationed themselves a short distance away on another of the fancy and incredibly uncomfortable wrought iron benches much favored in cemeteries. In the shade of an elderly juniper tree, they watched covertly as Mary and Troy sat under a large oak tree, their heads close together like the lovers they had once been. The tree was already shedding its leaves like tears as autumn moved toward winter, and Kelly suddenly had a vivid image that the tree was weeping for the dead who rested all around.

Troy Matthews was indeed a handsome man for his age, Kelly thought. Dressed in a sober black suit and a spotless white shirt, thick white hair brushed right back from a high forehead, he looked far too classy a guy to have jilted his bride at their wedding without good cause. Although what good cause there could possibly be for his years of silence, Kelly couldn't begin to guess.

Her eyes filled with tears as she watched Troy and Mary talking, touching, gesticulating with their hands as they talked and finally—as the tears now slipped down her own cheeks—hugging each other as though they never intended to let go ever again.

Through the emotion of it all she heard a low growl from Brett. "That son of a bitch needn't think he's going to move in with Aunt Mary, live off her, and rip the heart out of her again!" He half rose from the bench, fists clenched, but Kelly grabbed his hand, and he sank reluctantly back down beside her.

"Face it, Rambo, your aunt is a grown woman. And she's no dummy—it won't take her long to figure out if this guy's a perennial loser and she'll kick him to the curb without a qualm."

Brett looked unconvinced. "It's going to take me some time to trust him. You haven't seen the way she's lived her life, all because he dumped her in that extraordinarily cruel way."

Kelly bit her lip, but she didn't let go of Brett's hand. "No one's asking you to call him Uncle Troy, but just be pleasant for Mary's sake. If everything goes well, she'll be one happy woman, and I know you want that for her. If it goes badly, well, she will need to know she can turn to you without any 'I told you so's'."

He slid back on the bench, relaxing against its solid back as he pulled her into his arms and held her close with an intensity that spoke volumes about how he felt. "How did you come to be so wise?"

****

Sitting there in the growing chill of the autumnal late afternoon, Brett thanked his lucky stars that he had found Kelly. Who'd have thought that walking into that wedding store prepared to do battle with a conniving entrepreneur he'd find such a gem instead? As he held her close to him, he felt a wave of sadness that Mary had missed such simple joys of holding and loving and being loved in return.

And then it hit him. He really, really was in love with Red. A woman who was still wounded by the ex-fiancé who had cut her in the most despicable way. If he told her now that he loved her, would she shy away, turn tail, and run? Or would she have the courage to return his love without fear? Worse, was she still, in some corner of her heart, in love with Wayne? Had Wayne damaged her for life? A woman who had faced life-or-death in the desert, who had been strong enough to rescue a wounded fellow soldier, surely she would be emotionally strong enough to trust?

He sighed and dropped a kiss on her flaming red hair. Now wasn't the time to ask the questions that were burning in him.

****

Kelly sighed as Brett's hand slid over hers, and his warmth telegraphed itself all through her body as her flesh remembered the night they'd just spent together. She leaned toward him, laying her head on his chest, and smiled as he dropped a kiss on her forehead.

"One thing is really bothering me," he surprised her by saying. "I mean—a cemetery has lots of capacity for restless spirits. How come you aren't being besieged right now by ghosts wanting their problems solved?"

Because I have my eyes tightly shut, she thought for a moment before replying. "I think it's because there has to be some kind of connection between myself and the spirit, something they can use as a conduit to me," she said slowly. "In this case, there were two lead-ins: the first was that cursed wedding gown that hung in Wedding Bliss's window; the second was that I had experienced being left at the altar, too. At least, I think that's what it is. I don't know anyone here, and it seems like I don't have anything in common with anyone here, so there's no way through for them. I don't really know…"

As she spoke, she steadfastly ignored the pale, gray figure in a long old-fashioned dress who was staring at her with heartbreakingly intense longing from under a nearby maple tree. She thought Brett probably wouldn't want to know, and she wasn't ready to deal with another unearthly problem, either. Maybe one day she'd return to the cemetery when she felt stronger.

She was grateful when she saw Mary and Troy rise from the bench and start toward them. Kelly smiled to see they were holding hands, although she would have preferred to see Mary bop the man on the nose a few times before reaching the hand-holding stage.

"Oh, look—they're coming this way!"

****

Even Brett could see the happiness that radiated from his aunt. "She looks like a different person," he whispered, his expression incredulous. "I've only ever known her to be this reclusive, bitter, and rather sad and sometimes angry person. Now she's glowing."

Reluctantly, he stood to face his smiling aunt and the man long thought to be dead. *And who would wish he was, if he caused Mary any more pain,* Brett vowed.

Brett and Kelly were both eager to hear Troy's story, but they were to be disappointed. Mary insisted that they all go home and meet up at the Atwell mansion the next morning for breakfast, when all would be revealed. No amount of protest would move the couple. "Other than telling you that Troy and I now completely understand each other, you'll have to wait to hear his story," Mary said firmly, adding, "Let's make it brunch rather than breakfast. Nothing too early, so we can all have a lie in." Mary spoke to Brett, but her eyes never left Troy, and she was twinkling as she spoke.

It was obvious that Troy was going back to the Atwell home with them. Brett started to protest, an angry flush across his cheekbones. "Aunt Mary, just think what you're doing. You've only just met this man and you can't…"

"Goodness, Brett—you sound exactly like I did when I admonished your sister Sasha not to bring strange men home." She sighed. "What a prude I must have sounded. Anyhow, Troy isn't a strange man, and we have a lot of talking and catching up to do." Mary gazed up at the tall, white-haired man who couldn't seem to take his eyes off her.

"I can hardly believe this is real," Troy murmured, reaching for her hand.

Brett opened his mouth to protest again, but Kelly squeezed his shoulder and stood on tiptoe to whisper in his ear. "They're grownups, sweetie. As Mary said, they have a lot of catching up to do."

Distracted by her sweet breath wafting warm against his ear, Brett forgot what he was going to say.

"Now, you young folks get along. We have to go back to Troy's house to pick up some things, and then we'll see you in the morning," Mary told them. "Don't wait up for us," she added over her shoulder as she walked away hand in hand with the man she had thought lost forever.

"I don't understand any of this." Brett opened the car door for Kelly, but he was looking down the street. "How can she just..."

"Shhh, love." Kelly put her arms around his neck. "She still loves him, and judging by the look on Troy's face, he's still pretty well besotted, too. Let it go, Brett. Soon, as Mary said, all will be revealed."

"But not until tomorrow. Anything could happen..."

The wicked grin Kelly gave him was so full of promise his knees went weak. "Anything can and should have happened by tomorrow. Fifty years is a long time to wait to get lucky." Her grin widened at Brett's scandalized expression. "Frankly, I'm having problems waiting for a couple of hours in hopes of getting lucky myself."

She had his full attention then as he drew her into a kiss that sent tingles all the way down to her toes, pausing to light little fires in many other places along the way.

Chapter Twenty

They awoke early the next morning, all tangled up together like a couple of cats in Brett's bed, basking in the warm sunshine flooding in through his bedroom window.

"I'm looking forward to hearing the story of why Troy didn't make it to the wedding," Brett said as he lazily stroked Kelly's back. "That should be an epic."

She yawned and purred as his hands worked magic on her spine. Turning around and pressing against him, she layered little kisses on his face until he groaned and captured her lips with his mouth. His hands roamed from her spine to her breasts and down along her belly.

"I'm really glad Mary insisted on meeting for brunch," she murmured lazily. "It gives us time…"

"Time for what?" Brett's breath was warm against her neck.

"Time for…" Her lips curled in a knowing smile. Actions speak louder than words, so she set about showing him.

Later, much later, they decided to take a stroll along the wharf and see if any of the food stands were open for a quick snack. They found one that sold mouth-wateringly fresh lobster rolls served by a plump, cheerful man who whistled an old love song melody as he handed them the white paper bags of food and paper cups of steaming hot coffee. They carried the food to a nearby bench with a view of the bobbing boats and choppy sea toward the horizon.

"You're very quiet," said Kelly as she cast a worried glance at Brett. She hated losing the sense of intimacy they had built up, and his abstracted silence worried her.

"Hard to speak when I'm wolfing down these delicious lobster rolls," he said, flashing a smile.

They ate in silence for a while, but she still felt that he was holding back on her. It was hard to still that quiet voice in her head that told her something was wrong, but she sat staring at her own bright pink flip flops and waited. *Stop being so insecure,* she admonished herself. *I'm not going to ask. I'm sure he will tell me in his own time if there is something wrong. Like, if he's regretting the hot sex we just had...or is he simply worried about his Aunt Mary?*

She was relieved when Brett cleared his throat. "What would you do if Wayne came back and pleaded with you to marry him?" He made the question sound like idle curiosity, yet she heard something in his voice that made her pulse jump.

"It kind of depends, I think."

"On what? I mean, do you still think about him?"

"Sure, I do." She smiled at the question. "I've thought about him a lot over the years, fantasized scenes about him coming to find me."

Brett studied the wharf and the lobster boats with an unwarranted intensity. "Are they the kinds of fantasy scenes that would do Mimi L'Amour proud?"

She was fighting to keep a straight face now. "Actually, they usually start with him on his knees..."

"I'm not sure I want to hear this." Brett stood and

went to lean on the white painted steel railing. The bright morning sun outlined his lean, muscular frame and his black jeans pulled tight across his butt as he propped his elbows on the cold metal. Kelly leaned back to admire the view. A seagull swooped down to catch the scrap of lobster roll he threw for it, its triumphant cry bringing a host of its brothers and sisters to beg and bluster for scraps, too. She got up and followed him to the railing, tossing a few more scraps to the birds.

"Yes, they start with him on his knees. Then I slowly undo my buttons…"

Brett's deep-throated moan sounded like a wounded animal.

"…and I open my jacket..."

Now he stared fixedly at the pewter colored waves, but she could see his Adam's apple bob as he swallowed hard.

"Then…" She paused, enjoying the tease. "Then I pull out my service revolver and shoot him in a variety of different body parts."

Brett turned, his eyes twinkling. In a swift stride, he closed the space between them and pulled her into his embrace. After he claimed a deep, heated kiss, he murmured, "Well, then, I guess I just have to be glad you no longer have a service revolver."

She stepped back and took a last bite of the lobster roll, smiling as his eyes watched her mouth, before replying, "What makes you think I don't?"

****

The Atwell mansion seemed to have undergone some metaphysical changes since the day before, Kelly thought as she and Brett entered for brunch. The old house, which had seemed so cold, now had a completely different atmosphere. *Almost homey.* For one thing, there were two plump and fluffy marmalade cats sitting among the delicate antique crockery on the dining room cabinet. Obviously, the kitties were among the 'things' that Troy had needed to pick up from his house. Feeling guilty about leaving her own feline alone, Kelly phoned Noelia and asked her to look in on Sullivan and give him a little love. "He should have lots of food left in his dish, but I don't want him to be lonely," she explained after filling her friend in on the events of the previous day. Noelia agreed and sent her good wishes to the happy couple. "What an exciting story," she said. "I am so looking forward to hearing the rest."

Brett was rubbing two pairs of feline ears. The purring rose to deafening proportions.

"Aunt Mary never allowed cats—or pets of any kind—in the house. Said they were dirty, caused too much damage, and required too much care," Brett whispered to Kelly. "As I got older, I began to think she was afraid of having anything around that she might get to love, in case it went away."

Kelly squeezed his hand. "She loved you and Sasha."

"We only came for holidays when we were kids. It was like she was borrowing us. I moved in after our folks died, and then when I was eighteen, Auntie insisted I have the apartment so that I'd have privacy. I think it meant I wasn't actually living with her."

"But she let Sasha live here?"

Brett grinned. "Sasha is a force of nature. You've met her—she's here and then not here, like a zephyr.

And she and Aunt Mary had frequent spats. Sasha is hard to love."

Kelly bit her lip. She'd thought Brett's sister a spoiled, self-centered, ruthless brat, but now wasn't the moment to start trashing his family. Especially as the spoiled brat in question had just wandered into the room. She wore a rich blue mini dress that accented her fragile blonde looks and showed off her long, slender legs. Kelly wished she'd worn something more elegant than white capris and a blue and white striped tee shirt. Maybe she could get Mary to teach her a spell that would cause a big red zit to appear on the end of Sasha's pert little nose…

"Brett! How are you, big bro?" Sasha air kissed her brother, sent a distracted smile at Kelly, and plucked up one of the cats. "Isn't it wonderful to have these little guys in the house? I always wanted a cat, and now there are two."

"Don't get too fond of them, young lady. No doubt you'll be off with another beau and heading for heartbreak again." Mary Atwell issued the warning as she walked into the room.

Sasha's face broke into a wide grin. "Oh, no, Aunt Mary. I'm sworn off men for good. You're stuck with me."

Mary responded with a 'we'll see about that' look. "You're getting ginger cat hairs all over that pretty dress—which, by the way, is much too short."

"Oh, Auntie, minis are back in fashion now. I bet you wore one way back in the seventies!"

"Never mind that. We're not talking about me now, you cheeky monkey." Mary's voice was strict, but Kelly was sure the older woman had a twinkle in her eye. She noticed that Brett's aunt had dressed in a casual, soft pantsuit in a lavender color that complemented her skin and eyes. The outfit was much different to the tailored skirts and twinsets she usually favored.

Mary hugged Brett and then turned to Kelly. "I want to thank you, Kelly—if it hadn't been for you and your special gift, I might never have found such happiness again." She directed a shy smile at Troy, who'd followed her looking ten years younger than the man they first saw standing at his father's grave. He was relaxed in dark blue casual slacks and a cream fisherman's sweater.

"You have a special gift? What is it?" Sasha asked, wide-eyed.

Kelly deadpanned. "I see dead people."

"Oh. Whatever." Sasha immediately lost interest and turned back to cuddling the cat.

****

Breakfast was a strained affair. Even Mrs. Patrowski seemed tense as she placed muffins, scrambled eggs, bacon, sausage, and home fries on the table, enough to feed a small army, added a coffee pot, and escaped quickly from the room.

Mary insisted that there be no talk about the last days' events until everyone had eaten. Warm glances between her and Troy indicated that all was well with the happy couple, but everyone else ate in a tense silence after a few attempts at small talk.

Finally, Mary suggested they take their coffee into the small parlor. When everyone was settled, Troy spoke for the first time, bolstered by Mary's hand slipping into his. "I think it's best if I tell you everything that had happened, why I…why I didn't show up for our wedding all those years ago."

"I'm looking forward to hearing this," Brett said, his voice hard and earning him a sharp look from Mary.

"Me, too—I thought only creeps did something so unforgivable." Sasha spoke up defiantly. "Honestly, Aunt Mary, I can't understand why you—"

"That's enough, Sasha." Mary cut her niece off sharply. "Wait and hear what Troy has to say; perhaps then you'll understand."

Troy, looking pale and tense, got up and made his way across the room to the ornate fireplace so that he could stand like an actor on stage, easily visible to everyone in the room.

"All he needs is a freaking podium," Brett muttered under his breath. Kelly shushed him and shivered as if a cold hand touched her shoulder.

She should have known the Old Man on the Bench, a.k.a. Peter the Friendly Ghost, wouldn't miss this particular get together. She saw Mary shiver, too, and Troy looked momentarily distracted. She noticed again that he walked with a slight limp, although he seemed to be trying to hide it.

He took a deep breath, filled his cheeks with air, and then blew it out with a sound like a sigh. "First of all, I want you all to know that I never intended to hurt Mary. I think I've been in love with her since she put paint in my hair during finger-painting in senior kindergarten." He smiled over at her. "So, here's the story of the biggest mistake I made in my life.

"Before the wedding, Peter Arnt—my best friend then, although I don't know what I'd call him now…" He paused, pulling down the rolled-up sleeves of his sweater. "Is it chilly in here or is it just me?"

Kelly wondered how Troy would react if she told him his old and now ghostly best friend was standing right beside him and breathing chilly sighs as he reacted to Troy's words.

"Anyway, Peter and I and a few friends from our classes at Harvard were having a kind of joint celebration. Finals were over, and we were about to go out into the world and make our mark. I was going to marry the woman I loved. It seemed like everything was perfect, and the future looked like more of the same."

Brett pulled the letter he had received from Peter Arnt from his pants pocket and handed it to Troy. "We've heard some of this from Peter. I'm sorry to have to tell you that your old friend died shortly after he wrote this."

Troy took the letter and unfolded it slowly as if he couldn't bear to read the contents. He pulled a pair of dark-rimmed reading glasses from his shirt pocket. Tears stood in his eyes when he looked up after reading his friend's words. Kelly was sure that the restless spirit standing next to Troy also wiped away a tear. *Could ghosts cry? She'd wondered that before…*

Mary crossed the room and handed Troy a glass of water. She gave him a gentle kiss on the cheek and returned to her seat.

"Thank you for showing me this, Brett." He placed the glass down carefully on a small glass topped table. "In those days, drinking hard was a sign you were a man, and I wanted to be a man desperately. So, I kept up with the guys and pretty soon was as drunk as a skunk. We'd also smoked a bit of weed and, frankly, we were really living in another dimension by then! When Peter came up with that great idea—that we'd literally go out and paint the town, not just red but all the colors of the rainbow—well, it sounded like a real adventure."

"What do you mean by 'literally painting the town'?" Sasha asked.

"We got some aerosol paints in every color you could imagine, found us a large wall on the side of a downtown store, and set to work." Troy paused and took a deep drink from his water glass as if the telling of his story was parching his throat. "Somebody must have spotted us and complained to the police, because the next thing was, we heard sirens. I wanted to finish the words I was spraying—'I love Mary,' in multi-colored spray—and delayed leaving when the others ran off."

"Oh, Troy—you did that for me?" Mary smiled, and then shot a hard glance at Brett who had snorted derisively.

"So, you didn't run fast enough, and the police caught you. How did you wriggle out of that?" Brett questioned.

"That's the whole point—I couldn't. I was so out of it I didn't even sober up until much later, so I don't think I really understood what was happening when they put me in a jail cell. It didn't hit me until I woke up in the drunk tank the next morning, feeling like hell. Then I saw the time and panicked, pleaded with them to let me get to the church for my wedding."

Troy took another gulp of water. Kelly could tell it was hard for him to go through these details in front of everyone, and suddenly she found herself feeling sorry for the man. "Who hasn't done something stupid when they were that age?" she whispered to Brett.

"I don't know anyone who'd have done something like that the night before their wedding," he retorted.

Obviously Troy heard him because he looked Brett right in the eyes and said, "I know it was stupid. I've kicked myself a million times since for being so dumb. The police charged me with vandalism and being drunk in a public place. I kind of lost it then, shouting that I was getting married and needed to get out, which was even more stupid because then they told me to calm down or they'd book me for causing a disturbance as well. They didn't have much sympathy for spoiled rich kids from Harvard who defaced the town with their crazy nonsense."

In desperation, Troy had called his father to come and post bail, but Mr. Matthews had no sympathy for his son. "I was pacing up and down in my cell, desperately waiting for my father to come and bail me out so that I could get to the church. Time passed, and I got more and more desperate. He showed up after the wedding was canceled, absolutely furious with me and saying I'd shamed the family name and that I didn't deserve a wonderful girl like Mary." Troy paused and bit his lip. "Mary was in pieces, and her family had forbidden me to go anywhere near her."

Behind Troy's shoulder, Kelly could see Peter's ghost looking paler than ever and very distressed. *And he should feel guilty!*

"Dad brought my enlistment papers for Vietnam and told me that the only way to redeem myself would be to go and do my duty for my country. If I didn't, neither he, my mother, nor any member of the Atwell family would want to see me again. *Ever.* I said I needed to go and see Mary to explain, but Dad said the war would be over in a few months, that I could come back with some discipline and backbone, a better man. Maybe then and only then, might Mary consider seeing me."

Mary used one of her tiny lace handkerchiefs to mop her eyes. "I knew nothing about this. It seems everyone made the decision I was too delicate to know any of it and so they 'protected' me. It was a huge mistake. Their misplaced concern made everything worse."

Troy gave her a brief smile and continued. "As we all now know that war didn't end quickly or well. I was wounded a couple of times. My last tour of duty, a land mine blew my foot off. Gangrene started to set in before I could get to a hospital, so they took off most of my leg below my knee and fitted me with a false limb. I can show you if you wish." He moved to start rolling up his right trouser leg but stopped when a chorus of "No, really, that's okay" sounded from his audience.

"Well, when you got back stateside, why didn't you do something then? You must have known how hurt my Aunt Mary would be because of you," Sasha said.

He looked gently at her. "I was in the hospital for several months. It seemed to take a very long time for my leg to heal well enough to wear the false leg…and I was suffering from what is now known as post-traumatic stress disorder. Back then, they'd started to call it Vietnam Syndrome.

"I was a mess. I wasn't sure if I'd ever be able to hold down a job and certainly something like the law, which would require a lot of people contact, was out of the question. I just couldn't handle talking to people. Plus, I had blackouts and sometimes flew into rages for no good reason. I sleepwalked and didn't remember anything when I woke up. I seemed to be living on my nerves, hardly sleeping or eating, drinking too much. How could I go and see Mary in that condition?

"I felt she deserved better than a physically lame, mentally crippled husband. Even if she'd accepted me, I was afraid she would have done so out of pity and without understanding what she was taking on."

Mary was worrying her fingernail, a nervous habit Kelly had never seen her do before. Tears threatened to spill again down the older woman's cheeks. Kelly was struggling not to get weepy herself; what Troy was describing was a severe version of her own experiences, minus the restless spirit visitors. She knew too many good men who had survived the horrors of war only to live a life of misery with the aftereffects. Too many had given up the struggle to regain their former lives and happiness and had taken their own lives. She shivered. Brett put his arm around her as if he read her thoughts.

"It took me years, literally, but I finally became a certified public accountant and found a job where there was very little interpersonal contact. Years of therapy helped me control the waking nightmares, the flashbacks, the rage, the depression. I no longer thought of suicide, but I did think of Mary, just about every day. By then she was just a dream, something to hold onto but something that I'd never have."

Troy's voice took on an edge of bitterness as he recounted how his mother had died in the early eighties without ever seeing her son again. His father had lingered on, and when he became ill, he sought out Troy to be his caregiver.

"You remember Dad, Mary? Too proud and stubborn to have strangers around while he was growing increasingly sick. He wanted me to move back to Derry and live on the family estate, but I refused. There was too great a possibility of seeing Mary, and I couldn't bear to see in her eyes the pain I had caused her, or worse, to see her horror or pity at the man I had become. I persuaded Dad to move in with me in a house I'd bought in Bar Harbor.

"Dad's last lingering illness was awful; his death was a blessing in a way. The man was ninety-five when he passed last week. The elderly woman you met was our neighbor, Mrs. Aylesbury, who's in her nineties herself. She and her son have been a godsend over these last few months. Because you arrived on the day you did, she just assumed you were coming to my father's funeral."

He looked over at Mary, who by now was crying openly. "I thought I had lost my mind again when I saw you standing there, Mary—or maybe that I had died myself and gone to heaven and you were there, waiting for me. I want to spend the rest of my life making up to you the happiness we should have had from the beginning."

Mary got up slowly and went to him, turning to face her family with a tear-streaked smile. "Troy has asked me to marry him, and I have said yes. I don't care if it bothers any of you because it's simply time I caught up on my life while I'm still breathing. Oh, and if anyone is thinking Troy is after my money, or worried about your inheritances—" She glared at Sasha, who colored and looked away. "—well, you should know that Troy, despite the modest house he was living in, is wealthy in his own right from his own work and investments, and he will inherit the Matthews' estate when his father's will is probated."

She took Troy's hand, and they turned to leave.

Brett stopped them. "I have something I want to say, Aunt Mary, Troy." They turned back to the room, their expressions closed against the hurtful words they expected.

"Go ahead, Brett. Might as well get it off your chest now. It won't make any difference."

Brett smiled. "I just wanted to say congratulations to you both, and I want to be the one who walks you down the aisle, Aunt Mary."

Mary's face radiated joy as she went to hug her nephew. Troy's lips edged upwards into a wide grin, and the two men shook hands.

After the happy couple had left, Kelly got up and kissed Brett. "I am so proud of you," she told him. "You made your aunt so happy just now."

Chapter Twenty-One

Kelly was thrilled that Mary and Troy had hired Wedding Bliss to organize their wedding, although they'd given her just three weeks to get everything done. Even self-absorbed Sasha forgot about herself and had gotten into the wedding mood. Kelly and Noelia had been run off their feet trying to put together a society-style wedding and reception with such little notice and were grateful for Brett's sister's willingness to be a gofer. She showed there was more to her than a good-time girl or the bimbo that Kelly had first dubbed her.

"Is everything going to be ready?" Mary asked shyly. She was in her elegant green and gold bedroom at the Atwell Mansion, dressing for her wedding with the help of Sasha and Kelly. Mary had been busy rebuilding friendships with people she had shut herself away from after the wedding fiasco. To everyone's delight, two little girls, the grandchildren of one of Mary's closest friends from back in the day, were acting as flower girls for her.

Mary's eyes filled with tears as she watched as the girls, dressed in pink and white dresses, giggled and jumped on the bed. "If everything had gone right, Troy and I might have had grandchildren like these two sweeties."

Kelly put her arms around her. "The past doesn't

matter now. This is a day for celebrating that you and Troy have found each other, not a day for sadness."

"We've had to be innovative in a few ways, but you're going to have a wedding that will set folk talking for more reasons than the obvious Matthews-Atwell romance," Kelly assured her. She'd been delighted when Mary chose the small Marina Grove church of St. Christopher's for her wedding rather than having the ceremony in Derry.

"It was here in Marina Grove that Peter first contacted you, it was here that my old bridal gown landed after Sasha sold it...and I certainly don't want to marry in the old church where the first service was to take place."

"Oh, Auntie..." Sasha was blushing a deep red.

Mary surprised her with a rare hug. "It's okay, dear. It's all water under the bridge now."

Her niece sniffed. "If you think about it, if I hadn't sold your wedding gown, then none of this would ever have happened."

"Don't push it, Sasha—what you did was wrong, and you can't wrap it up as anything else," Kelly murmured, getting a dark look from the other young woman.

The wrongs and rights of the story soon fled from her mind as she and Sasha helped Mary into the beautiful pale-pink brocade afternoon gown with its matching deeper pink jacket. Her silver-white hair had been skillfully restyled into a modern easy-care cut which fell softly around her ears and framed her pixie face.

Between the new style and the old love, Mary looked radiant and years younger than when Kelly had first met her.

"Is the limousine here yet?" the bride asked for the tenth time, admiring her wedding regalia in the long cheval mirror.

"Most brides want to follow tradition and be fashionably late," Noelia said as she brought the bridal bouquet and attendants' flowers into the room. Sasha was to be Matron of Honor.

"Not me," Mary declared." After all, I'm over fifty years late already. Is that fashionable enough for you?"

"Plenty so," Noelia answered as she handed the little girls their pretty flower baskets and stood back to admire the cute youngsters in their pink gowns and white ribbons. She gave Sasha her bouquet, which was a miniature version of Mary's pink roses, trailing ivy, and white baby's breath.

Confident that everything was in order, Kelly slipped out to poke her head into the room down the hall where Brett was helping a nervous Troy to fasten his tie. He looked handsome in his formal white tie and tails, but Kelly's eyes were fixed on Brett. She'd only ever seen him in jeans and shirts or sweaters, and to see him in such elegant formal wear made her pulse race.

Tearing her eyes away, she asked, "Is everything all right?"

"Fine, except that Troy has the worst case of wedding nerves I've ever seen," Brett replied. Kelly smiled. Brett had got over his suspicion of Troy in the three short weeks since Mary and he had announced their intention to marry. In fact, he'd been very supportive of the older man.

"Oh, Troy, you are going to show up at the church, aren't you? Because I won't be responsible for what

Mary will do to you if you don't. Especially now she's learned how to use computers to hunt people down." Troy went so pale that Kelly regretted her teasing.

He gave a weak laugh. "I wouldn't be half so nervous if I was sure she won't change her mind. Is she okay? She isn't going to back out, is she?"

"No, there's no chance of that," she assured him. "She's very sure that this is what she wants to do and that you are who she wants to be with. Stop worrying and get yourself over to the church so you can be waiting at the altar. Remember, it's a bit of a drive to Marina Grove."

"I'll make sure he's there," Brett said.

"You'd better, or Mary will hold you responsible, too. Remember her threat to turn us into frogs?"

****

Now that everything seemed to be going smoothly, Kelly slipped out on a special mission of her own. She drove herself to Marina Grove and checked in at the church where she was surprised and delighted to see that people were already arriving. This was certainly going to be the wedding of the year. It was a day for resolutions and promises.

Mary and Troy had finally found each other again and were going to swear to love, honor, and cherish each other for the rest of their lives, which Kelly hoped would be long and happy.

Early that morning, at Mary's request, Kelly had invited Daria and her fiancé, Drake, to the Atwell Mansion for breakfast. It was the first time Kelly had met Drake, and she liked him immediately. He was a tall, distinguished looking man with silver streaks at his temples and a confident bearing. When he smiled, his whole face lit up. He seemed the perfect match for Daria.

"So, you are the young woman who is going to wear my wedding gown to the altar," Mary said, holding Daria's hand and smiling. Then she reached out and held Drake's hand, joining the two together. "And you are the young man who will be waiting for her in the church."

"Yes, ma'am."

"I know there has been a lot of fuss about this wedding gown and I admit that, in the throes of a terrible grief and abandonment, I did curse those yards of silk and lace. I know it sounds horrible, but I never wanted another bride to be happy in that dress."

Daria leaned forward to give Mary a one-armed hug. "I am so sorry for what happened to you, and very glad it's been resolved. I don't really believe in curses, but...?"

"But we'd like you to lift it from the gown, anyway," Drake spoke up.

Mary smiled. "I think the deep love you both obviously have for each other is enough to defeat any curse. Still, if you feel you need a ceremony...?"

The young couple looked at each other, their faces radiant with love. "No, ma'am. I think your good wishes for our wedding will be more than enough to end this dress's strange history."

Then Mary had kissed them both and wished them well. Kelly had wiped away a surreptitious tear from her eye, and she was pretty sure both Mary and Daria did, too.

She smiled at the memory.

Time was passing, and there was still one more

thing to cross off her list. She rushed away in the direction of Wedding Bliss.

Sure enough, he was there.

Peter Arnt's ghost sat in his usual spot on the street bench at the side of the park across from the store. He seemed to Kelly to be even paler than he had been, as though he were fading away from this earthly plane.

"So, you know that Mary and Troy are together again and getting married today?' she asked as she sat down beside him.

He turned to her with a huge smile on his ghostly face. "Yes, and I have you to thank for that. You went above and beyond the call of duty to find Troy and bring the two of them together, and I will be eternally grateful. I can leave now, knowing that they are together and happy. It doesn't erase the wrong I did, but it does restore the balance."

"The balance?"

His smile grew larger. "Yes, there is a balance in all things, including human relationships. People are meant to find each other, fall in love, and be together. When that happens, it's balance. You should know that."

"I'm not sure…"

"Yes, you are. You deserve some happiness yourself, my dear. That nephew of Mary's, he's a good man. The two of you are in balance."

"I think it's too soon…"

"No, don't say that. Don't wait too long to allow yourself to love."

"What happens now?" She had to speak around a lump in her throat. With a small shock, she realized she was actually sad to know that she would probably never see Peter the Friendly Ghost again. *At least not in this life.*

As if he read her thoughts, he said, "I am leaving now, it's time. And there's someone I love waiting for me…can you see them? My lovely Elizabeth and the child? My daughter?" The ghost's voice cracked a little as he realized his only daughter was there, waiting with her mother. The child he thought lost forever.

Kelly had to swallow around the lump that came into her throat as she realized she could see Peter's family. A beautiful woman she recognized from Mary's photograph stood some distance away, her arm around a little girl. They cast that eerie glow that all ghosts have. She was smiling and holding out her hand and, as Kelly watched, Peter walked toward his wife and daughter. As he took her outstretched hand in his, they shimmered for a moment and then slowly faded away completely.

Kelly's cheeks were wet with tears. "Safe journey, Peter," she whispered. "I hope you find your balance again with Elizabeth."

****

The church was packed with well-wishers, including some old friends of Mary's with whom she'd lost touch when she went into her splendid isolation after Troy's disappearance.

There were quite a few townspeople there, too, people who'd heard the story of the lovers who had finally found each other after all those years and had come along to support the couple. Daria and Drake were in the crowd. Daria, dressed in another of her designer outfits, waved as Kelly joined Noelia for a last-minute check of flowers and seating. Susie Lamont and her fiancé, Mark Turner, were also smiling from one of the pews. It seemed that the curse had truly been lifted.

She took a few moments to speak reassuringly to Troy as he stood at the altar and then slipped into a pew just as the organist began the Bridal March. Mary Atwell appeared at the entrance to the church, Brett tall and handsome beside her. She walked slowly and proudly down the aisle on her nephew's arm. Mary looked radiant in her dress of palest pink underneath a matching fuchsia pink coat, her white hair styled and sporting a jaunty little fuchsia hat with a small net veil. She carried the bouquet of pink roses and trailing ivy and baby's breath and glowed with love as her eyes focused on the dignified man waiting at the altar.

Troy Matthews stood straight and tall, his face alight with love as he waited for his bride to join him for wedding vows that had been delayed for over five decades. Brett kissed his aunt on the cheek before passing her hand to her groom. He took it and kissed her fingers tenderly.

There probably wasn't a dry eye in the church as Troy and Mary finally stood before the minister and promised to love, honor, and cherish each other for the rest of their lives.

****

"You and Noelia must be the best wedding planners in the world, to put something as exquisite as this together in three short weeks," Mary told them dreamily as she surveyed Noelia's garden.

If only she knew the hassle and the sleepless nights it took to get here, Kelly thought. There had been moments when they had doubted they could pull this very special wedding day together in the time they had. It seemed like Marina Grove had become a go-to spot for every wedding, every convention, and every family get-together in Maine. There was simply no suitable place available for a last-minute wedding reception.

In the end Noelia had said, "Well, blow this. Honestly, we could have a marquee on my lawn and…"

And that's what they did—complete with a wooden dance platform, a tent for a splendid meal, balloons, flowers, a band playing music from the 1960s and '70s so that Mary and her groom could dance to the music of their memories. There was a bar that flowed with champagne and every other beverage known to man or woman. Due to the generally warmer than usual weather, Noelia's garden was bright with late summer flowers and colorful shrubs blooming among the bushes sporting autumnal colors. The profusion of late summer roses added a romantic perfume to the reception. Even the weather cooperated, and the whole event was bathed in sunshine on a day that was warm for so late in the year.

"For a lady who's been pretty darn nearly a recluse for all these years, your Aunt Mary sure knows how to party," Kelly said to Brett as they watched the happy couple doing the twist to a Beatles number.

"Well, I guess she's got a lot of catching up to do."

Kelly nodded. "Yes, and there's something rather bittersweet about that, isn't there? That they should have been kept apart by a silly prank and by their parents…"

Brett pulled her in close, and she leaned against him happily. "I think Troy and Mary are going to be very happy, making up for lost time. They'll value the time they have even more."

"You're right. And I need some time to decompress. It's been hectic. Beautiful, but hectic."

"I know just what you mean, and I wasn't the one chasing around making the wedding arrangements. How about a walk along the pier to breathe in that lovely salty air? It'll be quiet down there at this time of the day…"

Kelly wondered again at Brett's ability to know just what she needed. Once more she heard the ghost's advice about the balance that existed between herself and Brett. As if sensing her conflict about leaving the reception, he said, "I can drive—I haven't had anything to drink because I promised Aunt Mary I'd drive her and Troy back to Mary's place so they can get a good night's sleep before they leave tomorrow."

Kelly smiled. "Yes, the honeymoon. Have they let out the secret of where they're going yet?"

Brett leaned down and whispered conspiratorially in her ear, "If I told you that, I'd have to kill you. That's how big a secret it is."

"Darn!" Kelly punched him playfully in the arm. "I thought you trusted me."

"I do, really. With all my heart. Just not with the secret destination of Aunt Mary's honeymoon."

Chapter Twenty-Two

Brett was right. Most of the tourists had gone home as summer had ended, and the Marina Grove seafront wharf and pier were almost deserted that evening. They walked along hand in hand, nodding to the occasional local resident or visiting conventioneer they met meandering along and enjoying the evening. As they walked, Kelly filled Brett in about her last meeting with the Old Man on the Bench.

"So he's really gone?"

"Yes. I saw them, Brett. It was so beautiful—Elizabeth held out her hand and he took it, then they were both gone. Their little daughter, the one who drowned, was with her." She sniffed back the tears that formed again in her eyes.

"Don't cry, Red—it doesn't suit you," Brett said as he tenderly wiped the droplets away with his thumbs. "There's too much fire in you for tears."

They found a bench and sat to watch the sky change over the bay as the sun set and dusk began to darken the sky. They talked and kissed and talked some more, and the minutes flew by.

Kelly sighed, snuggling into Brett's warm body. "I don't think I have ever been this happy," she murmured. Brett squeezed her tightly to him. Soon the sky was full of stars, a perfect setting for lovers. The breeze from the sea was cool, and Kelly began to shiver in her thin peach silk dress and short jacket. Brett slipped off his tuxedo jacket, placed it around her shoulders, and then wrapped his arm around her again as if he'd never let her go.

She had never felt so cherished in her life.

If only this moment could last forever.

But she knew it couldn't, had known it by the slight distraction in Brett's manner for the past few days. "You're going away again, aren't you? Overseas for the charity you work for?"

Brett turned and pulled her around to face him, dropping tiny kisses on her cheeks, and her head fit snugly against his shoulder. "How did you guess? Yes, I have to go. I wouldn't if I hadn't committed to this before I met you, before we...I...you see, it's a negotiation that's finally coming to fruition that will mean so much to some very poor people in..."

"Shhh." Kelly placed a finger over his lips. "I know you have a job to do. Let's take a leaf out of Troy and Mary's book and just enjoy the time we have." She planted a kiss filled with longing on his lips, a kiss that he returned eagerly, holding her so close against him they could feel the thud of each other's hearts.

"Let's go back to your place," he whispered huskily in Kelly's ear.

"Won't they be missing us at the reception?"

"Right now, I don't care, and I doubt if Mary and Troy are aware of anyone but each other at this moment..." He pulled out his phone and hit a button. "I have to make a quick call. Noelia?"

Kelly's eyebrows shot up. Why was Brett calling her assistant?

"Yes, just as we'd talked about. Could you see to it

that the limo is waiting for when Mary and Troy are ready to leave? Give my apologies to Mary and tell her I'll see them before they leave tomorrow. I'm driving them to the airport.

"And is everything else…? The lights came on as planned? And heaters in the tent? Yes? Thank you. Perfect. I'll let you know how it goes."

"I thought you were driving them back to Derry? Is there some kind of conspiracy I'm missing here?"

"You'll see," came the very cryptic reply.

"So where is this secret honeymoon destination?"

"You know there's an old superstition about keeping the honeymoon destination secret?"

Kelly gave a mock shiver and placed her hand on her throat. "I've had it up to here with superstitions and curses and all sorts of mysteries."

"You're the one who made all this happen, so maybe I can tell you." He leaned over to whisper in her ear, his breath a soft caress on her skin. "They've rented a cottage on a private beach in Jamaica. To hear Mary's glowing description of the place, I think it's possible they might never come home."

She laughed out loud. "Really? It sounds absolutely lovely!"

Ten minutes later Brett stopped his vehicle outside Kelly's little shoreside house. She stopped on the path, amazed to see the windows of the house lit up with softly glowing white fairy lights.

"Oh, my goodness, Brett…don't tell me there's…"

He laughed, that deep rolling sound she'd grown so fond of. "No, no restless spirits tonight. Just you and me and…" He threw open the door to reveal the interior of her home filled with the seductive light of candles. A log fire burned warmly in the small glass-fronted wood stove. She gasped as she saw roses everywhere, huge bouquets of deep red roses, their scent filling the space with subtly sexy perfume.

And on the coffee table, a silver bucket with a cooling bottle of champagne.

"What's going on, Brett? I mean, it's beautiful…"

"Don't be so suspicious. Is there something wrong with my trying to have quality time with the woman I love?"

The woman he loves. She felt the words flow deeply inside of her to the spot it seemed only Brett could reach.

Brett shut the door firmly behind them, slipped his tuxedo jacket from around Kelly, and led her toward the sofa. She eyed the two champagne glasses with white and pink ribbons tied around them, the chocolate covered strawberries, the scented candles…and light dawned in her own desire fogged brain.

"So, that Noelia Russo helped you set all this up, didn't she? And she never said a word. Just wait until I see her…"

"Noelia's great at keeping secrets, isn't she?"

Kelly thought of her suspicions about her assistant being Mimi L'Amour and smiled. "She certainly is."

"Don't be mad at her. I asked for her help and…well, you're going to need her."

"I do need Noelia, at the store and as my friend, but…"

"More than that, you'll need her help in arranging our wedding."

"Our wedding?" Kelly sank onto the sofa, her heart beating dizzily as she tried to take everything in. She fought a smile as Brett dropped to one knee.

"If you laugh at me, I'll take away the chocolate covered strawberries," he threatened.

Kelly sat up straight. "No, whatever you're doing, don't stop. And leave the strawberries alone."

He pulled a blue velvet covered box from his trouser pocket, flipping it open to reveal the ruby and diamond ring nestled there. A ruby red stone for his Red. "Kelly Andrews, I love you more than I can put into words. Will you be my wife?" He paused, looking stricken. "Why are you crying?"

Kelly sniffed and blew her nose on the blue monogrammed handkerchief he hastily pulled from his pocket. "I'm just so happy," she sobbed and went into a fresh bout of tears. "Will you ask me again?"

"You just like having me here on my knees, don't you?" Brett grinned. "Kelly Andrews, you are the love of my life. Will you do me the honor of marrying me?"

She smiled through the tears and threw her arms around him. He moved up onto the sofa and held her tightly as she whispered, "Yes! Yes, Brett Atwell—I'll marry you!"

She raised her face to his as their lips met and melded in a kiss that promised forever.

****

It was still dark when Kelly awoke. She was far too languid and warm to check the time but guessed it was still the wee small hours. All was quiet in the little house except for the eternal rhythm of ocean waves against the shoreline and the gentle snoring of Sullivan the cat who slept in the chair by the window.

Earlier, they had extinguished all the candles before Brett clasped her hand and led her up the shallow stairs to Kelly's bedroom with its sand-colored walls and queen-sized bed covered in a fluffy, soft, white comforter. Now, the only light in the little cottage came from the waning moon which hung over the bay. It arced through her bedroom window and spilled over the bed in which she and Brett lay.

Kelly rolled onto her side to watch as he slept deeply, admiring the contours of the lean, muscular body that she had so recently explored with such delight. The moon spilling through the white lace curtains turned the pale hairs on his chest to filaments of gold.

She placed her left hand on the hard warmth of his ribcage and smiled as the rise and fall of his breathing caused the beautiful ring on her finger to twinkle and glow in the moonlight. Its weight felt strange and new. So unfamiliar and yet so beautiful.

A promise of a lifetime of love.

The gentle touch of her hand woke him, and he smiled up into her face. Sleepily, she luxuriously stretched and sighed and turned toward him again to plant a gentle kiss on his lips, a kiss he captured and returned with mounting heat. Pushing her gently back against the pillows, he raised himself on one elbow.

"I want to wake up every morning, with you, like this, for the rest of our lives," he told her.

Slowly he moved down her body, kissing the white scars and moving on to stroke her curves and then returning hungrily to her lips.

"I love you, Red," he murmured against her mouth.

"Call me Red again, and you know what will happen…" she warned as his arms went around her.

"Oh, I know what will happen. Let me show you."

His deep voice was filled with laughter and promises.

A word about the author...

Glenys O'Connell writes romantic suspense and comedy, sometimes with a touch of paranormal! Her interest in criminal psychology began when covering the crime beat as a journalist for a large daily newspaper . She holds a degree in psychology and is qualified as a counselor. As well as romance, she also writes non-fiction on mental health issues, children's books, and is an award-winning playwright. After years of travelling and working abroad, mainly in the UK & Ireland, she now makes her home in rural Ontario, Canada, with her husband, four grown-up children, and three spoiled cats. You can read more about her at her blog,

https://romancecanbemurder.blogspot.com/

Thank you for purchasing
this publication of The Wild Rose Press, Inc.

For questions or more information
contact us at
info@thewildrosepress.com.

The Wild Rose Press, Inc.
www.thewildrosepress.com